C000182436

Nights in the Asylum

Carol Lefevre

PICADOR

First published 2007 by Random House Australia Pty Ltd

First published in Great Britain 2007 by Picador
an imprint of Pan Macmillan Ltd
Pan Macmillan, 20 New Wharf Road, London N1 9RR
Basingstoke and Oxford
Associated companies throughout the world
www.panmacmillan.com

ISBN 978-0-330-44889-5

A CIP catalogue record for this book is available from
the British Library.

Typeset by Midland Typesetters, Australia
Printed and bound in Great Britain
by Mackays of Chatham plc, Chatham, Kent

Visit **www.panmacmillan.com** to read more about all our books
and to buy them. You will also find features, author interviews and
news of any author events, and you can sign up for e-newsletters
so that you're always first to hear about our new releases.

For the ones I love,
Christopher, Lorena, Rafael

Contents

Sometimes I forget completely
what companionship is.
Unconscious and insane, I spill sad
energy everywhere. My story
gets told in various ways: a romance,
a dirty joke, a war, a vacancy.

Divide up my forgetfulness to any number,
it will go around.
These dark suggestions that I follow,
are they a part of some plan?
Friends, be careful. Don't come near me
out of curiosity, or sympathy.

Jelalludin Rūmī

The Photograph does not necessarily say *what is no longer*, but only and for certain *what has been*.

Roland Barthes
Camera Lucida: Reflections on Photography

PART ONE
Camera Obscura

MIRI

Miri had bitten off half her tongue, or thought she had. She kept coughing out slivers of flesh and catching them in her hand, and the pieces were bluish, like raw meat sliced for a stir-fry. All one side seemed to be missing and her saliva was sweet with the blood, while the knob of tongue that remained swelled to fill her mouth each time she swallowed. But when she slid a finger into her mouth to probe the damage, the tongue appeared intact.

Her body sagged and she lay for a long time in the dark. Then, quite suddenly, it was dawn and the morning of Alice's funeral.

She rose and watched the gradual fade-in of the gardens: pale gravel paths lacing the black slabs of lawn, a row of slender cypresses bordering the drive. As the sky lightened, a flock of pink cockatoos landed on the topmost branches of a Norfolk pine. Miri leaned her forehead against the glass of the small window overlooking the street.

As a child, Alice had been forever watching out the window, waiting for her father — and Jack was always late.

Miri touched a fingertip to her swollen eyelids where the skin was damp and tender. This was Alice's window. Alice's bed.

Alice.

Alice.

If she remained quiet and still as a stone this day might slide over her without a ripple.

The morning was close and humid, the white sun buried behind layers of cloud. By eight o'clock she was showered and dressed and walking up and down in her black linen dress. Her arms felt weighted, and she could not think what to do with her hands. At ten o'clock a hired car and driver arrived to take her to the church. The streets teemed with traffic but for once other cars kept their distance, as if the black car with Miri perched on the spongy grey uphol-stery carried some visible taint of death. As they passed a row of shops she remembered the prescription for tran-quillisers, but when she tapped on the perspex screen the driver seemed not to hear, and the car carried on up Oxford Street.

Jack was waiting for her outside the church. The sight of him momentarily disabled her, and he had to lean into the car and tug her out. His palm at the base of her spine steered her down the central aisle towards a front pew. Polished wood under her hands. The scent of hot wax overlaid with the sweetness of lilies. Cobalt and crimson flaring in the stained-glass windows and the swaying dan-delion heads of women wearing hats: for one confusing moment Miri imagined there must be a wedding, until the sombre clothing of the congregation, the texture of her own black dress against her skin, reminded her why she was there.

She could not seem to hold onto the truth about Alice. It came and went a thousand times a day, the shock of it surging through her like an electric current with each remembering. They were halfway through the first hymn before she could bring herself to look at the coffin, ridiculously small to contain their long-limbed daughter. Her eyes slid over it and away and she squeezed Jack's arm.

'There must be some mistake.'

Her husband's face, when he turned towards her, was blurred and unfamiliar, his answer lost in the rustle of hymn sheets.

The vicar's voice rose and fell and bounced off the whitewashed walls.

They shuffled to their feet as the organist's hands moved like a pair of pink-shelled crabs over the yellowed keys. Miri's sole request for the service had been that no stringed instruments be played, but she wondered now if anything could be worse than the breathy groan of the organ.

And then they were outside, people they knew avoiding eye contact as she and Jack walked with their heads bowed under the pearly sky.

In the flat open field, the coffin looked exposed and vulnerable. The sight of it suspended by ropes and the mound of newly dug earth triggered a pain behind Miri's breastbone. Jack slid a hand along her waist, a warm patch in the cold currents eddying around her, as she forced her eyes to follow the coffin down. She didn't want to look, but this was the last glimpse of Alice. A blur of milky petals on the pale oak lid. The gritty soil clogged Miri's nails as she scooped it up. Jack had to nudge her twice before she could open her hand to let it fall.

The shocking clatter of earth on wood; the perfect flowers bruised and coated with dust. She turned away as a tear slid from beneath Jack's sunglasses, crossed his jaw and seeped into the network of creases on his neck.

Miri's breathing quickened and she looked up, giddy with nausea, to where the frosted disintegrating trail of a jet was embedded in the tilting sky. The pain in her chest was not so much spreading as forming crystals. She needed to close her eyes, to rest her cheek against something cool and smooth.

By keeping her head very still and moving carefully as if on ice, she thought that she would make it to the car. But halfway down the long paved walkway with the rows of weathered gravestones on either side, Miri felt herself slipping and did not resist. A whining sound spiralled around her. Even when she pressed her hands over her ears she could hear it, a note as hard and bright and constant as a wet finger rubbing over the rim of a glass.

They had taken her to St Vincent's Hospital in Darlinghurst. It was where they brought the overdosing drug addicts, the raped and murdered. She had been there almost a week. A week of nights like so much black air scratched with static. A week of days through which she counted people rushing along the hot silvery pavements outside her window. A week of thunderstorms and sudden steaming downpours, of muted conversations that never quite cut through the wooziness in her head.

Each dawn she had followed the escalating clatter of the hospital as it stirred to life after the long night and, this morning, looking out at the streaky grey sky, she felt a new and unbearable restlessness in her limbs, as if she must move and keep on moving or lose the use of them. At seven o'clock two nurses arrived. The plump one took her temperature and pulse, while the thin one flicked at creases in the bedclothes with the back of her hand. The rattle of a breakfast trolley brought tea and two slices of stiff white toast cut into triangles.

'Try and get something down, love,' the plump nurse said.

They backed out of the room, and the lock clicked once like a camera shutter. Miri's hand shook and she set the cup down in a puddle of tea. Visits from a bereavement counsellor had left her craving privacy, and yesterday she had asked to go home. From an edge of apology in the fat nurse's smile, she wondered if there was going to be a fuss about her leaving.

Later in the morning, a woman with coarse grey hair springing back from her forehead introduced herself as a social worker.

'I'm Jean,' she said. 'Do you have time for a chat?'

Miri shrugged at the empty room and nodded.

'How are you feeling today?'

'I'm feeling lousy, how about you?'

'Ah, well. It's you that concerns me, Mrs . . .?'

'Passmore.'

'Good,' Jean beamed an encouraging smile.

Miri gaped at her. Had there ever been any question of forgetting her own name? Clearly, the woman thought it a possibility. Would that be proof of madness? Did mad people abandon or mislay their names like lost umbrellas and winter gloves? Miri would have been glad to forget, but forgetting was not an option. Perhaps she should have said her name was Kissack, seen where that took them.

The social worker asked if there was anything that Miri would like to share.

Miri was flustered by this offer of intimacy. 'I'm not sure . . .'

'It's just that you've asked to go home, and before we can discharge you we must establish that you're going to be all right. Will there be anyone at home?'

The woman's eyes were earnest, beady. Miri had to say something, although she knew she was never going to be all right.

She said, 'I once read a book about an actress named Maria who spent her days driving on the freeway.'

'I see,' Jean said.

'I am an actress,' Miri said, struggling to order her thoughts, to pinpoint the connection with the novel and how it proved she was okay. 'Although these days we call ourselves actors.'

'And what is it about this Maria that you relate to?'

'Have you read the book?'

Jean shook her head, quick little shakes.

In the book, Maria was going through grief, but she was stronger than she looked. Miri wanted to explain to this woman that sometimes she acted Maria. That's all it was, acting. They really mustn't worry. But her throat was tender, and her tongue refused to form the right words.

A pucker appeared between Jean's eyebrows. She opened a file on her knee and scanned a page of notes.

'Does it say how I got here?' Miri said.

'You don't remember being admitted?'

Miri knew they wanted her to remember, as if that could somehow make a difference. So, give them what they wanted. 'Some of it,' she said.

Jean closed the file. 'I'll have to ask Dr Byrne to speak with you,' she said.

'I *need* to go home,' Miri insisted.

The social worker gave a noncommittal smile and rose. 'The doctor will be around in an hour.'

From the woman's doubtful face as she edged out the door, Miri knew that mentioning Maria had been a mistake.

When Dr Byrne arrived she pretended that she hadn't been fully awake when she spoke to Jean. She acted her heart out. All her fuses might be blown, but she could still do that. The scene lasted twenty minutes, and at the end of it the doctor signed her discharge.

MIRI

She would go back to the beginning, or as close to the beginning as she could get. It took her half an hour to pack, pressing random garments into a suitcase, tossing in scarves and unmatched pairs of shoes. Then, with her luggage at the door, Miri pulled a pile of laundered sheets from the linen press. The telephone rang but she ignored it, shaking out sheets and draping them over chairs and sofas. Already the white rooms full of stale air looked unfamiliar and abandoned.

In the study she flapped a sheet until it cracked, lifted her arms high and let it drift over Jack's desk like a parachute descending. Papers slithered to the floor but she left them where they fell and stared for a moment at the snowy cotton with its grid of creases. When she had last bothered to iron bed linen, the world had been so different.

With the car keys in her hand, Miri hurried through the apartment flipping switches, closing curtains, checking window locks. Then she opened the door of Alice's bedroom.

Miri had slept here on the night before the funeral, and the feather pillow still held the imprint of her head. A crumpled sheet lay under the window. If Jack had come home in her absence he had not bothered to tidy up — or perhaps he would not have thought to look in Alice's room; after all, it had been months since their daughter had lived at home. She wrapped her arms around her chest. It seemed to her that the still room waited for something, that it was poised in silent expectation, as if at any moment the world might change colour and all would be well. She spread the sheet across the single mattress, tucked it in and flattened the blue woollen blanket with her palm. Before Alice had adopted Gothic black, her favourite colour had been this clean sea-washed blue.

It was Friday night, the end of a scorched week in December, and cars were caught like flies in the web of streets leading out of the city. Rows of hard-edged candy-coloured houses lined the inner-city pavements. Further out, the suburbs were all glare and glitter and strung-out drivers punching car horns in the snarled traffic. Every few miles she passed a vehicle stranded at the side of the road with its bonnet propped open and steam whistling from the radiator, and her eyes flew to the dials on the Ford's dashboard.

By the time she reached Parramatta the sun had set, but the sky still glowed blood-red above the junkyards and second-hand car lots. Gaudy advertising banners and lines of fluorescent bunting flapped in a hot wind. The night air, spiked with sirens, tasted of smoke.

Beyond Penrith the traffic eased, and the wind buffeting the car cooled her skin. In the mountain townships, smug stone houses nestled in the beam of her headlights.

Christmas trees shimmered in the windows. Miri could not look without a welling pain in her chest. The sight reminded her of a ceramic Christmas lamp they'd had when Alice was small, a cone-shaped tree covered with tiny pink birds, a bit kitsch for the brittle white spaces of their apartment, but Alice had always pleaded for it to be set in the window. 'So that Daddy knows we're home when he comes around the corner.' Now as she passed through empty streets beaded with sleeping children, with capable mothers and patient fathers, other people's happiness fluttered at the edges of her vision.

One a.m. She smoothed the creases in her trousers. In the rear-view mirror she was red-eyed and dishevelled, but the receptionist only yawned as she swiped her plastic card and handed over a key.

Everything in the small square motel room was brown and ugly. All sound, even her own breathing, was absorbed by the dull brown surfaces and, beyond them, by the unimaginable void arching above. Miri stood motionless under the stark overhead light. When she could bear silence no longer, she crossed to the window and pulled back the curtain. The other units were unlit. She peered at the bonnet of her car outside the window, but its silver duco revealed no trace of the miles she had covered.

She let the curtain fall and turned up the air conditioning, peeled back the sheets on the double bed and examined them: they looked clean enough. In the end she shrugged off her clothes and fell exhausted onto the mattress with the spare pillow hugged into the curve of her body.

The moment when a life began to fall apart, Miri thought, was never obvious until it was too late. Arriving home after a performance at the Matchbox Theatre, she had opened the front door of the flat and found Alice sitting on the floor in the hall. Only later would she recognise this as one of those undetected moments of disintegration. Her daughter's arms were full of soft toys collected through childhood. Alice was eighteen, but the toys still crammed a shelf inside her wardrobe.

'Hey,' Miri said. 'I thought you'd be asleep.'

Alice stood up and shook plum-coloured hair, flicked at it with a knobbly shoulder. The new spiky cut barely brushed her collarbone, but her body still spoke the language of a girl with a velvet headband and flowing locks.

'Where *were* you?' Alice said, her white face floating in the darkened hallway, and her voice stretched taut as a tightrope.

Miri was shrugging off her coat, and as her head swivelled towards this strained sound Alice opened her arms and the soft toys fell and bounced around their feet.

'What is it?' Miri said.

Her daughter still clutched a teddy bear. 'You never see what's going on!'

Miri raised her eyebrows. 'And what *is* going on?' she said.

Alice's bottom lip quivered, but her eyes sparked as she mimicked her mother's voice. '*Oh, whatever is going on,*' she drawled. She hurled the teddy bear and reeled away into her bedroom. Miri stumbled forward over the toys, but the lock clicked as her hand closed on the doorknob.

'Alice, please let me in.'

'Go away!'

Miri heard the violin strings in contact with the bow, two staccato passes over the open strings, followed by a barricade of scales that repelled her anxious questions.

Next morning she found a note stuck with a magnet to the fridge.

I'm moving into a friend's flat. It will just be easier. I'll ring you with the phone number. Don't take it personally, all right? Love, Alice. ××

She read the note twice. Why had Alice needed to make an early morning getaway? The note ended with two tiny kisses, but the paper had skidded sideways and when Miri levelled it they looked like crucifixes.

Jack was in the shower, but Miri tapped on the glass screen and held up the note.

He stepped out of the spray, flecked with foam. 'Which friend?'

'It must be Jessica, she's the only one flatting.'

Jack screwed his eyes shut as shampoo slid down his forehead. 'Well, Jessica's not such a bad kid.'

'But Alice can't afford to move out.'

'Then she'll soon be home,' he said.

Their voices boomed in the tiled bathroom. Miri rubbed a hand across her mouth as Jack stepped back under the shower spray. Bubbles glided down his neck and shoulders, following the contours of his arms and torso. Miri watched the creamy residue collect in the coarse black hairs on his chest, on the down that divided his belly below the navel.

Jack opened his eyes and grinned at her, shouted over the hiss of water. 'So, remind me again what age *you* left home?'

Seventeen. She had left home at seventeen. But it was different with Alice. Their daughter had dreams and ambitions, she was halfway through her first year at university, and Miri understood how a sudden change of venue could spin a life out of kilter.

She went out to the hall and stared uneasily at the soft toys still scattered there. In the end she gathered them into a plastic bag and replaced them in Alice's wardrobe. Afterwards Miri sat hunched over a cup of bitter black coffee, the first she'd drunk in months, and stared at the crosses on Alice's note, one each for her and Jack.

Saturday. Hour after hour, under a feathered sky, the landscape drained of green in barely perceptible stages until at last a dun colour settled over the car like silt. Miri winced at the light bouncing off the bone-dry plain. The towns she passed through were dying, tin and spit outbuildings with their ribs protruding, collapsing houses, broken-down cars, shops with shattered or boarded-up windows. Weathered billboards advertised internet cafes, and on one main street, where the spaced out houses leaned like loosened teeth, a flurry of youngsters loitered outside the service station. Only the pubs looked rooted and flourishing.

Groggy with heat and with the car's motion buzzing through her, Miri pulled off the road and slept, but her sweat-drenched dreams left her dazed and gasping. She sipped warm water from a bottle, revved the engine, and as she eased back out onto the highway she thought of Maria driving on the freeway. Maria had been right: it was better to keep on moving.

In the afternoon, on the outskirts of an unknown town, she came upon a massacre of galahs in the wake of one of the road trains. Rosy feathers mashed with flesh for fifty yards along the bitumen. So much wasted beauty. She shivered as a flock of live birds flashed pink and silver overhead, and it was all she could do to hold a straight line and not veer off wildly into a field of stubble. Further west, the map emptied to a few red lines snaking across the buff-coloured paper. The day stretched endlessly ahead and sometimes she felt herself free-falling, the car gliding on a tide of hot air. Whenever her eyes brimmed and over-flowed she picked up the map and repeated words she found there — Dubbo, Narromine, Mungeribar, Trangie, Cathundral, Nevertire, Belaringar, Mullengudgery, Warrigal, Nyngan, Canbelego — until the scattered black dots turned one by one into the towns whose names released a nasal droning music.

By evening the desert air had cooled. Now the chill falling off the windscreen soothed her as she pulled onto a side road and curled up on the back seat with her jacket folded underneath her cheek.

With Alice gone the flat had felt flimsy and less structured, as if some vital stabilising element had been removed. Miri pondered their choice of a city flat over a solid suburban house. A household. Why had they never considered the suburbs? Bricks and mortar, shrubbery, some crazy paving, a rumpus room where Alice could have hung out with her friends.

But it was too late. One Friday evening Alice called to collect some belongings, and her hair was dyed a seething metallic black, her nails glossed to match. It had only been three weeks but already she looked older, thinner, more knowing than the girl who had waited in the hall with her arms full of teddy bears.

Miri had stood sipping a gin and tonic in the kitchen while Alice packed up her bedroom. A Sarah McLachlan song they both liked started up and was extinguished. Miri wondered if her daughter would take the CD or leave it. Alice sidled into the kitchen clad in floating layers of black, and Miri watched as she opened the fridge. Her daughter's smudgy purple lips and eyelids took on an opalescent gleam in the blue light of the fridge. Goth fashion. Alice's new friends dressed the same way, although their pierced chins, cheeks and even nipples were more repulsive than her daughter's tiny nose stud and the new rose tattoo inside her ankle. Thankfully, Alice was squeamish. Miri stared at the powdery white shoulders glowing through the razor slits in Alice's shirt. Was her daughter always this thin? Yes, of course — how could she have not noticed?

'Looks like you haven't eaten since you left home,' she said.

Alice shut the fridge without taking anything. Miri leaned against the sink. The gin and her daughter's fragile shoulders made her want to cry, and she fumbled in her purse.

'Buy groceries,' she said as she handed over a bundle of crumpled notes.

Alice slid both arms around Miri's waist, and her lips pressed a warm purple kiss against her cheek.

Breakfast at the Caltex roadhouse in Castaway. Toast two inches thick, bacon, eggs sliding in a slick of butter. Miri dipped a corner of toast in a mug of black tea. It was the taste of her late teens, days when modelling work was scarce and often toast was all she ate in a week, gas-scorched slices of white bread dipped in tea. Hand-to-mouth days before she met Jack, nights when hunger would prod her awake with a craving for rare meat, or for that Cuban dish of black beans her Auntie Con used to simmer on the stove in winter.

The early light was piercing, bouncing off chrome and scratched laminex, while beyond the petrol pumps the empty blacktop glittered. A radio pumped out country music that ricocheted around her as she hunched over the greasy plate. Heartbroken lyrics wrapped around a jaunty tune. A waitress with foundation in a line along her milky jaw brought the bill and hovered beside Miri's table. *Ask me, I might say Yes* was punched out in diamante studs across her chest, and in the neck of her T-shirt a chain of silver letters spelled *Chandelle*.

'Don't I know you?'

Miri shook her head and fumbled in her handbag for her purse.

'You definitely remind me of someone.' Chandelle fingered the letters at her throat. 'It's on the tip of my tongue.'

Miri laid a twenty-dollar bill in the saucer. As she rose to leave, the waitress pestered to know where she had come from, where she was headed.

Crows flapped around the red and grey-furred carcasses of kangaroos that littered the roadside. Red soil clotted with saltbush and bluebush stretched across a vast treeless plain, with the sky a blue glass paperweight pressing everything flat. Miri was careful not to look at the sky; any sudden movement, even a flickering eyelid, could make it crack and shatter. Once she spotted a fox, its slender shape, muzzle to bushing tail, trapped for an instant in the wavering amber light before it turned and merged with the desert. Occasionally a wedge-tailed eagle coasted above the power lines. The purple broken-backed hills on the horizon never drew nearer, however many miles she covered, while the sky and land merged, infinite and empty, until Miri felt she might have reached the edge of the earth.

The man materialised by the side of the road as naturally as if he had always been there, isolated and abandoned, as incongruous as the lidless lavatory bowl Miri had noticed some miles back, dumped among the stunted clumps of saltbush. The sight of him sitting calmly in the dust made her heart pump with fright even as her foot eased off the accelerator. He sat with his legs folded under him and his hands resting on his knees, as if in meditation or prayer. The crystalline surface of a saltpan flashed in the corner of her eye in the instant before she passed him. Then the back wheel slipped off the blacktop onto the verge, and she peered into a rear view of dense red fog.

Maybe the heat was playing tricks. She accelerated, but the question mark of the man's bowed head disturbed her. Those hands folded on the knees of his trousers, his utter absorption. Despite his calm demeanour he had looked unwell, and the vision stayed with her. If he collapsed no-one would see him, and anyway, she had not passed another vehicle for hours. The kilometres ticked over: two, three, four. Miri slowed the car, wishing she could forget the kneeling figure but knowing she could not. She sucked in the dry air, checked her wing mirrors and made a perfect three-point turn.

He walked towards her along the edge of the bitumen, a scrap of cloth folded over his head to protect it from the sun. Close up, the first thing that struck her was his beauty, an impossible softness in the tilted corners of his mouth, in the curve of his eyelids and the springing curl of his hair. Beauty was a commodity she understood, and this sudden manifestation made her draw breath, made her register her own surprise. As the car idled forwards she caught the glimmer of the saltpan where he had been kneeling; his slow shuffle had not brought him far.

With a sigh, she wound down the window and shouted, 'Have you got water?'

When he didn't answer she waved the plastic bottle. He stared at her as if puzzled, then raised his arm and pointed along the road. Miri did not want company. She definitely did not want a stranger, a man, in her car. But they were miles from anywhere. He had no hat, no water, there was no shelter and he looked about to drop. Then again, his skin was dark, the colour deeper than could be accounted for by exposure to the sun. Miri's hands tightened to fists on the wheel and her feet tensed against the clutch and brake. It was the isolation that bothered her, aggravated, she had to admit, by the colour of his face beneath that flap of washed-out cloth. This unexpected streak of prejudice flooded her with embarrassment, and the momentum of it flung her across the seat to unlock the door.

Her passenger was silent. When his head drooped she wondered if he was asleep but didn't want to look. The light was changing, thickening, gathering colour from the red desert, and Miri strained to keep the road in focus, to separate the shapes of animals from the landscape.

When they hit the roo she felt a sudden glancing knock in the region of the front bumper, was still absorbing it when his hand darted to the steering wheel, just brushed it, and then pointed to another animal bounding alongside his window. Miri braked hard as it skimmed the bonnet and bounced away. She pulled off the road, and they clambered out. There was no sign of the animal she had hit, but the front mudguard was crumpled and the headlight glass broken. How could a mere bump produce so much damage?

Back behind the wheel she felt defeated and the breath whistled out of her. When he turned towards her she stiffened, but he did not touch her, nor make eye contact, and after a moment she relaxed. Without his warning the car could have been one of those crumpled wrecks they had passed with its nose embedded in the desert.

'Thank you,' she said, and heard her own voice, formal and nervous.

At around four in the afternoon, the town where she had been born appeared as a disturbance in the heat shimmer on the horizon. Soon the shapes of ancient slagheaps solidified and then she saw the first houses, late sunlight glancing off their corrugated-iron roofs. They passed a welcome sign that had been sprayed with black and red graffiti. In the town's heyday, twenty thousand people had lived here; there had once been talk of city status. Now, with the mining all but over, the population had dwindled. The town was small enough that you could not walk down the street without bumping into someone you knew; it was big enough to get lost in, if that was what you wanted.

She let her passenger out beside the entrance to a new shopping mall on the outskirts. He raised his hand, fingers curling towards her once, before he turned and merged with the stream of people heading into the shops.

Miri nudged out onto the wide main road. There was no traffic and she let the car crawl along at twenty-five as she stared out at the rows of square tin houses, the broad flat streets of the town. She had not been home for years, but the ragged shape of it had held steady in her mind.

AZIZ

The prayer beads slipped through his fingers without a sound, thirty-three smooth glass globes the colour of honey, on which he recited the Ninety Nine Beautiful Names of Allah. *Ar-Rahman*, the Merciful. *Ar-Rashid*, the Guide, *Al-Mumit*, Bringer of Death. He shuddered at the memory of the desert prayers. Without water for the cleansing ritual he had knelt and brought a handful of red dust to his face. He still could feel the gritty malignant heat of it against his skin, three times down the right arm and three times down the left. He had been lost and knew it, everything stripped away but an insistent thirst that pressed at every cell in his body and swelled in his mouth. Another hour and he would have choked to death on his own salty tongue.

That day he had travelled for miles on the back of a truck, crushed against the tender underbellies of sheep, panting beside them in a slurry of urine and dust until the driver — stopping to urinate against a wheel — discovered him and, with a rough shout, dragged him out and drove away. He had stood clasping his head, watching the receding truck with its cargo of gasping animals until it was no bigger than a beetle in the distance. Then he trudged for hours with the diamond sun drilling the back of his neck, but the landscape continued flat and waterless.

Few other places had been as inhospitable. He recalled kneeling to say his prayers among the sick and dying, in charred fields, in black soggy soil with the water in the ploughed furrows turgid with pollution. This time he had been tempted to lift his arms and wail that prayer was useless, but instead he went through the motions of prayer because of the promise to his father.

And then, like a reward for faith, he had noticed a speck of movement, something no bigger than a dust mote gliding towards him. When the car drew level and then passed by, he closed his eyes and flung himself into his prayers with all the ferocity his weakened body could muster. He prayed as if it was his last moment on earth, prayed knowing that his life depended on whatever happened next, for he had no hope of walking to safety.

His vision had begun to blur with dehydration, so when the car returned for him the figure behind the glass was indistinct. He had not realised the driver was a woman until she spoke, words he could not understand, but the invitation was there in her voice as she held up a bottle. He feared she might offer him a drink then drive away, but instead she had leaned across and opened the door of her motorcar.

He had wanted to offer an apology for the soiled state of his clothing, but the woman's expression was so disoriented that his halting English words evaporated. She handed him the bottle, apparently indifferent to the sheep stink that clung to him, and when the water touched his lips he'd had to force himself not to drain it in one swallow. As she turned to look along the highway he glimpsed the sad arc of her mouth, her shoulders curled towards the steering wheel, shoulderblades bunched like stunted wings beneath her shirt.

When exhaustion overtook him his head sagged against the window. Soothed by the car's motion, he dipped from consciousness into shallow pockets of sleep. The upholstery cupped his spine as he dreamed of ice-cream flavoured with bitter oranges, a soothing *sharbat* made from snow that dissolved with a tingle on the tongue. He dreamed, too, of a memory game his sisters used to play, a game that began with the breaking of a wishbone and continued for days or weeks, until one of them forgot to play.

Mara yad, tura faramush, the winner would cry. Memory for me, forgetfulness for you.

Perhaps he dreamed for hours, perhaps even for days, but when at last he opened his eyes and saw the town, Aziz did not know whether to be thankful or afraid.

PART TWO
Diorama

CHANDELLE

When Jude Moran and his wife walked into the Castaway roadhouse and sat down at separate tables, Chandelle Burns handed them a menu each and avoided making eye contact. The wife, Suzette, carried a baby in a sling around her neck, a tiny blob in a pink romper suit with a fuzz of red-gold hair on her scalp. It was the first time Chandelle had seen the baby. Jude was in civvies; moleskins and a checked shirt instead of his cop gear. Without the holstered gun clamped to his belt, the two-way radio and nightstick, he looked almost naked, Chandelle decided. She preferred the uniform.

Suzette Moran sat with her back to her husband. Her bare arms were freckled, and as she bent to pluck the baby's bottle from a bag she tossed aside red curls that reached to her waist. Chandelle shook her head self-consciously; she was growing her hair but it would be years before it was anywhere near that long, if ever. Once the baby was plugged into the bottle, the wife lit up a cigarette and stared out across the rectangle of concrete towards the road. After a couple of minutes a chair scraped, and Jude moved to stand in front of the window, blocking her view.

'Zett,' he said, 'why d'you want to make a scene?'

His wife stubbed out the half-smoked cigarette without answering, fumbled in her handbag for a tissue and dabbed the baby's mouth.

After looking at her for a minute, Jude whacked the plastic menu on the table. 'Steak sandwich and coffee, times two,' he called to Chandelle.

By the time their food came through the hatch from the kitchen and Chandelle clattered towards them with the tray, the Morans were sitting together, though not talking much. As she slid the plates onto the table Chandelle felt big and clumsy beside Jude's wife, plus she suspected that the fluorescent lighting transformed her new foundation into an unflattering orange. Then, setting down the cutlery, she noticed with regret that her nail varnish was chipped back halfway up her nails. She should have reapplied it last night. It was true what that old beauty book of her mother's said, that every morning you should dress and leave the house as if you expected to bump into Mr Right, because one day you would. Chandelle sighed; waking each morning in the slabby little tin and asbestos place behind the roadhouse it was hard to take advice like this seriously.

Suzette Moran ignored her husband, her gaze fastened on the tabletop as if trying to memorise its pattern of scars and scratches. When she looked up suddenly, Chandelle was staggered by the colour of her eyes, green as a pair of frozen peas.

'I want you to know,' the wife said, 'that I've never seen this bloke before in my life.' Her voice was steady with a strand of venom running through it.

'Christ, that's a good one!' Jude said, but when he picked up his knife and fork and started on the steak sandwich, Chandelle saw that he looked peeved.

His wife bounced to her feet, hugging the baby to her chest as she stalked out through the double glass doors and headed for the road. From behind the counter Chandelle watched her go, a tiny figure in a skimpy skirt striding along the yellow verge beside the blacktop. Jude and his wife lived fifty kilometres away in town, but she was marching in the other direction, and the sun would set in half an hour.

Excitement rippled through Chandelle, and she turned to see how Jude was taking it. He'd been in last week for coffee after the Rigby kids rolled a stolen car, and again after nudging the bumper of some troublemaker he was encouraging across the border into South Australia. Jude had a way of standing up close when he talked, and Chandelle liked his aftershave. *Brut*, he'd told her it was, dead macho. Now the wife had gone she hoped he'd stay, but Jude Moran didn't linger over the meal, although he didn't hurry either. When he had wiped the plate with the last chip he called for the bill.

Chandelle stood close to his shoulder while he peeled notes from a wad, disappointed when he gave no sign that he remembered her, though from the tightness of his mouth she could see he was preoccupied with the problem of his wife.

Outside at the bowser, the Castaway patrol car had pulled in for petrol. When Chandelle hurried out she noticed that Jude's wife was already out of sight. Jude ambled out of the servo and crossed to the police car; it was Mickey Murphy driving.

'Just picked up the wife from hospital,' Jude said. 'She's been having some tests.' He tapped his fingers against the side of his forehead.

'Where's she gone to?' Mickey asked, looking around.

'Marched off towards bloody Sydney,' Jude said. 'I gotta round her up.'

Chandelle watched the dollars and cents click up as the tank filled.

'Give you a hand,' Mickey said.

Jude walked over to his car and when Chandelle withdrew the pump, Mickey's car pulled out onto the highway followed by Jude's red Land Cruiser.

An hour later Mickey gave Chandelle the details when he came back to sign for the petrol.

'So I pull up beside the silly bitch,' he said, 'and ask her to get in the car with her husband and go home.'

Shania Twain was whooping it up on the radio; Chandelle reached over and turned it down. 'And what'd she say?'

'She says to me, "You don't own this fucking highway!"'

Chandelle crossed her arms and leaned on the cash desk until her boobs bulged in the scoop of her T-shirt. Mickey stared appreciatively.

'And?'

'And I says, "Missus Moran, I own this highway all the way to Sydney, and if you don't get back in the car I'm going to do you for drunk and disorderly." So she says, "But I'm not drunk, or disorderly."'

'"Who says?" I ask. "Way I hear it you've just come out of Hillcrest and been hitting the bottle."'

Chandelle smirked. Hillcrest was a loony bin, she knew that much, but Jude's wife hadn't been there that she'd heard of.

Mickey went on. 'Then she stops walking and looks at me. She's a bit of all right, Jude's wife, but a redhead's temper. Baby's a coppertop too.'

Chandelle had seen Jude's red Land Cruiser streaking away towards town so she already knew the outcome. She asked Mickey anyway.

'What'd she do?'

Mickey grinned. 'Her language was ripe, but she went over to their car and hopped in beside hubby.'

Chandelle could hear the clatter of the dishwasher out back. The roadhouse was empty, leaking fluorescent light into the night air. Time to turn on the outside spots and put the takings in the safe. Mickey was still staring at her breasts. Maybe there was just time. She shivered. Last week they'd done it standing up in the storeroom, cartons of Heinz sausages and beans supporting her buttocks and the tip of the fake Christmas tree tickling her ear. Mickey had to be quick because his house was only quarter of a mile away, and if the patrol car was parked too long outside the servo his wife would want to know why. Once she'd come storming down the road to find him, a tough dried-up little blonde with two snot-nosed kids — mini clones of Mickey — trailing behind her.

'Tea's on the table getting cold,' she'd snapped at Mickey, who was sitting at a table spooning foam off the top of his cappuccino. 'So what are you hanging around here for, as if I didn't know?' She'd stood glaring down at him, her fists planted on her hips.

'Come on, Sharon,' Mickey'd said in his slow soft way, but he'd drained the lukewarm coffee and left with her.

For an outpost, and one with so much space around it, the truck stop was claustrophobic. Chandelle knew almost everyone she met by name, and never in her wildest dreams were any of them Mr Right. She should move into town before she shrivelled up like Mickey's wife, before she could no longer raise the energy. In town there'd be more scope.

You only had to look at Jude Moran to know that town living made a difference. Jude wasn't bothered by what people did or thought and, unlike Mickey Murphy, he wasn't under his wife's thumb.

Jude Moran had once offered Chandelle a ride into the desert in a police car, and the things he'd done with his handgun terrified and excited her. She never knew people did stuff like that in real life, like they were starring in a porn video or something. With his missus acting up, perhaps he'd take her out again. She reached behind the till for the tube of cherryade lip gloss, opened her mouth wide as she used her little finger to spread the sticky stain across her lips. From the look of things, Jude might get divorced.

Chandelle twirled once on the scuffed lino, her hands caressing the imaginary drift and sway of a billowing white dress. In the bridal catalogue under her bed she had her favourites numbered once in order of preference and again in order of what she might be able to afford. Well, she could live in hope — but in the meantime, there was Mickey.

MIRI

She stepped out of the car into tepid air. It was dusk, and the sudden silence settled with a weight that made her stagger. Miri leaned against the flank of the car and looked up at the house, more dilapidated now than when she had last seen it. Some of the upstairs windows were lined with newspaper, and the balconies sagged under their load of iron lacework. *Havana Gardens.* The tin nameplate was still wired to the flaking front verandah. Locals had always called it 'the Cuban's place'. For all Miri knew, they still did.

For decades, the Kissacks had lived in clusters on streets named for minerals and metals. They were Anglo-Saxon miners, scalded and freckled, scabbed and blistered by the sun. Then one year her grandfather, Max Kissack, had come home from a world trip with a suitcase full of banknotes and a Cuban wife in tow. He'd won her in a card game, he said. It could have been true. Max was a professional gambler, good at winning. The woman's name was Esperanza. In photographs she had a snake of black hair draped over one shoulder, smudged charcoal eyes and a dancer's legs. One look at those legs and it was easy to imagine how the Kissack men had nudged Max in the ribs, how their sparrow wives had frowned and averted their eyes. Essie spoke no English, so what she made of the town and its inhabitants was anybody's guess.

The house stuck out in a place where anyone with money soon moved away. Set on the last block of residential land on the racecourse road before the Starlite Drive-in, it was the town's only extravagant mansion and a local landmark. Even before the building was finished, Max Kissack had hired a machine to push the red soil into dips and mounds then planted it with palms and creepers, tropical trees with pods and waxy flowers. With heavy watering, the mineral-rich soil soon produced an oasis where Esperanza, pregnant with twins, took siestas in a hammock slung between two young coconut palms.

Max and Essie were long gone, but their house, perched above the olive-green surface of the river, still overlooked a square more thickly planted and profligate with green than the town's War Memorial Park, or the beauty spots — funded by the mining companies — that were dotted along the river. In the waning light the garden was a dense mass, its edges spilling flowers. More than house or family, it was this memory of a leafy refuge that had drawn Miri back. At the hospital she had rehearsed running her hand along the black wrought-iron spokes of the fence; she had leaned on the gate, anticipating its protesting squeal. As a child she had taken the garden and her Auntie Con's struggle to water it for granted, but standing before it now it struck her as luxurious, an intoxicating, rustling, liquid presence, its fragrance spreading outwards in waves to merge with the scent of fish and mud and water that drifted up from the river.

That river smell. When she'd first left home it had nearly knocked her over every time she opened her suitcase. She'd overcompensated with patchouli oil and, later, when she had the money for it, French perfume. Now she felt it settling in her hair and clothing and the pores of her skin, an insistent swampy odour that she supposed still clung to every surface inside the house.

Miri walked up the steps and onto the verandah to peer through one of the panes of dimpled glass beside the front door.

'Anybody there?' she shouted, with her lips against the crack between door and doorframe. Her voice, thin and uncertain, echoed along the hallway and the feebleness of the sound was a shock. Perhaps she was barely visible, a haunting ghost or an alien blown off course. Behind her lay the garden with its swaying palms and papaya trees. She closed her eyes, visualising its root system. The trees and shrubs had roots like muscular arms, digging into the soil. Fern-like filaments of flower roots were delicate but strong as silk thread. The underground network was larger than the garden. It spread further, reached deeper. It had anchored the garden through hurricane-force storms, through seventy-five scorching summers and everything the desert had thrown at it.

Alice had played in the garden. In one shady corner it held a fig tree with her initials cut into the silvery bark.

Suddenly shaky, Miri hurried down the front steps and took the side path.

At the back of the house the flyscreen sagged open on its hinges, but the inner door was sealed tight. Maybe Auntie Con had made one of her rare trips to an out-of-town race meeting. Tears slipped down her cheeks. The sky was purple, streaked with clouds; the desert air carried a bite. Her Aunt Lois and Uncle Dig lived on the far side of the gardens, but if she knocked on their door they would ask questions. She would find somewhere else to stay the night.

Back in the car, she mopped her eyes. Then, turning to gaze up at the house, she saw that the weathervane, a flattened angel, still pointed resolutely east. She tipped back her head to stare at its secretive tin smile. The angel had always faced away from town towards the impossibly distant coast. Con said it was because the prevailing hot wind was from the western desert, but Miri had taken it as a sign not to linger and, at seventeen, had left with a guitar-playing hippy who had blown into town on his way to Sydney.

Warren Moore. He had called to collect her in a purple kombi, a deathtrap with a leaky radiator and a gearbox so sick it was a wonder they even made it to the Sydney turn-off. Miri shook her head; she had married and divorced Warren the following year and the angel had been watching for her two years later when she rolled back into town with Jack.

She had met Jack for the first time in Zaza's, a basement nightclub beneath a tattoo parlour on Oxford Street. Throughout the winter and spring of 1983 Miri worked part time at the club, and even when her modelling work began to pick up she was reluctant to quit. The dimness of the bar soothed her nerves after the popping flashguns of the photographic studio, or, less frequently, the casting director's indifferent stare. All these years later, she still remembered walking home in the early mornings, intoxicated by the knowledge that for the first time in her life she was anonymous. With anonymity came the feeling that she owned the city with its salt air, its constant sirens, its bedraggled back lanes and the bakery smells that mingled with the stale cigarette smoke of the night just ended and the fresh day nudging the horizon. Although she was always weary after her shift, she sucked in the humid air as if she could never absorb enough of the city's energy after the dust and lethargy of home.

Adele, the canny drag queen who owned Zaza's, had taken Miri under her wing. 'You've got to get out of this dungeon and find yourself a real job,' Adele said, as Miri cashed in her tips. 'Although Christ knows why I should be encouraging you to leave.' She circled Miri's wrist with her fingers, lifted it to the light to inspect the long fine bones of her hand, the perfect ovals of her nails.

Miri smiled at her boss's fluttering two-inch lashes as Adele finished counting the change and handed over a fifty-dollar note and a twenty from the till.

'Listen, Twiglet, leave the clearing-up and eat something,' she said. 'You're way too thin, even for a model girl.'

She had carried her plate of food to a table near the kitchen door. There were still three tables drinking in the bar, though they were slowing down. The women in the nearest group were dozy with drink, and the men, ties askew and shirts rumpled, sat jammed close to them on the velvet seats. The women were all blondes, their heads and necks and arms reflecting planes of ivory and pearl in the mirrored walls and ceiling. Their muted colouring made Miri feel over-vivid. (Years later, when she visited California with Jack, she would discover other women who looked the way she did; in California, the maids, the waitresses, the prostitutes, could have been her sisters. Jack acted as if he'd always known this, but the surprise lingered on her face in photographs taken months after they got back home.)

The night she met Jack, her black hair was swept up high on the back of her head and fell in a thick plait that brushed the base of her spine. Under the shaded lights her olive skin merged into the retro flocked wallpaper; the black lace shirt and miniskirt she wore disappeared behind the apron with *Zaza's* embroidered in lipstick pink across the pocket. In the mirrors, her eyes and mouth were blank with exhaustion, which gave her the look of a sleepwalker or drug addict. She eased off her high-heeled shoes under the table and stirred the congealing food. When a man at the furthest table stood up and moved towards her she waited for the usual slurred invitation, but he stood before her without swaying. 'Jack Passmore. I was at the audition this morning. It's a shame you didn't get the part, you were good.'

Audition. The morning seemed like decades ago, but yes, she remembered hurrying to get ready, light-headed from lack of sleep as she dabbed concealer under her eyes to mask the shadows. She had snagged her tights on the ripped vinyl of a chair in the waiting room when she stood up for her turn to enter the airless gymnasium where they were casting *A Streetcar Named Desire*. She remembered him now, a lanky figure hovering in the background with a camera.

'They said I was too young to carry off Blanche.'

Jack nodded. 'You'll be old enough before you know it.'

As he said this he smiled and lifted his chin, and a down light struck his eyes, making them shine.

After three months at Zaza's, she had a jaded view of customers, but this man's untidy black curls and direct blue gaze appealed to her. Or maybe she was just low because she hadn't got the part, and he was being kind about her talent. She smiled at him and fumbled with one foot for her shoes.

'All you need is a good agent,' Jack said, 'and it so happens that one of the best in Sydney is sitting at my table. I've just been urging him to sign you up.'

She was opening her mouth to say she never sat with customers when he slid a crisp business card onto the table.

'Whiley Marsden. Ring him during office hours,' he said.

Before she could reply, he was gone.

For the rest of the week she had looked for Jack in the club, but he didn't return. After the next unsuccessful audition she found the card in the bottom of her handbag and dialled the number. Whiley booked her for a rock music video with a young band called Snakebite. Jack Passmore was the cameraman. In the final cut, Miri discovered that fragments of her body — the long taut muscle of her inner thigh, the sole of her foot, an arc of skin that might have been an underarm or the hollow behind a knee — formed a fluid counterpoint to Snakebite's frantic rhythms and slamming guitars. As the mass of her hair unravelled against a wall of sound, Miri saw that Jack was gifted. She adored his work and from there it was only a short step to adoring Jack.

The first time he kissed her she felt like a child jumping into a swimming pool at the deep end, down down down, breathing suspended until she could go no further, until the world was erased by water, until her feet struck the bottom and kicked away, until the moment of fear when the surface seemed hopelessly distant and her lungs flattened beneath the weight of the water. And like a child, as soon as she broke the surface, drew breath and scrambled out, she could not wait to jump back in.

In the morning, Havana Gardens was still locked tight. Puzzled, Miri bit her bottom lip and stared up at the blank windows. In sunlight, last night's impression of gentle decay looked closer to dereliction, especially on the upper floor, where the bulk of a grapevine had partly collapsed the iron lacework of the balcony. Vine leaves and pendants of black grapes meandered over curls of flaking iron. The tin roof was held in place by a massive slab of sky. On the far side of the garden stood two small houses, jigsaws of corrugated iron and wood and the pressed tin that was the signature of the town. Miri gazed at their patched rooftops glinting between the trees. Despite the town's frontier swagger, she was struck by the fragility of its houses.

In the front yard of her uncle's house, a concrete pelican stood beside a birdbath on the frizzled tufts of grass that might once have been a lawn. A cane chair on the verandah had been warped by the sun, but the building was not as run-down as others Miri had seen, houses with patched fences and rotting car seats propped out front. She was about to knock at the screen door when her aunt, Lois, peered out. The fierce light defined pouches underneath her eyes and bounced off the pink sponge rollers in her hair. She wore a leopard-print satin dressing-gown and heels, and her toenails were painted the colour of smoke.

'God, you nearly gave me a heart attack!' Lois lurched forward to hug her. 'I haven't even got me face on yet!'

Miri had never thought of Lois Kissack as an aunt. She was something more exotic, more dangerous. Now, at sixty-three, she still had the figure of a young girl.

'You haven't put on an ounce, Lo,' Miri said.

'Well neither have you, doll!' Lois kissed her on the

cheek. 'You should of rung me that you were coming.' Her aunt waved towards the collapsing front steps. 'I'd like to say you could stop here, but we've lost a few rooms to the white ants.'

Miri shrugged. 'The caravan park had a cabin. I stayed there last night.'

Her aunt's kitchen opened out to a pergola from which hanging baskets dangled. Beyond the pergola lay the clothes line and a patch of shade under a lemon tree, where a blue heeler scratched among a scattering of beef bones. By the back gate, in a concrete and wire kennel, a black greyhound wagged its tail. Lois said, 'You've seen Con?'

'She's not home.'

Her aunt paused with her hand on the kettle. 'Didn't you know?' she said. 'Con's in hospital.'

'What?'

'Been there a week. Dig rang you, but he got the answer machine every time.' Lois shrugged. 'You know him. S'pose he never tried to leave a message.' She held the kettle to the tap. 'Con was fooling around with that old racehorse of hers, galloping out along the back straight. Fell and did her hip.'

'But she's going to be all right?'

Lois screwed her mouth into a pout. 'Ask me, you go galloping round on horseback at her age and you're begging for trouble. Anyhow, it's good to see you.'

When she had made tea, Lois took a key from a nail on the wall. 'This is Con's spare house key. Better look if your old room is still respectable. She wouldn't want you paying tourist prices up the caravan park.'

Miri cupped the key in her palm. When she had lived at Havana Gardens the house was never locked.

'Do they still call it the Cuban's house?'

'Not so much since Essie died.'

'At least it's still standing.'

'But falling around Con's ears. She won't repair any-thing. Still pours every penny into watering the garden.' Lois pushed a mug across the table. 'Lately she's been pestering the council to give her the water for nothing. Claims it's a tourist attraction.'

'Are they going to?'

'Not last I heard. When the council bloke came around all the gates were locked. Con went through a spell of padlocking after some kids from the river flats ringbarked a couple of trees.'

'So how's she pay for it?'

Lois laughed. 'A few years back there was a racing scam. A friend in Melbourne would phone with the race results before they were broadcast here, and Con'd be hot on the phone to her bookie. Small bets, nothing flashy, but the winnings kept her in tap-water.'

Miri made a face. It was the sort of deal her aunt would pull without a second thought.

'Thing is,' Lois said, 'the local station's had an overhaul, so there's no delay between the racing and the broadcast. Con's water fund has dried up, but Dig says she's run illegal piping down to the river and siphons at night.'

Lois Kissack reached up and plucked a curler from the front of her head, leaving a spring roll of bleached hair.

'And how's Jack?'

It caught Miri by surprise, but of course they would want to know about Jack. 'Oh, Jack's fine.' She picked up the mug of tea and pressed it between both hands to keep them steady. It was difficult to breathe. 'Busy, you know.'

'His film was on a while ago. I saw it twice.'

Jack's feature film was about teenagers adrift on a drug-spiked Gold Coast. It contained scenes that had made Miri blush when she first saw them on the big screen. For Lois to sit through it twice in the company of others was an act of devotion. Lois had met Jack a few times during his bohemian artist phase: Panama hat, crumpled linen jacket, floppy silk scarf. Lois adored style, and Jack had always had enough to go around.

'It's been nominated for a prize,' Miri said.

'Violent, but that's how life is these days. Jack should win.'

'He probably will.'

As soon as she could, Miri made a tentative move towards the door, anxious to escape before Lois moved from Jack to Alice. Her aunt followed her down the hall, tottering a little on her heels.

At the front door Lois captured Miri's face between her hands. 'You look so washed-out, honey, you okay?'

'It was a long drive.'

Lois let her go with a pat on the shoulder. 'And I hit you out of the blue with bad news. Dig should of left a message about Con. Maybe Jack would of come with you, done the driving.'

Miri forced a smile. 'Visiting hours still the same up at the hospital?'

Lois nodded. 'You're a class act, doll,' she said. 'Nobody round here dresses well anymore. It's disgusting.'

As her aunt fussed around her it occurred to Miri that until she broke the news about Alice, until she made it definite, Lois would continue to believe that there was a hazy point just over the horizon where Alice lived and breathed.

When she thought of Alice unexpectedly, Miri saw a girl with a flesh-coloured lace slip worn over a tie-dyed dress.

A girl with string-thin legs thrust into heavy boots. This Alice wore black and green striped stockings and a violin case lay open at her feet. Her hair was not yet black but a burnished cherry that made her bronze eyes greener, her brows more emphatic. When Alice settled the violin against her shoulder it pushed forward a small double chin; there was enough flesh for that. On the neck of the instrument, Alice's fingers were long, her nails bitten. The sun printed her shadow onto smooth white tiles. The pattern of the tiles reminded Miri that this image came from a photograph taken during Alice's last summer at high school.

She'd found the print in a drawer after Alice moved out and had tucked it into the frame of the dressing-table mirror, a snapshot of a woman-child with sleep-dazed eyes, a chrysalis. The picture had the diffused flicker of an early calotype. Entering the past at this point, there was the possibility of change. Everything could be different, it was only a question of effort, and all the broken china could be mended.

In the end she slid the picture between the pages of a book plucked at random from the bookcase, hoping that by the time she rediscovered it the picture would have altered, or Alice would. Because this Alice, who effortlessly extracted *Spanish Dance in E Minor* from a violin, felt less like a girl photographed in sunlight, more like something ineffable and precious that had preferred to flee their marriage.

Miri fitted the key into the lock. Blisters of blue paint flaked onto her hand as she pushed the front door open and swung her suitcase over the threshold. It was almost a surprise to find the hall empty. In the old days, Havana Gardens had been full of hungry ghosts, strangers who drifted in and camped in the upstairs bedrooms. Miri was used to brushing past unknown women on the stairs, or finding them spooning porridge into their children as they smoked hand-rolled cigarettes in the kitchen. There were regulars, women whose names and habits she got to know over frequent visits. Others would arrive in the night lugging a suitcase or clutching a swaddled baby, only to be gone by morning.

'Why do they have to come *here*?' she'd moaned once when a rowdy batch of kids was making life uncomfortable.

'Where else is there?' Con had said.

It had started back when Max Kissack was shot dead at a two-up game and his young widow, cast adrift, began to take in lodgers. They were mostly girls, a few of them hard cases who had nowhere to go and didn't want to get up early in the mornings or work in the hot afternoons. Gradually, Havana Gardens had become a place men drifted to on pay nights. Grandma Essie was dead by the time Miri went to school, but the house had gained an unsavoury reputation that persisted. Older kids said puzzling things, and the ones whose mothers went to church never invited her home to play. Even when she was old enough to understand, Miri hadn't wanted to ask Con about it, but had tackled Lois instead. Lois was straightforward as always.

'I think money changed hands quite often, if that's what you're getting at,' she said.

'You mean it was a brothel!'

Lois had shrugged and pursed her lips. 'Not as such,' she said. 'No, I'd say it was more a place of consolation. And sometimes that consolation resulted in cash and sometimes it didn't.'

'Was my mother one of them?'

'One of what?'

'You know, one of the sort who turned consolation into cash?'

Lois had howled with laughter. 'Of course not.'

Later, Miri came to understand that the women arrived at Havana Gardens via a string of bad decisions. They gravitated towards disaster. After Warren, she had decided to pay attention to that tendency in herself, like she had some say-so in the matter. Now, she saw the women had been battlers, doing their best to dodge the debris of their lives, and was stunned to find she had become one of them.

Sunlight pierced the wide hall and illuminated a fine red dust on every surface. Even when she lived here as a child the mouldings were coated; Con declared she had better things to do than brush the outback off skirting boards. Halfway along was the curtained alcove under the stairs where she had rocked her dolls, out of sight and mind, a witness to the arrivals and departures, the sobs and whispered confidences, the confrontations that erupted when men came looking for their women. She stroked the rotting velvet, remembering the cupboards packed with surprising jumble, lurid dresses Grandma Essie had brought from Cuba with their dank fruity smell, the scent of books with yellowing pages and the endless sticky jars and bottles, veterinary remedies for Con's dogs and horses.

In a niche at the foot of the stairs stood a statue with peach-coloured cheeks and faded blue eyes, one of the saints brought by her grandmother from Cuba. Its chipped pink smile was demure, its palms open and facing upward as if seeking a blessing. Miri wrinkled her nose at the scuffed skirting and the threadbare runner on the stairs. With her hand on the banister she peered up into the well of the staircase. The heart of the house was as dark as it had always been, a warm conspiratorial dark.

Miri hoisted her suitcase and climbed to the first floor landing.

The rooms she poked her head into were dusty and neglected, the air so stale and thick she could have stirred it with a stick. Windowpanes were clouded so that the landscape appeared at a distance, pale and indistinct. She felt the tightness she had carried in her chest all the way from Sydney ease fractionally. These frosted windows erased the world, or at least held it at arm's length, and just at this moment distance was what she needed.

MIRI

She woke in the night to the sound of a baby crying. Half past three, hot and still. Perhaps the crying belonged to her dreams. That, or a hungry ghost was making its presence felt. Havana Gardens ticked and groaned, its roof and floors improvising a symphony of tin and wood. She was in her mother's old bedroom overlooking the gardens, a room where lumpy tub chairs and a mottled swing mirror that had once belonged to Grandma Essie cluttered the corners. She had chosen this room rather than her own out of yearning for a time when she had climbed in beside her mother in the night. It was strange to be a grown woman and feel this way. She switched on the bedside lamp, casting a circle of light over the sheet, and touched a finger to the shade's bobbled trim. It was possible Con had never even opened the door of this room since Candela died, but the comfort Miri craved, the memory of warmth and her mother's familiar body, had evaporated.

She frowned and reached for her cigarettes on the

bedside table, but before she could light up, the crying resumed. It sounded close. The protesting squall of a young baby. Three coughs and a stretched cry, then a pause as tiny lungs gathered wind. Miri flung back the sheet and padded over to the window. Beyond the gardens, Lois's windows were unlit. If anyone was nursing a colicky baby they were doing it in the dark. She was about to climb back into bed when a new wail seemed to come through the ceiling.

Miri crossed the hall to her old room and felt for the lamp inside the door. The room looked gloomy, as if the bulb was weak or the electric current not strong enough. She stared at the bedclothes thrown back on the single bed; perhaps she had left it that way twenty years earlier. The house was silent again. Miri frowned at the plaster rose in the centre of the ceiling. It was almost four and she wondered if Jack was asleep now. Wondered where, and if he was alone.

Jack Passmore was famously impatient. It was the first thing that struck Miri, the ardent whoosh of his enthusiasm like a skyrocket leaving the bottle. His mother dying when he was seven had left him needy, he said. Miri understood the charged space left by dead mothers. She and Jack had been lovers for months, but on their honeymoon they were only halfway to the south coast when he swerved off the road at Bird's Hotel and tugged her from the car. Ignoring the landlord's knowing smirk, Jack paid in cash and led her along a corridor to a room the colour of custard, where, despite the thudding heat, goose pimples rose on her arms as he unzipped her dress and propelled her towards the bed.

They had stayed in the shabby hotel room until they could no longer face the room service menu of greasy burgers and steak sandwiches. By the time they reached the coast, Alice was already tucked into a fold of Miri's body, a fragile shoot, something the size of a lupin seed or a tiny mung bean, unfolding in the dark.

Jack was eating strawberries and cream when Miri told him. They were back in Sydney in a bistro by the water, surrounded by laughter and popping champagne corks. She patted strawberry juice from her lips with a linen napkin. Over Jack's shoulder she could see herself reflected in a mirror, her face calm, radiant. She couldn't understand why he hadn't noticed.

'Guess what?' she said.

Jack paused, a spoonful of strawberries raised halfway to his mouth.

'What?'

She smiled. 'I'm pregnant.'

His face dropped. He lowered the spoon. 'Are you sure?' he said. Just that. No spontaneous pleasure, no flush of pride, just feeling for the bottom line. Seconds later, he tried to gloss over his lack of enthusiasm with glib remarks, but Miri had read all she needed to know from that first flat look. Afterwards, she would wonder why she hadn't realised that Jack's plans had never included children.

A week before her due date, Jack had left for New Zealand, promising to return in time for the birth. 'Two, maybe three days. Keep your knees crossed,' he'd said.

But three days stretched to five, and Alice arrived early. Miri endured her twelve-hour labour, cursing Jack between contractions, but as soon as it was over she knew she could do it all again. From the moment she clapped eyes on her daughter's crumpled face Miri understood that Alice was the good true part of their marriage. The intensity of maternal love rocked her.

She was still dazed when Jack turned up. As he kissed

her, Miri saw him reaching into his jacket pocket for the light meter. Jack's photographs of Alice's newborn hands and feet were the catalyst for a rash of pregnancies among women of their acquaintance. But four days after Miri left the hospital he had dragged her to a film company dinner, where she sat wedged uncomfortably close to strangers with her breasts tingling and leaking and a high-pitched whine of anxiety in her head.

Havana Gardens swarmed with unseen spirits: her mother, her aunt, herself in happier days. It was a long walk down the hall in the dark, and as her fingers pulled the light cord Miri stumbled into the stair rail and scraped her shin. The pain made her cry out, and she sank onto a step and rubbed the skin, tempted to give in to full-blown sobbing. Instead, she fixed her eyes on a row of framed photographs on the wall above her head. They showed the river in flood, limpid water and sky with a tiny strip of shoreline. Her mother had taken the pictures on an old Box Brownie. All sky and sticks, faded, they looked almost like modern art.

Miri went downstairs, hearing her own breath, feeling her way through the lower hall. The stale biscuit scent of the kitchen nearly knocked her over as she pushed open the door.

She stood blinking under the yellow kitchen light, then froze as the pantry door swung open.

A woman stood in the doorway.

Miri jumped as if she'd been stung.

The woman was small and freckled with red hair that drifted about her shoulders and fell to a point near the waist of her pyjama pants.

'I was going to wait till morning to introduce myself, but I guess you heard Opal.'

Miri's breath eased out of her, disbelief and relief mingled.

'Opal would be the baby?'

The woman nodded. 'I'm Suzette Moran,' she said. 'Everyone calls me Zett.' Her wide grin rearranged the delicate freckles around her mouth. 'And you'll be Miriam Kissack.'

'Have we met?'

'I stayed here once as a kid, but there were mobs of us, you know? You won't remember. Con showed me your photo, though. She said you're in the movies.'

'You've been staying with my aunt.'

Zett shook her head. 'Not exactly,' she said. 'Your auntie'd already gone to hospital, but I knew she wouldn't mind me and Opal stopping here for a bit. She was always good in the past.'

Miri moved to the sink and filled the kettle. She knew now where the crying came from. 'That attic room will be roasting,' she said.

Zett smiled and shrugged. 'We're used to doing without aircon, and there's a fan in the dining room if Opal gets too hot. The best thing is the attic staircase. No-one would find it unless they knew where to look.'

The east bedroom was a lost jigsaw piece, its entrance easy to overlook among the maze of hallways on the top floor. At first glance the attic entrance appeared to be a broom cupboard. Miri wondered who this elfin woman was hiding from.

She flicked on the kettle. 'Are you avoiding anyone in particular?'

Zett Moran's smile faded. 'My old man Jude is the local chief copper, so I guess you could say I'm hiding from the whole bloody New South Wales police force.'

Later, they sat on the uneven floor of the attic with their

backs against a red plush sofa that had been underneath the tiny single window since the days when Miri had bagged the room as a den, defending her privacy with booby traps and trip-wires on the stairs. Zett had made the attic comfortable by raiding some of the unused rooms for furniture. The walls were a raw-plaster pink, all the more faded against the richness of the Persian rug spread across the floorboards. Miri watched Zett rock Opal in her lap as the night at the window grew less dense.

She poked a tuft of horsehair back into a wound in the sofa. 'The springs are sticking through,' she said.

'I've slept on worse.' Zett sucked on a cigarette and blew the smoke away from the baby.

The sofa was so big it must have been built in the room, or squeezed upstairs in pieces and then assembled. Miri ran a thumb along the frayed arm. 'I used it as a trampoline,' she said. 'I'd have gone easy if I'd known.'

Zett shrugged. 'Opal loves to snuggle down next to me. At home she has to sleep in her own room.'

Miri wanted to ask if Opal was hiding from the police too, or if it was just Zett. She looked at the woman's hands. They were freckled and soft, but capable looking, and it occurred to her that maybe this fragile woman had slit somebody's throat, or worse. But if she was bad news, Con wouldn't have given her refuge.

'Hey, have a look at this.' Zett up-ended a small red leather handbag on the carpet and from the contents picked a pot of eye shadow. 'What do you think?' she said, lowering her eyelids for Miri's inspection. 'My sister sent it from Surfers. It's got flakes of real gold.'

'It suits you,' Miri said.

'Yeah,' she giggled, 'all brass and no class. Time to start a new life.'

'I know that feeling,' Miri said.

'Yeah?'

Miri nodded and traced with her fingertip the paisley shape in the border of the carpet.

Zett said, 'From that picture Con showed me, I'd have said your life was perfect.'

'Pictures lie,' Miri said.

To her relief, Zett changed the subject by starting in on the town.

'It's where everyone comes who has failed. All the losers, the perverts, the no-hopers waiting to latch onto something or someone. This place is an ashtray,' she said. 'You want to watch yourself.'

'I'll bear it in mind,' Miri said.

Zett ground out her cigarette and eased a new one from the packet. The room was filled with smoke, and Miri's eyes and throat began to ache.

'Nothing makes me happy anymore, 'cept for Opal.' Zett stroked the child's cheek. 'I hate to ask, but you never heard of us if anyone comes looking, right?'

'You mean the police?'

Zett nodded, chewing at her thumbnail. 'Sooner or later someone will knock on the door. Jude can't stand losing. He'll be going apeshit right now.' Her voice, with its husky tone, was brave, tough even, but her eyes were fearful. She gathered the baby into her arms. 'We'll be going to Adelaide the day after tomorrow, I hope.' She brushed her lips against the golden fuzz of Opal's hair. 'A mate of mine is finishing a fencing contract and then he's coming to pick us up.'

Miri had been studying the baby's waxy eyelids and the moist pink circle of her mouth. 'What will your husband do if he finds you?'

Zett turned and tucked Opal into a corner of the sofa. When the baby was settled she straightened and looked over her shoulder at Miri as if wondering how much to tell. After a moment she reached down and peeled up the front of her T-shirt.

'Finish this, I reckon, or maybe worse.' Her torso was mottled with bruises, some fresh and livid, other older hurts fading to a limey yellow and disappearing under the edges of her bra. 'I'm not saying I didn't deserve some of it. Sometimes I say things just to piss him off, and one time I got a couple of broken bones for my trouble. But look!' She lifted the singlet from Opal's chest and the two of them stared down at a single butterfly-shaped bruise. 'Jude reckons it was an accident. Opal was falling and he had to grab her. Reckons he must have held her too tight. Accident my arse! Jude always marks where it won't show.'

Looking at the purple flowering on the tiny chest, Miri felt sick.

'There are laws . . .' she said.

Zett eased the baby's singlet down. 'Survival is the only law that operates round here.' She turned her candid green gaze on Miri. 'Opal 'n' I have to skedaddle, you know? I mean, what else can you do when the bloke who's supposed to protect you is the bugger you need protection from?'

MIRI

Light pooled on the polished linoleum floors so that Miri felt afloat on the broad green corridors of the hospital. The wards, with their floral-curtained bays and the dry chemical smell that was a mask for something more organic and rotten, seemed unchanged since childhood, when her mother had been the patient.

'Your aunt is asleep,' a nurse told her. 'But she dozes on and off, so just go in and wait.'

Miri slid onto a plastic chair beside the bed. On the pillow Con's plait lay like a short dark taproot attached to the bulb of her head. White hair in the centre parting made the dyed hair appear detached from the paler scalp, and it was this half-inch of regrowth, rather than her surroundings, which made Miri realise she had stayed away too long. While she had been gone, her tough energetic aunt had been transformed into an old woman, perhaps not so much by the accident as by its aftermath of inactivity. Con had always despised idleness.

Under the sheet, her aunt's chest softly rose and fell. Even in sleep she exuded determination. If Connie Kissack had wanted to keep a horse and ride it, no-one could have stopped her. Miri saw that now, at almost seventy, Con's high cheekbones and finely moulded eyes — of which her own and Alice's were a tracing — were barely lined. The Hispanic beauty handed down by her Cuban grandmother was a valuable legacy, but with Alice gone the genes would peter out. Essie had cut the pattern for all of them. Her twins, Candela and Consuela, had inherited her elongated thighs and dancer's ankles, her olive skin and smoky colouring. Candela had passed the Mendez looks to Miri and she, in turn, had handed them on to Alice. Even the way the Kissack women moved was somehow a rhythm from a place she knew Con could barely have located on a map. Jack claimed Miri had hypnotised him with the Mendez walk, like the first steps of a dance that never quite materialised.

Over the years, Miri thought bitterly, Jack had put her walk to good use. His clip of her climbing a staircase in stiletto heels — ankles criss-crossed by snakeskin straps and silver chains — sold thousands of pairs of shoes. Jack judged people by what they could sell, and along with snakeskin shoes Miri could sell musky perfumes and beaten silver, she could sell cigars and chocolate, and she had lost count of the foreign cars she'd sold for Jack, the bottles of lethal dark liqueurs.

Con opened her eyes and stared at Miri for a long time without blinking. 'I've been dreaming,' she said, 'such a complicated dream.'

Miri's smile was crooked. 'I only wish that I could say the same, Con.'

The muscles and tendons in her throat and face ached; something elastic inside her was about to snap. She toppled forward to lay her cheek against the bed's starched sheet. Perhaps after all she would not be able to hold up.

Con stroked Miri's hair. 'So,' she said, 'you've come home.'

Miri registered with a tremor that her aunt assumed she was back for good. Until that moment she hadn't known she planned to stay, but now it seemed obvious. She might hate the town, but home wasn't a place you could choose any more than you could choose your parents or the colour of your eyes. She had called Sydney home for twenty years, but it still felt foreign, still let her know she was an outsider.

'How are you?' Miri asked.

Con's voice was pitched low as if someone might overhear them. 'Bored to death,' she said. 'But don't fuss about the hip because it's nothing that can't be mended. Tell me about Alice.'

There was a silence, which, to Miri, seemed to stretch to Sydney and back as the warmth of Con's hand spread across her scalp. At St Vincent's Hospital, the bereavement counsellor had talked about the phases of loss, but she had not thought to lay her hands on Miri's hair as her aunt was doing. The laying on of hands. Con was a believer in ancient cures.

Miri struggled to control her voice, but only managed a series of incoherent sounds.

Her aunt sighed. 'You've lost her then,' she said. 'I thought so.'

There was another long silence, out of which Miri finally said in a small muffled voice, 'How did you know?'

Con's finger and thumb squeezed Miri's earlobe. 'On Alice's birthday, a magpie appeared in the gardens. You remember that patch of grass beside the lavender hedge where Alice sat and read her magazines?'

It was during their last visit, when Alice was thirteen. Con had prised her from the pages of her teen magazines to go horse riding. Miri sat up and looked at her aunt.

'The magpie wouldn't be shooed away. It hung around day after day, cocking its head at me. *One for sorrow*, the saying goes.' Con opened her hands and spread them wide. 'Then, you didn't send me a birthday picture, like always. So I put the two together. Something bad had happened to Alice. The details weren't so important.'

'I should have rung. I just couldn't bear . . .' Tears welled in Miri's eyes, and she leaned forward and put her cheek to the sheet again, grateful for the sensation of cleanliness and order offered by the crisply starched surface. If only she could stay like this, suspended between the smooth white sheet and the warmth of Con's hand.

Con said, 'It's times like this I'm thankful Candy isn't here. Of course, there was a magpie for your mother, too. Don't you remember it pecking at her bedroom window, watching its reflection in the glass, preening its evil self?'

The weight of feathered bodies flapped around Miri's losses.

She shook her head. 'I don't remember any bird.'

Had there been a bird? Con believed her premonitions and omens came from her mother, Esperanza. They had been arriving in a constant stream, foretelling troubles large and small, for as long as Miri could remember. Hadn't Essie's own mother communicated with her all the way from Cuba? And wasn't Cuba further from Havana Gardens than anywhere on earth? Compared to the distance between Cuba and Australia, the transmission of an omen from heaven to Havana Gardens was nearly negligible, according to Con.

'You were only little. Probably I didn't point it out, so as not to frighten you,' Con said. 'Anyway, the magpie came for Alice this time, though not the same bird. I shot the one that came about your mother.'

What link could possibly exist between a sharp-beaked bird appearing in a garden and the death of a girl who had not visited that garden in years? Miri sat up and blotted her cheeks with the backs of her hands. She badly wanted a cigarette, and a physical pain she had been ignoring all morning now registered as hunger. When had she last eaten? Con was waiting, her eyebrows raised and pushing wrinkles of concern into her forehead, but Miri had no idea where to begin about Alice.

The flat Alice had moved to was on the second floor of a run-down terrace in Glebe. On Miri's first visit she unfolded the scrap of paper and checked the address, pressed the security buzzer at the front door while children shrieked in the playground of a primary school along the street. The double espresso she had drunk in a cafe on Glebe Point Road had left her wired. She checked her wristwatch and buzzed again, and this time the front door clicked open into an entrance hall painted a chipped emerald with matt black skirtings. Miri climbed two flights of stairs and found the flat's door ajar. Didn't these girls ever ask who was calling? She could have been anyone.

Alice stood with her back against the window that overlooked the street. Sunlight backlit tendrils of hair and the handkerchief points of her black chiffon dress.

'Hi,' she said.

Miri looked around at the rumpled divans with their batik throws, at the charcoal sketches thumbtacked to the walls and the overflowing ashtrays, as she struggled for calmness against the caffeine circulating in her system. The long bones of Alice's arms and legs were solid spindles, X-rayed against the light-box of the window. Miri blinked. Her daughter was almost transparent.

'I have to drop off some pictures near here, so . . .'

'More airbrushed publicity shots?' Alice said.

Miri flushed with annoyance. 'Some photographs I took. They're going to be in an exhibition.'

Alice's head nodded on the poppy stem of her neck. 'Cool,' she said. 'You should do more of that.'

Miri picked up a pen and wash portrait from the coffee table. 'I hope to,' she said. 'Is this one of yours?' The head and shoulders study showed a young man with Asian eyes and straight black hair gathered in a loose ponytail.

'Jessica's. She was up all night sorting out her portfolio. She must have decided against that one.'

'I saw a cafe up the street if you've got time for lunch.'

As Alice turned towards the window her eyes were vague. Traffic moved in slow motion on the street below. The net curtain billowed in a draught that set a billion dust motes flickering around her slender body.

'If you want,' she said, without enthusiasm, 'but I'm not that hungry.'

Miri left the package of photographs beside her chair and led the way downstairs. The cafe was a hundred yards away on the opposite side of the street. Alice's black skirt swirled about her knees and her jewellery jangled as they crossed the road.

'This is the place,' Miri said.

They sat at a pavement table and she handed Alice a menu.

'I said I wasn't hungry.'

'They do great mango sorbet.'

'I know, but I'm not hungry.'

'You don't have to be hungry to eat sorbet.'

Alice said, 'I'll have a Diet Coke.'

Miri ordered a salad sandwich and two Cokes, and they sat in silence staring at the traffic. How did conversation get to be so difficult, she wondered. When the food arrived, the layers of the sandwich were held together with a wooden skewer, and the plate was piled with chips and a pyramid of salad. It was more food than Miri had ordered at lunch for years. Alice reached over and picked a chip from the plate.

Miri stood. 'I need to wash my hands.'

When she returned she checked the pile of chips, but it was hard to tell if it was any smaller.

She cut the sandwich up the middle. 'Take some,' she said.

Silver bracelets clanked as her daughter flipped the lid from the sandwich and poked at the filling. Sparkling particles clung to the razor edge of Alice's collarbone. It was a struggle for Miri not to plead.

'So where's this gallery that's showing your pictures?' Alice said.

'Paddington.'

Alice poked a shred of lettuce into her mouth. 'Not exactly next door.'

Miri took her time eating a slice of cucumber as Alice picked up another chip. 'No, but I wanted to see you,' she said. 'How's uni?'

Alice dropped the chip on the plate and leaned back in the chair. 'The usual,' she said. 'You know, bitching classmates, groping tutors, that kind of thing. Look, I just took a couple of days off. I've been feeling under the weather, okay?'

Miri glanced uncertainly at her daughter. 'But you are going back, right?'

'Going back, oh yeah.' A closed looked settled in Alice's eyes.

Alice could be stubborn and self-contained. She could go a week without speaking, not a single word, not even yes or no, if pushed. Miri looked away along the street to where a group of women were talking outside the school gates. She suppressed a sigh: small children, small problems.

When she had done her best with the food and paid the bill, Miri walked back to the flat with Alice to collect her photographs. As she picked them up she saw, on a low table between a stack of CDs and a dirty ashtray, Alice's violin. A hole had been drilled in the body and a silver jack plug jutted from it, joining the instrument, by a snake of pink fluorescent lead, to a black box on the floor.

Miri said, 'You've gone electric.'

'What?'

She pointed at the violin.

'Oh, that. I've started doing some gigs with this acid croft band.'

'Was it really necessary to drill?' Miri knew her anger to be futile but was unable to retreat. 'Surely drilling a hole in the body has ruined its value, maybe even the acoustic tone.'

Alice's eyes widened. Her voice was tight, exasperated. 'I'm sorry, I thought it was *my* violin. I thought you *gave* it to me.'

Miri stared at her daughter's pinched face. 'Alice, what's happened?' she said.

Alice stood motionless.

'You're not eating. That's why you feel unwell.'

'I *am* eating. That's not why.'

'Then what?'

'Nothing. I'm fine.'

'You're too thin.'

'Look, why did you come all the way over here just to pick on me?'

'I'm not picking,' Miri said, eyeing Alice's fragile wrists, 'but if you feel unwell you ought to see a doctor.'

Alice was silent for another long moment, then raised her chin and looked straight at Miri with the black kohl melting from the lower rims of her eyes onto her cheeks. 'But I am seeing a doctor. Your shrink friend, Laura Petit. I asked her to send the bill to Dad.'

Turning from the hospital towards the main street, Miri kept an eye out hoping for a vacant cab, but none came by. For reasons that were now beyond her she had walked from the house to the hospital and had not even thought to wear a hat. While she had sat with Con, the day had heated up, and she wished now that she had brought the car. After ten minutes she reached the intersection of Galena and Main, where a wounded soldier on a pedestal gamely held his bronze rifle aloft. Miri skirted the statue and looked along the main street. Halfway down the block, a bus idled at the kerb; a crowd was gathered on the footpath, and beyond that she saw a couple of taxis parked in the shade of a jacaranda tree. As she moved towards them, a woman passed her, grinning.

'Someone's been chucked off the bus.'

There were hoots and whistles, and through a network of legs and shopping bags she glimpsed a figure crouched beside the front wheel of the bus. Miri hesitated. Fights here sometimes escalated from fists to guns. The sun thumped at her shoulders, and the pavement was gritty. To reach the taxi rank she would have to skirt this commotion by the bus.

Reluctantly, Miri edged closer. The bus stood with its engine chugging, and beside it she saw the bloated figure of the driver.

She hadn't forgotten Mervyn. At primary school he had been a bully in the playground and, judging by his belligerent expression, nothing had changed.

The figure on the ground was kneeling just as she had first seen him by the roadside, only this time in the stained concrete gutter. A cut beside his right eye dripped blood, and he was shaking his head in a slow, dazed way. Perhaps Mervyn had punched him, or he might have fallen from the bus and struck his head, but the body language of the onlookers told Miri this was a violent confrontation rather than an accident.

She saw that his trousers were too heavy for the time of year and peppered with holes, the bottom half of some charity shop suit by the look of it. His arms jutted from the sleeves of a T-shirt, dark and wiry. Compared to the Anglo-Saxon faces in the crowd his face was fine-boned and foreign-looking. He reminded Miri of a stray dog: underfed, experienced at dodging stray boots.

'So, you gunna say sorry?' Mervyn flexed his shoulders and squeezed meaty hands into fists. Four pencil-widths of fat rippled up the back of his shaved skull.

The man gazed up at the people on the pavement as if they were not quite in focus. A big sun-dried woman in a straw hat smirked at the bus driver. 'Cat's got 'is tongue, Merv,' she said.

'Probably doesn't speak the lingo,' shouted someone else, 'by the look've him.'

Mervyn's eyes were mean as he wiped his nose with a

finger and scanned the crowd. 'It's a nasty wog,' he said. 'A real grubby little grill.'

What first struck Miri about the onlookers was their apathy. But then, studying the blunt faces, she recognised here and there a spark of willingness to go along with whatever brutal act was about to unfold. Perhaps bloodshed even seemed somehow authorised, as if the bus driver's malevolence had behind it the authority of his Department of Transport uniform.

'Gets on my bus without a ticket,' Mervyn growled. 'Least he can say's please.' A smile hovered at the corners of his mouth.

'Fair go, Merv, he would've had a ticket if you'd handed it over!' It was a man's voice, fretful and nervous.

Mervyn swivelled to see who it was, but the speaker edged out of sight at the back of the crowd.

The woman with the straw hat grinned. 'I'd say sorry if I was you, mate, else Merv'll have your balls for bhajis.' She folded her arms and backed her neck into a double chin, pleased with herself.

But the man kneeling in front of them swayed gently as if to music. His mouth was dry and cracked, but the top lip had a delicate line and tilted corners that gave the lower half of his face an almost feminine beauty.

Miri's jaw tightened. The town had never tolerated softness; it might have been nothing more than the slant of his smile that had kindled the bus driver's fury. She edged forward until she stood poised on the kerb. The top of the man's bowed head, dust-coated, made her want to pick him up and brush him down, but, at the same time, the urge to disappear before she got involved was overwhelming. Along the length of the street the afternoon had drained to a painful glitter, while around her the crowd shifted restlessly, a smeary mass of colour.

So he had ridden in her car for an hour – the man on the ground was still a total stranger. No-one could blame her for walking away. From the distant mine, a siren blast signalled the end of a shift. Miri raised her chin. She was turning to go when he suddenly looked up. He was not quite present, she saw, perhaps a touch delirious or suffering from sunstroke. Certainly, he was disoriented, but his eyes warmed with recognition as they settled on her.

AZIZ

He sensed rather than saw the blur of the arm arcing towards him, heard the driver shout, 'Hey!'

The coins he had handed over for the fare struck Aziz's chest and bounced away into the gutter. Heads ducked in reflex as people fell back and then surged forward. He sensed the tautness of the crowd, like a cordon surrounding him, as the driver circled. At other times, in other places, when he had expected to meet his death at any moment, terror had sharpened his senses until his eyes became a camera. He was in trouble now, but he did not expect to die. The fat man might inflict a beating and the onlookers, with their squinting speculative eyes, might join in, but he did not believe they would kill him.

He braced his body to absorb a blow, was struggling to focus, when the woman who had stopped for him in the desert stepped down off the pavement. Her eyes were still empty-looking, but her mouth was tight as she slipped between him and the bus driver.

'Leave him alone.'

Her words stood stiff as a fence, shutting out the fat man.

He saw the driver's eyes bulge as he turned towards the woman.

'Well, haven't we got ourselves a little Care Bear!'

Aziz felt himself drifting. It had been two days since she had stopped her motorcar and saved him, and in that time he had explored the town: its centre and also its unlovely outer edges. But the surfaces of the town would not absorb him, so when the bus with grey plush seats had pulled in beside him the coins were in his hand for the ticket. Then the fat man had begun to shout and push him backwards down the steps. He could not tell what the fat man wanted, but he was familiar with unfocused loathing. Sometimes he felt the same swill of bile in his own gut towards people who were unlike himself, which was everyone in this forsaken desert. He scanned the crowd, not lingering on faces; their mouths made shapes, but he could not grasp what these stiff pale people were saying, what they expected.

Silence. As a child he had chattered until his mother laughed and clapped her hands. 'Peace, Aziz! Just for one moment,' she would cry.

Now, adrift among strangers, he had been silenced indefinitely.

The woman bent and retrieved his coins, wiped the dust from them with the hem of her shirt and pushed them into his hand. 'Here,' she said, as she closed his fingers over the money.

He swayed at her touch, about to faint, and at this moment of weakness came a flash of those in the camp who had sewed their lips. The ugliness of their mute deaths surged through him. Since his escape, he had counted the days of their suffering. Perhaps he should have joined them. His tongue flapped like parchment in his mouth. The sun lapped his ears, and the pattern of red staining the gutter in front of him polarised and turned turquoise. He clasped this blessed colour with a swooning sigh. For Aziz, the colour turquoise billowed with the smoke of fresh kebabs. The resonance of turquoise released a flurry of doves, scraps of purest white that formed erratic, shifting patterns above the dome of the mosque.

His lip split as he smiled, and the blood moistened his tongue. The bus driver moved closer. There were mutterings in the crowd. Remembered sounds rattled in his head: whispered blessings, the clink of coins, prayers that passed over him with the ease of water over stones, the hubbub of the market. His uncle had once traded from a market stall. Aziz stared at the ground, remembering his uncle Faisal, busy with a customer.

Again the fat man spoke, but it was more important to remember the mad patchwork of the bazaar with its stalls of goods, glorious in their usefulness — lengths of string, batteries, soap, spectacles and other humble necessities — so unlike the glittering waste piled in the plate glass windows of western stores.

The shop of his uncle had been a shawl spread on the pavement. Sometimes there were second-hand socks for sale, or shoes, or a round loaf of bread. Sometimes bowls of hard-boiled eggs marbled with spices, bags of chickpeas and rice, or the herbs and roots that Aziz could still name but whose flavours were beginning to elude him. It was the same with memories of his family. Names and faces were clear, but voices, the sound of their laughter, ebbed with every day that passed.

There was pushing and shoving at the edge of the crowd, then a young woman in a baseball cap held out a bottle of water.

The woman from the car supported him while he drank. Beside them, the driver cleared his throat, shifted his weight onto the balls of his feet as he looked for a way back in. But the spell had been broken, and the crowd was losing interest. A few passengers with shopping bags climbed back onto the bus. The driver spat and wiped his mouth with the back of his hand.

The two women turned from the blob of yellowish spittle at their feet and glanced up at the driver with disgust. Inside the bus, a passenger tapped on the window and pointed at his watch. With one last glare, the driver lumbered on board.

Aziz pushed air from his lungs, a sigh so deep his chest felt punctured. He lifted his eyes to the empty sky, momentarily lost.

O Allah, we ask of Thee the good of this town and the good of its residents. We seek refuge in Thee from its mischief.

He shook sweat from his eyes. When he swallowed, his mouth and throat and then his gut softened with the water. He took the air of the town into his tired lungs, air infused with red mineral dust, with zinc and lead, with tobacco smoke, with alcohol, with horse sweat, with human sweat, with hopelessness, with decay and despair. He breathed all this in and resolutely pushed it out.

Inshallah. God willing, I live.

MERVYN

In the side mirror he saw the two women hovering as the grill slugged back water. The Wood girl had pulled her baseball cap so low he couldn't see much of her face but, as usual, her tits were on show. The way she was leaning over him, wog boy must be getting a decent eyeful. Mervyn snorted; the girl's mother was a goer, and it wouldn't surprise him if a liking for dark meat ran in the family. He watched the grill stagger to his feet. He was bowing and waving his arms, thanking the women, by the look of it. Mervyn scowled at the mirror. He was supposed to pick up anyone, shit, he even stopped for drunks, but buggered if he was going to pick up some filthy little foreigner who stank like a polecat.

The Kissack sheila had started walking. No wonder she had jumped in — she was part dago herself, and the other part was anybody's guess.

As the bus pulled away, the figures in the mirror dwindled. The bus stop at the corner of Bauxite and Main was right outside the betting shop. There was dog racing in Melbourne, and Mervyn planned to park and place a bet. But as he swung the bus towards the kerb he spotted the pumped-up shape of Sharkie White, the bookie. Sharkie stood beside his silver Mustang feeding coins into a parking meter and, without thinking twice about it, Mervyn accelerated. The bus veered away from the kerb, amid protests from punters up the back who were heading for the TAB and to sink a few beers in the Queen Vic next door.

'Where the hell are you going to, Merv?'

'Hey, you missed the stop!'

Mervyn fired a filthy look at the rear-view mirror. The blokes on the back seat were half standing, waving their arms. 'Get over it,' he growled. 'You're a bunch of losers, anyhow.'

A voice called, 'Can't've lost more than you, mate, not with that black turd you call a dog.'

'When's it going to stop fighting and chase the fucking lure?'

'Yeah, that last start, you shoulda been rubbed out.'

Mervyn's jaw bulged. 'As soon as I can pull over I'll come down the back and you can tell me more about my dog, all right?'

There was silence from the back seat. Mervyn was sweating. He didn't think Sharkie had spotted him, being busy with the parking meter and jawing to Diego-the-dago Kissack, who'd just emerged from the betting shop. If Mervyn was scared of Sharkie, his brain boiled at the thought of Dig Kissack. Dig's bitch, from the same litter as his own, romped home at every start, while his dog, identical in every way, was a dud. And didn't his customers bring it up every fucking time they set foot on the bus. Mervyn had something up his sleeve, though: a dog-swap and a quick start at an unregistered out-of-town track that would net him enough to settle up with Sharkie.

He craned his neck to check the wing mirror. The silver Mustang was growing smaller, and he couldn't see Sharkie now. Mervyn pulled an old bath towel from beside the seat and mopped his face. The next stop was the Sip'n'Save Liquor Store and the supermarket, where a bunch of old tarts waited with their shopping bags and walking frames. Christ, ever get to the stage he needed one of those things he'd be happy for Sharkie to shoot him. The back doors opened with a hiss, and the would-be punters got out, grumbling as they headed back towards the betting shop.

MIRI

The man from the bus followed her as she walked along the main street. For two blocks it was mostly houses, with a few small shops set back from the footpath. As she passed a crash repair workshop Miri noticed him keeping a steady distance behind her. When the shopping blocks drew closer, she tracked his progress in the long reflective facade of the ANZ bank. His walk was effortless and fluid, like he could keep it up forever, but in the droop of his head she saw that he was weary too. Something about him troubled her. There was an element of disguise about the shapeless clothing. He reminded her of a circus clown whose clumsiness masked a gymnast's skill.

The taxis she had spotted earlier had all vanished. Miri glanced back along the baking pavement at the stripes of shadow cast by shop verandahs, at shots of sunlight exploding off parked cars in sudden blinding bursts like machine-gun fire. She wished again that she had brought the car. Overhead, the sky was a faultless blue, a finish so even it looked spray-painted, and for a moment she could taste it in her mouth, a dense metallic colour that made the saliva run. She badly wanted a taxi, wanted the security of the house, its stone walls, its dim sheltering rooms. But the thought of a taxi driver making conversation — the intimacy of his eyes seeking hers in the rear-view mirror, of him turning out to be someone she had gone to school with, someone whose name she ought to know — filled her with panic. A small town could drive you nuts in no time.

A row of red brick shops across the street had the look of an overdone roast. Behind their rooftops, the slagheap glinted. The town felt oppressive; the weight of it, its blunt edges, made it difficult to think, made her feel dull-witted and clumsy, made her crave sugar. Miri slowed her pace, looking for a cafe. She had in mind an old-style joint with a jukebox, lino and laminex decor, but the first eatery she came to was a noodle bar, the next a Thai restaurant with crisp tablecloths and a minimalist menu. Miri had almost given up when she spotted Bernie's, crushed between a card shop and a hardware store. A ute with a cattle dog straining over the tailgate slowed and the driver whistled as she crossed the street.

It was cooler inside the cafe. She ordered a Coke at the counter and settled on a vinyl seat. The vintage decor was only marred by three computer terminals fitted against the back wall, where a handmade sign announced Bernie's internet rates. Overhead, red and green Christmas balls twirled in the air-conditioning draught. She sipped the cold drink, keeping an eye on the street, but there was no sign of the man who had been following her. In the plate glass she saw that a woman had appeared from the back of the cafe and was propped behind the till studying her. Sure enough, when Miri unwisely turned, the woman flashed a chummy grin.

'Miriam Kissack,' she said. 'Reckon you'll see some changes round town.'

Miri summoned an automatic smile. It did not matter who a Kissack woman married, or how many times, in this town she would always be a Kissack.

'The Thai restaurant is new,' Miri said, resigned to making small talk.

The woman came out from behind the counter. 'Thai, Greek. There's a few fancy restaurants, now that we get more tourists passing through.'

Miri nodded. Through the cafe window she could see across the street to a colonial building with a clock tower.

'They've fixed up the town hall,' she said.

She and Jack had been married in one of its whitewashed offices. Con in a red straw hat, pastel confetti from an earlier wedding swirling around their ankles as they stepped from the air conditioning into the blast furnace of the midday street.

'That was done a while back.'

The woman's head tilted expectantly. Her skin was like used wrapping paper. They were about the same age; it was what the town did to women.

'I see your auntie Con out shopping sometimes,' she said. 'Always stops and asks how Stella's going.'

Stella Dutton: Miri grasped the name with relief. She pictured a woman with a doughnut of fat that encircled her like one of the inner tubes kids used to keep afloat at the city baths. When her husband went on a bender, Stella used to show up at the house with her daughter, a skinny kid called Joy.

'And how is Stella?'

Joy shrugged. 'Oh, married again after Dad died. But they're not getting on too well, you know how it is.'

Miri thought she probably did.

By the time she left the cafe the man had disappeared. Relieved, she crossed the road and turned into Swann's Pharmacy. It was cool inside and a kitchen chair was propped beside the counter. Nobody was serving. She could hear the pharmacist out the back chatting to someone; they were swapping racing tips for the trots on Saturday night. In the shadowy laneway across the street, a man in dark trousers leaned against the side wall of the fruit shop. Miri turned from the window, sank onto the chair and closed her eyes. It was only Monday but it already felt as if she had been back for years. Soon she would look as lined and desiccated as the other women in town, women with fat-smoothed shoulders and bosoms that flowed on into their waistlines, with cracked heels jutting from their sandals and scrappy fly-away hair. It had been her destiny from the start, so why fight it?

'You all right?'

A woman in a light-blue tunic was bending over her.

'Fine,' Miri said, straightening her spine.

'You look pale. Stay there and I'll bring you a glass of cold water.'

'It's okay, I only came in for nappies.'

'Oh!' The woman planted a hand on her hip. 'How old is your baby?'

Miri hesitated. 'Five or six months,' she said.

The woman frowned and moved around one of the display units where feeding bottles and dummies were lined up under glass.

'Boy or girl?' she said.

'Girl.'

The blue cotton strained across her back as she reached into a low cupboard and plucked out a pack of nappies. 'These should be the right size.'

From the woman's skewed expression Miri guessed she

had said a wrong thing, but couldn't isolate it. She handed over the money and slipped her sunglasses from the top of her head onto her nose, feeling the woman's eyes on her as she stepped into the street.

Outside, cars and people stilled and floated; everything quivered and blended with the shimmer of the bleached street. The pavement, with its mineral sparkle, was melting at the edges. Miri felt her body suspended in a dream of heat and light, only anchored by the weight of the nappies in her hand. Perhaps the man still followed her, or perhaps not. She didn't have the energy to turn her head or to feel apprehension or feel anything at all. As she walked, the harsh light scoured all thought and feeling from her, as if her flesh had dissolved somehow, exposing the dry white bones. Memory, too, was numbed by heat. In the hospital, she had longed for this state of meltdown. It was why she had come back — the certainty that she would be able to walk along a street and feel as weightless as an astronaut, or a figure on a screen in one of Jack's slow-motion film sequences.

Six months earlier, she and Jack had been at a party in a garden beside the harbour. Jasmine flowers and waxy white frangipani floated on the surface of the swimming pool and candles in pink glass shades shimmered in the trees. Waiters circulated with champagne. Miri was almost sinking in the swell of conversation when a young woman walked towards them. She wore a dress made of some glittery transparent material held together with half-a-dozen safety pins. Miri's agent, Whiley Marsden, was guiding her to their table.

'Miri! Jack!' Whiley's portly figure quivered with excitement. 'Meet Nell,' he said, and he gave the girl, who had her arm hooked in his, a nudge of encouragement.

But Miri could tell that Nell and Jack had already met. Nell grinned, offering her hand; Miri glanced down at her wrist and the web of violet veins throbbing below the surface. The hand felt smooth and pliable as plasticine, and Nell's white skin made her own appear swarthy and coarse. When Nell turned to say something to Whiley, Miri wiped her palm down the side of her dress, but could not erase the imprint of the girl's silky flesh with the dense little bones inside.

Jack was planning a twentieth-anniversary video with Snakebite and within minutes he had offered Nell a part, telling Whiley to block off at least a week for location shots and a couple more days at a studio in town.

'Oh, wow!' Nell said. 'My mum's, like, Snakebite's greatest fan. She'll be rapt when I tell her.'

Miri's gaze wandered. Jack had never said she was too old for his music videos, but at some point he had stopped asking and she tried to remember when that had happened. She'd worked with Snakebite since before their first album. The drummer and guitarist had long grey hair, but the girls in their videos were getting younger.

She turned back to the conversation. Nell was animated but her eyes never quite connected with Miri's. Whiley puffed out his chest and beamed like a proud father with a precociously talented child. 'Little Nell's been working in London,' he said.

Shakespearean actor, or barmaid, wondered Miri.

'What brought you back?' Jack said.

Nell raked her fingers through her pale tousled hair. 'Oh, I just got homesick.'

A watch with a wide band slid on her right forearm and Miri tried to recall what a psychic once told her about left-handed women. Underneath the glitter Nell looked about twelve. A shimmering fish.

Whiley cupped Miri's elbow and whispered that they must do lunch.

'Soon,' she said, watching as Jack leaned close and whispered into the tentacles of tawny hair above Nell's ear.

Back at the house, Miri found Zett curled in a corner of the sofa in the attic with Opal asleep beside her. Judging from her damp and puffy eyelids, Zett had been crying.

Miri dropped the pack of nappies on the rug and fumbled in her handbag for cigarettes. 'What's up?'

Zett shrugged. 'Sick of myself, that's all. It's Christmas soon and I'm getting nowhere.'

Miri had seen the decorations in the shops and managed to ignore them. Even at Bernie's there had been coloured baubles and tinsel around the window and the till.

She passed Zett a cigarette. 'You didn't hear from your friend?'

Zett stuck the cigarette in her mouth and reached for her lighter. 'Craig? Not a sausage, so he can't be keen.' She lit the cigarette and studied the flame a moment. 'Probably I should just get it over with and give myself up.'

Miri frowned. 'You mean to the police?'

Zett sank back into the sofa and closed her eyes as she blew smoke.

'To fate,' she said. 'Which in my case just means Jude.'

In bed, unable to sleep, Miri rolled onto her side and stared at the pattern of shadows on the wardrobe. As a child she would creep into the bedroom and open it when her mother was out, but Candela always knew if anything had been tampered with. Once she brought home a stuffed monkey and hid it in the bottom among the shoes to give Miri a fright. Oozy the monkey had a grotesque felt face and fake-fur limbs and for a while he kept Miri out of the wardrobe. But the contents exercised a magnetic pull more powerful than fear and soon, armed with a scarf to cover Oozy, Miri was turning the key of the door and reaching past the monkey to examine her mother's belongings. Now it occurred to her that there was nothing and no-one to stop her looking in that wardrobe.

On the left side, dresses hung under heavy plastic covers. Miri slipped her hands in, skimming the hems of taffeta, satin and bubbly nylon. Three pairs of high-heeled pastel satin shoes were lined up below; under a layer of fine dust they looked like new. Behind the right-hand door were shelves where Candela's cameras lay sealed in plastic bags. Miri remembered the shapes of some of them pointing in her direction.

Look this way a little minute, Mimi?

Candela had loved the unexpected corners of her daughter's childish body: sharp elbows jutting from summer dresses; the smallest of her toes, shaped like a jellybean; the straight, silky hollow of her spine. Her mother had cajoled angles and images out of her, and later, when she earned her living in front of cameras, Miri's instinct for how to position her body was infallible. The photographers she worked with only had to hold their breath and keep on clicking. Most of them were easily satisfied, but Jack had found the pieces of Miri that had been mislaid since Candela's death. Jack had celebrated her adult beauty, but she reminded herself that even if the genes were good, beauty had a shelf life.

Miri took her mother's old Pentax from the plastic bag and put her eye to the viewfinder. The bedroom leapt at her in all its shabby detail, the sheet thrown back from the bed, her suitcase open and spilling clothes onto the carpet. She lowered it and turned it in her hands, peered at the frame counter where the number eleven showed the camera contained half a roll of unused film.

Miri dozed and woke again just after daylight, knowing five hours of sleep was the best she could hope to extract from the night. She rolled out of bed and pulled on bits of clothing she found strewn about the floor. Then, with Candela's camera around her neck, she felt her way downstairs. The house was a cave, still warm and stuffy after the night. In the kitchen a panel of sunlight spilled across the linoleum picking out dents and cracks, places where things had dropped and broken over the years.

Warm air flowed over her bare arms as she pushed through the gate and into the gardens. The morning was dewless. She was fiddling with the camera settings, squinting through the viewfinder and twisting the focus on the zoom lens when she saw him curled in the sheltering roots of a Moreton Bay fig. Miri let the camera dangle on its strap and stepped closer. The faint accordion wheeze of his breathing reached her. His mouth was soft in sleep. She stared at the eyelashes fanned across his cheek and without thinking lifted the camera. As the shutter clicked, his eyes snapped open.

He gazed up at her without moving, the shapes of fig leaves stirring on the bright reflective surfaces of his eyes. Bronze-tinted brown eyes that reminded her of Alice. His skin was tightly wrapped around his bones, with a napped texture. A young man's skin. Delicately tinted at his throat, darker on his arms and darker still at his elbows and neck. Dry leaves rustled overhead. The sap-rich scent of the early morning gardens contained a pungent note that rose from his skin like the fleshy tang of Con's horses after a hard gallop. He looked undernourished and feverish and the shoulder of his T-shirt was stained red from the soil. He was so still that she thought he might be injured. As she bent over him, the muscles of his face tightened until the mask of strain and exhaustion he had worn in the street was back in place.

Again, something in the way his shoulders tensed under her gaze reminded her of Alice.

'You look like you could do with breakfast.'

He stared back without blinking.

She touched his arm. 'Food?'

He swallowed once, then scrambled up and followed her inside.

'All this pretending not to understand,' Zett whispered. 'He could be playing games.' She was at the sink in her pyjamas, filling a bottle with boiled water for Opal.

Miri pushed two slices of bread into the toaster and shook her head. 'What would be the point?'

As Zett backed out of the kitchen door into the hall her expression was severe. 'It doesn't bother you to pick up a hitchhiker and next minute he's found out where you live?'

Miri glanced across to where he sat meekly at the table. He must have followed her home. And yes, there had been that moment of alarm when she'd first noticed him keeping pace with her along the main street. But after the ugly scene at the bus she'd been on edge, surprised too that she had interfered when all she'd really wanted was to get away. There had been something about the look of him then that had unsettled her, but this morning he seemed crumpled and rather ordinary, the only striking thing about him being his lack of English. Still, Grandma Essie had spent more than half her life in this house without uttering a complete sentence in English.

'Con would have something to say if I didn't fix him up with breakfast,' Miri said, but Zett had disappeared upstairs.

When he had eaten a plate of fried eggs with four slices of toast and a mug of tea to follow, Miri went into the pantry and returned with a pencil and an old sheet of Christmas wrapping paper. He leaned his elbows on the table and watched as she laid the paper plain side up, smoothed the creases, and began to draw the shape of Australia. She drew the whole continent with one nonstop line, making quick squiggles for the indentations of the coastline. He watched as she carved it into states and added Tasmania. Then, away to the right, the north and south islands of New Zealand. He leaned closer to the paper, concentrating on the drawing, frowning over it as if it were a treasure map.

Miri smoothed the expanse of the Pacific Ocean with the side of her hand. She sketched North and South America, biting her lip as she struggled to make recognisable shapes. When she was satisfied, she returned to South-East Asia, to the bulb of China, the lizard head of the Malay peninsula, the pendant of India. The map grew fuzzy as she moved towards the Middle East. How these countries related to Africa was a mystery.

He took the pencil from her and drew the slab of Iran and Iraq and marked the borders with a fierce dotted line. Then he added the jigsaw of Russia, Europe, Scandinavia and the ragged shape of Great Britain. He seemed to be charting winding rivers, lakes and inland seas, scrubbing at the paper with small strokes that might represent pine forests or mountain peaks. When he threw the pencil down, his hand was shaking.

As tears leaked from the corners of his eyes and dripped from his chin onto the paper, Miri noticed that the wound beside his eyebrow had scabbed over. He swiped at his eyes with the back of a hand, and his breathing grew agitated.

Miri bowed her head over the map in silence. When he was calm again she took up the pencil and marked a dot for Sydney on the east coast. Beside it, she drew a square house with sloping eaves, a front door, windows.

'In the car, I came from here.' She pointed to the map and to herself, then handed him the pencil.

His eyes roamed back and forth across the paper in confusion.

Miri tapped the table, took the pencil from him and marked a spot where she judged the town must sit. 'Now, we are here.'

He studied it for a long time.

At the top of the page Miri drew a question mark and passed the pencil to him. As he stared at the mark on the paper she watched his confusion escalate into panic. For a moment she thought he was going to shout, but instead he threw the pencil down. It was still bouncing across the lino as he leapt to his feet and wrenched open the back door.

Something about his furious departure was so very like Alice.

He was not where she had first found him, but deeper in towards the centre of the gardens where beds of blowsy roses ringed an overgrown patch of lawn. He was face down, his fingers tearing out clumps of couch grass as he burrowed into the dry red soil. When Miri moved closer she saw that the cut beside his eye had opened; blood was beginning to matt his hair and travelled in a messy line across his cheek. The opening of the wound felt like her doing and, after hovering over him for a moment, she turned back to the house.

Con's medicine cabinet was crammed with half-used bottles, mostly animal medications for things like ear mite, along with worming tables, vitamin pills, herbal remedies and painkillers. It took a couple of minutes to find something useable, but when she returned to the gardens with a jar of calendula ointment, the man had gone.

AZIZ

Aziz no longer slept in solid slabs of time but punctured consciousness with naps, taken on the run. And these bursts of sleep embraced debilitating dream patterns that set his mind and body writhing. Sometimes he woke with his arms and legs flailing. Rather than confront the harrowing material of his dreams he would choose, if he could, for all the bones in his body to be broken one by one. But flesh and blood demanded rest.

In sleep, he swooped in from above, bounding over razor wire to zero in on buildings clustered at the centre of a compound. The scene floated like a raft on ripples of red sand. Sometimes it was midday and the glare bouncing off the desert battered his eyeballs until they threatened to implode. More often it was night, and then he shuddered and struggled to twist from the grip of the dream path.

This time it began with the throb of a car engine far out in the desert. Inside one of the huts a young woman knelt on a grey blanket with a wide blue stripe. He peered at her through the barred window, watching as she set out her possessions: broken comb, tin plate, plastic cup, a crumpled fabric flower, which she propped against a photograph of a couple in the costume of her country. He tapped to attract her attention, mouthed her name as she slid her hand beneath the blanket and extracted a long metal spoon, shiny and finely sharpened.

Outside the perimeter fence, figures wearing balaclavas worked with wire-cutters. He leapt towards the door of the hut, shouting, but in the time it took to test his weight against the wood he knew he would not be quick enough to save her. Images of unspeakable damage pranced and jostled in his head as he hurtled towards the duty office. The guard with the tattooed wrists was in there with the television blaring. He sat with his feet up on a low table and a plate of sausages and mashed potato in his lap.

Aziz flung up his arms, cried out in his own language and beckoned.

The guard jerked his bullet head towards the door. 'Out!'

Aziz pressed his hands together, pleading, mimed the razor-edged spoon slicing the soft skin of Jamila's arms and neck. He subdued his panic for long enough to grasp the slithery English. 'Help me so much, please?'

The guard threw his head back and laughed. Again he shook his head. 'Out! Out!'

Aziz reached this place many times and the figures outside the fence never broke through in time to save her. He clenched his fists, resisting, helpless, as the dream dragged him deeper. Scuffles and shouts exploded as inmates burst into the compound. Ignoring the tugging current of bodies, he kicked at the door of the hut where Jamila flopped on the soiled blanket. The splintered wood gouged his arms as he clambered through. Her eyelids were puffy and the edges of her lips blueing. Blood pumped from the wound beneath her chin. Aziz looked away but not quickly enough. He touched a fingertip to her forearm, to the new mouth with crimson lips that had opened on the inside where the skin was unbearably tender. He folded her into the blanket, wrapped her like a child, so that the coarse fabric hid the pooling blood. Tears spurted from his eyes and splashed his hands as he floundered from prayer to prayer.

O Allah! Grant her protection and have mercy. Pardon and wash her with water and snow and hail. Clean her of faults. Allah have mercy. Allah have mercy.

He was dragged from the hut and pushed towards the fence. Days he spent in the red desert, stumbling through his prayers with the bloodstains on his clothing turning black and images of the Iranian girl, Jamila, festering behind his eyelids.

MIRI

She stood at the sink, miles away, her wrists coated in clusters of iridescent bubbles as she washed coffee mugs and the bowls rimmed with the tomato soup she and Zett had eaten for dinner.

'They're talking about your hitchhiker on the radio,' Zett said.

Miri turned to find Zett with her ear pressed to Con's old wireless.

'Reception's crap.' Zett spun the dial in disgust. 'But I heard there was a break-out from a detention centre last week. Seventeen escaped and all except one have been picked up.'

Miri glanced at the sheet of wrapping paper still folded on the table.

Zett said, 'Where'd he get to, anyway?'

Miri shook her head, trying to think. The man hadn't seemed like someone on the run, not furtive, only sad and exhausted. But she could see there was a story. If they could have talked he might have told her, but whatever language he spoke sealed him in another world. She didn't even know his name.

'No wonder he looked completely shagged,' Zett said. 'Do you know how far from anywhere they pitch those camps?'

'It mightn't be him.'

Zett pulled a face. 'Pig's bum it mightn't! Why else was he staggering around in the middle of nowhere?'

'There could be lots of reasons.'

Zett said, 'Yeah, well, he's come to the right place, anyhow.'

'But he's gone,' Miri said.

'Oh, I reckon he'll turn up.'

Miri wiped her hands and sat down at the table. 'What will you do about getting to Adelaide?'

Zett tugged at her fringe. 'Ring my friend again tonight. See if I can find out what's up.' Her gold eye shadow intensified the bronze rim of her irises. She looked tired tonight, and very young.

'And if he comes, then what?'

'I've got a cousin there who'll give us a place to sleep for a few weeks. If I can swing some kind of job, Opal will have to go into child care.' The corners of Zett's mouth drooped. 'She'll hate it. But it's a case of getting a roof over our heads.'

'I know a couple who own a cafe. I could give you the number. Cafes always need staff.'

'Yeah?' Zett lit a cigarette and her eyes drifted to the baby, who was sucking on a finger of toast. 'This would've been a piece of cake without a kid,' she said, 'but how the fuck am I supposed to juggle both our lives without dropping all the balls!'

Miri was searching for something encouraging to say when Zett surprised her with a throaty chuckle.

'The minute I start feeling sorry for myself I hear my mother's voice paying me out something rotten. Mum was never a whinger, I'll say that for her.' Zett funnelled smoke from her lips as she brushed Opal's toast crumbs from her lap. 'I could invest in a pair of hotpants,' she said. 'After all, what's worked once can work again and the one thing I know for sure is that there's money in sex.'

'Try the cafe first,' Miri said.

Zett grinned. 'It's amazing what women will do when they have kids to raise,' she said. 'Up half the night and still turn out in the morning to slap fritz and sauce between two slices of bread for a school lunch.'

'Shiftworkers.'

'Yeah.' Zett laughed her chalky laugh. 'You could call them that. Women with the brains to have been accountants and lawyers, if only they'd done their homework. My mum was smart, but the only way she could bring up four kids was by selling herself half-a-dozen times a night outside Liquormart.'

Miri stared at her in silence.

'Give Sadie her due,' Zett said, 'she never worked on a Sunday.'

'That must have been hard for you kids.'

She shrugged. 'We didn't know any other way,' she said.

The baby dropped the toast and began to suck her fingers.

Zett's voice was wistful. 'I hope it'll be different for Opal.'

Miri thought of the nocturnal traffic at Havana Gardens, the muffled moans and shrieks. 'Did your mother ever bring men home?'

Zett's plucked eyebrows shot up an inch. 'Shit, yeah!' she said. 'The downstairs front room was where she did the business. Sometimes we crept out of bed and watched through the keyhole. When I was small I thought it was what mothers did at night. Once we got to school other kids told us Sadie was a whore.' She stubbed out the cigarette. 'A bloke shot himself dead in that room. It was a wonder the welfare didn't take us off her after that.'

Miri glanced uncertainly at her. 'Did you see the shooting?'

A wry smile flashed across Zett's face and faded as quickly. 'No. For once we did as we were told and went to bed by ten. The shot must have woken us, though all I remember is this huge twanging sound. The bullet went right through his head and into the upright piano, snapped one of the strings. It was still ringing when Mum came racing up the stairs with blood all down the front of her blouse. She had thirty dollars in her hand and told us to stick it under one of the mattresses. Her view was he'd had the goods and she was owed the cash.'

Miri thought of times she might have used a gun if she'd had one, wondered if she would've had the courage to pull the trigger. She doubted it. When she had confronted Jack about Alice's therapy sessions, she'd let him wriggle away without revealing his role in the arrangement. She remembered how he had stared at her uncertainly; for a moment he'd seemed about to explain, then he must have seen that she was so distracted, so weakened by anxiety, that he could safely evade her.

Miri had been to Laura for hypnosis when she was trying to quit smoking. Laura did not come cheap and Alice had been seeing her regularly. The visits were costing Jack a fortune.

'If Alice gets her head straight, it'll be worth it,' he had said.

But what was *wrong* with their daughter's head, Miri had wanted to know.

'Look, some girls just get hung up at this age,' Jack had said. 'Who knows why?'

The outer door of Laura Petit's consulting rooms was painted a deep quiet reassuring green with polished brass fittings. Miri had rung the bell and waited. When the door buzzed open, Miri slipped inside and explained to the doe-eyed receptionist that she had no appointment but needed to talk to Laura.

The receptionist rose, shaking her head.

Miri leaned across the desk and fixed the girl with a resolute look. 'I absolutely must see Laura today,' she said.

In the pause that followed, Miri backed towards the waiting room. She knew that Laura Petit was behind the door at the end of the corridor and would have to appear sometime. Miri settled on a sofa beside a pile of glossy magazines. People came and went and the afternoon stretched on until the last patient departed. Laura appeared a moment later. 'Miri!' she said. 'It's been a long day, but come on in.'

Laura had eyes like sea-glass and white blonde hair scraped back from her face and held with black lacquer combs. It was as if the beech fittings and mint-green walls had been deliberately chosen to offset Laura's pale Nordic beauty. She ushered Miri into her office and pointed to a chair, then sat quietly with her hands folded in her lap.

Miri's anxiety bubbled over and she plunged straight in. 'Alice tells me she's been seeing you.'

The therapist shifted in her chair and raised a hand towards the kitchenette tucked from sight behind white shutters. 'Coffee?'

Miri dismissed the offer with impatience. 'I'm so worried about her.'

Laura leaned forward. 'You know my sessions with Alice are confidential. Without that trust between us there's no way I can help.'

'I understand that, but I'm her mother.'

Laura nodded. Her practised smile was sympathetic but she gave nothing away.

Miri said, 'Look, anyone can see she has an eating disorder. She's got so thin.'

'Have you discussed your concerns with Alice?' Laura said.

A feeling of heat began to spread upwards from Miri's chest. 'I've tried, but she won't admit what's happening.' She brought her hands to her cheeks. 'Ever since she was a baby she's been surrounded by film and theatre people obsessed with how they look, how they photograph. It must have affected her. Or is it the friends she's hanging out with? Or—'

'Laying blame is never productive,' Laura said. 'It's tough, but you just have to trust Alice.'

Miri stared at Laura's narrow hands, her ringless fingers. The soft cool slush of the therapist's voice made her long to shriek and stamp her feet. Did this woman even know what she was talking about? After the hypnosis sessions Miri had only lasted ten days without smoking. Okay, so deep down she hadn't really wanted to quit. But did Laura have the skill to divine Alice's feelings? Because Alice's need to eat was urgent.

'She can't go on the way she is much longer,' she said, and her voice cracked.

Laura gazed steadily at Miri. 'Sometimes a crisis can show the way forward.'

Miri was beaten into silence by Laura's whitewashed beauty, her calm demeanour, but rising to leave she had longed to slap the therapist's smug face.

Gasping with dreams, Miri came up from the mattress like a drowner gulping for air to find Zett standing in the doorway of the bedroom with Opal wriggling under her arm.

'What's wrong?' Miri said.

'Craig. The bastard left for Queensland two days ago! His mate just decided to tell me. He didn't want to come to the phone at first, so I reckon Jude's been out and put the fear of God into them.'

'Does he come from Queensland?'

'Yeah.'

'Well maybe he got some bad news from home, you never know.'

Zett sniffed back tears and hitched Opal higher up onto her hip. 'Yeah, maybe. It's the same difference, anyhow.'

'What time is it?'

'About ten. I didn't think you'd be asleep.'

Miri's arms and legs were cold and she rubbed her hands together; it felt as though she had been asleep for hours. 'I need alcohol,' she said.

'Me too, but there's only some dodgy-looking bottles of wine,' Zett said. 'It'll probably kill us.'

'Let's open one and find out.' Miri climbed out of bed, opened the wardrobe and pulled out an old green overcoat that had been her mother's. It was impregnated with dust and camphor, probably also with the powdered wings of moths, but she dragged it on over her pyjamas.

The entrance to the cellar was in the scullery behind the kitchen, five steps down in the musty dark. 'There's a light switch on the back wall,' Miri said. 'You wait up here.'

She went down and found a wine rack that held two dozen bottles of red wine and a bottle of port, all covered with dust and cobwebs. A gecko zigzagged up the wall and turned the bead of an eye towards her as she blew the dust from a label and held it close to the light bulb.

'Made in France,' she shouted to Zett. 'Looks like good claret. I wonder how Con got hold of it?'

When Miri came into the kitchen, Zett was hunting through the cutlery drawer for a corkscrew. 'Don't ever say I looked a gift-horse in the gob,' she said.

They sat at the kitchen table with the bottle between them.

'Not my usual choice of couldn't-care-less juice,' Zett said, 'but it tastes okay.'

'Listen,' Miri said, 'you can make another getaway plan.'

'Oh yeah. It was no surprise, really. Craig was just doing us a favour for old times' sake. When a man wants into your pants but you haven't weakened yet, that's when he's reliable. Pity I let him have his way years ago.'

'My husband's like that,' Miri said.

'They all are. It's why monogamy is pointless.' Zett laughed and pulled a packet of cigarettes out of her pocket.

Miri screwed up her mouth. 'I think that's more or less Jack's idea. But I used to be the faithful type.'

Zett topped up the glasses. 'You're kidding! I didn't think anybody bothered these days.'

Miri stared at the ruby disc of the wine's surface, dipped her finger in and watched the wine drip back into the glass. She had not been completely faithful to Jack. At first it was revenge she wanted, until she realised that for revenge to succeed, Jack would have to care more. After such a passionate start, his eventual indifference had left her lost and free-floating. Opportunity had knocked and once or twice she had answered the door. That's all it was. But senseless coupling had made her feel a failure, so she stopped.

'I've had my moments,' she said. 'But they were nothing to write home about.'

'Whose were?' Zett had taken a notebook from her handbag and was thumbing through the pages. 'There must be someone left in town whose balls I've got a grip on,' she said.

A mouthful of claret slid down Miri's throat. It was her third glass and she was on the way to that warm, wide plateau where there were no sharp edges; the alcohol-softened light made the utilitarian kitchen look a little hazy. The baby had fallen asleep across Zett's knee. Miri reached out and stroked Opal's fingers and the contact sparked a tearing sensation in her throat. She folded her arms and stared hard at the yellow crushed-silk pattern of the laminex.

'When you look at married couples, it's a mystery why we keep on doing it,' Zett said. 'But then again,' she spun the cigarette packet on the tabletop, 'it says right here in big black letters that tobacco causes lung cancer and death. It couldn't be any plainer, but we keep on smoking, right?'

Miri shrugged. 'Some of us are committed to self-harm.' Blue light pulsed off a mirror in the hall and she tipped her head towards it. 'That's odd.'

Zett turned to see what she was looking at, then leapt up, knocking over her wineglass.

'Police,' she hissed, and she was off, bounding up the stairs two at a time with Opal bouncing on her shoulder.

Miri mopped up the spilled wine and rinsed Zett's glass. She was sliding it back into the cupboard when footsteps sounded on the back verandah. As she waited for the knock she checked the kitchen. Her own glass, half full, stood on the table beside the wine bottle. There was no evidence of Zett or Opal that she could see. She drew a long smooth breath and opened the door.

There were two of them. Young police officers with cropped heads and solid bodies packed into their blue shirts. They didn't wait to be invited in but brushed past her into the kitchen. One of them had ginger hair and his arms dangled wide of the hardware at his belt like an old-time gunslinger. He grinned at her as he crossed the kitchen. 'Always a shame to find a good-looking woman drinking alone,' he said.

Miri summoned a cool and indifferent tone and said carefully, 'I was having a glass of wine.'

He held up the almost empty bottle and turned towards her, eyebrows raised.

'I didn't drink it all in one go.'

His partner was peering into the hallway. 'This goes straight to the front door?' he asked.

'Take a peep, Robbo,' said Gingerhead.

Before Miri could protest, the second officer had disappeared down the hall. She listened to him moving about the two front rooms that faced the gardens.

'We had a tip you'd taken a young foreign gentleman under your wing,' Gingerhead said.

Miri's throat was dry. She could have drained her glass, but instead uncrossed her arms and projected a bland expression.

'I saw someone being bullied off the bus yesterday, if that's what you mean,' she said.

'This would be the guy you brought to town in your car?'

Doors opened and closed at the front of the house, followed by boots on the stairs.

That they knew she had picked him up did not surprise her. Someone would have spotted him getting out of her car in front of the shops, and news spread round town quicker than flu.

'He was stranded,' she said, 'so I gave him a lift.'

'In the habit of picking up strange men, are you?'

'I was brought up not to leave people in the desert without water.'

'So where'd you find him?'

She gazed at the cop blankly. Every stretch of highway was identical to every other stretch.

Almost absent-mindedly, he opened the nearest cupboard and stared at the rows of cups and saucers. 'How far out of town, roughly?'

'Thirty or forty kilometres. I don't remember.' Doors slammed upstairs. 'Your friend didn't ask if he could search the house,' she said.

Gingerhead shrugged. 'Haven't got anything to hide, have you?' He shut the cupboard, opened the next and peered in at the rows of glasses.

'That's not the point,' she said.

He ignored that. 'So this bloke you picked up, he told you what he was doing wandering around without water, right?'

'We didn't talk.'

He took a glass from the cupboard. 'Mind if I grab a drink?'

'Help yourself,' she said.

He moved towards the fridge. 'You mean he just got in the car and sat for forty kilometres in silence?'

'There's no cold water,' Miri said. 'No ice, either.'

As the fridge door swung wide she noticed one of Opal's bottles tucked into the side next to a carton of milk. Gingerhead reached in and flipped open the freezer door, exposing two empty aluminium trays furred with ice crystals.

'Look, I couldn't just drive off and leave him,' Miri said, careful with her diction because of the wine, 'but I had no desire for conversation.'

'You catch his name?'

She shook her head.

He shut the fridge door and turned to look at her. 'But the way I hear it, this same bloke came home with you after he failed to secure a seat on the bus.'

She said, 'I don't know where he is.'

Doors slammed again deep inside the house. Miri willed herself not to glance in the direction of the Christmas paper tucked behind a bottle of cough mixture on the sink, although the paper, with its pattern of small green trees, seemed to emit subliminal distress signals.

Gingerhead stepped close to her. Fruity aftershave wafted from his reddish cheeks.

'That your car parked out the front?'

She nodded.

His gaze dropped to the pyjama top showing beneath her overcoat. 'Done a few miles by the look of it, but still goes all right?'

It was an effort not to pull the coat more tightly around her chest. 'Yes.'

'Front right fender's been hammered.'

'I hit a kangaroo.'

'It happens. Still, even banged up it would have seemed like a Rolls-Royce to your pal. He's not an Abo, worse luck for him. Round here the government doles out grants to Abos. They get houses and cars. Did you know?'

'If you say so,' she said.

'Oh yeah. The lighter ones don't get as much as the darker ones, of course. But even a half-caste, say like the colour of your friend, can afford a nice four-wheel drive in this town.' His eyes wandered around the room, squinting up at the high ceiling where spiders hung motionless in the corners. 'Nice old place,' he said. 'What I remember, it's seen some action.'

'What's he done?' she said.

He shrugged. Standing too close to her in the centre of the kitchen, his fleshy lips curved in a smile that did not reach his eyes.

'Staying in town long?'

'I haven't decided.'

'Flash sheilas never last out here. They always get bored and head back to the smoke.'

Miri was silent, but Gingerhead persisted. 'Robbo reckons you're a film star.'

She said, 'I am an actor. Sometimes I work in film.'

'I'd like to see a film with you in it,' he said.

His partner appeared in the doorway and smirked at the sight of the two of them standing together.

'All quiet upstairs.'

Gingerhead touched her elbow. 'Thanks for showing us round,' he said.

Their muscled bodies blocked the doorway.

'You see that hitchhiker pal of yours again, give us a call.'

She held her breath, listening to the receding thump of their boots on the concrete path, the double slam of car doors.

The glass of wine felt tainted. When Miri was certain that they had gone she carried it to the sink. As she poured it away, the back door opened without a knock and her uncle Dig stood in the doorway scratching his head and smiling at her.

'Hello, stranger,' he said.

Miri smiled back at him. The lines in his face had deepened and his bulky frame was a little heavier than she remembered, but his black hair was barely threaded with grey.

'What brought the coppers round?' asked Dig.

'They're looking for someone,' she said.

'Anyone we know?'

The alcohol made her feel soft and dull. She shrugged. 'I don't think so.'

Dig shuffled into the room and pulled out a chair from the table. 'Seems like they put the wind up you, anyhow,' he said.

'Well, they came in so gung-ho.'

'The redhead is Eddie Doyle's boy. Nasty bit of work, just like his father.' He fumbled in his trouser pocket and pulled out a tin of tobacco and a packet of papers. 'I had to fight Eddie once after he called your aunt a loud-mouthed moll.'

Miri thought for a moment that Dig meant Con, and then she realised that it must be Lois. Who else but Lois with her teetering heels and blonde curls?

'Fair enough,' Dig said. 'It was a do after the Paddy's Day races and Lois was pretty loud that night. But I wasn't going to have him calling her a moll. So I went round early next morning and when Eddie opened the door I whacked him hard before he could do anything. When he was on his back on the carpet I told him why. If I'd mucked around he'd have pulled some trick or another. Eddie's a mad bugger.'

Miri had almost forgotten this world she'd grown up in where men knocked each other down to defend the honour of women they themselves took for granted.

She said, 'His son is creepy.'

'Yeah, Danny's a chip off the old block. Him and his friend Robbo turned up at the two-up a couple of weeks back, even though they're paid a fat backhander to keep away.'

'You still playing?' Miri said.

'Nup. Make a few bob keeping an eye on things, when it's running.'

The two-up games were played down one of the lanes that honeycombed the town, lanes put in place before any of the houses had plumbing so that the night cart could empty the outdoor lavatories. God! She had forgotten those outhouses, their smell of phenol and excrement, the squares of shiny paper cut from *People* magazine threaded on a loop of string.

Miri watched as her uncle worked tobacco between his palms, teased it out along the cigarette paper, rolled it and ran the tip of his tongue along the sticky edge. He had come across to see to Con's horse.

'How's the horse doing?' she asked.

Dig patted his pockets for matches. 'Should've been put out to grass years ago. But I'll keep on throwing him his feed and water until we see what's up with Con.'

'I saw her today,' Miri said. 'She's still the same.'

Dig lit the cigarette and held it with the lighted end cupped in his palm. 'Con'll get better if she wants to,' he said.

CONSUELA

On the second day after her accident, when a spate of admissions almost filled the ward, Con had been moved into a side room on her own. It was quieter there and a bit lonely, but any amount of loneliness was better than that dormitory of toothless women with their busted hips and knees, their complaining, wandering minds. She was particularly thankful to have left behind the woman who had shrieked all night that the nurses were pumping poison into her through a catheter.

By halfway through the second week Con was almost comatose with boredom. Through the open window she imagined she could smell the river, although it was so far from the hospital that it was unlikely. Still, its presence persisted, comforting her with a familiar marshy odour and even, so she fancied, sudden bursts of frog song. It reminded her of picnics long ago; she and her sister Candela eating sandwiches and cake in a latticework of light and shade under the willows, then crossing the muddy verge to swim, even though their mother had made them promise to wait at least an hour after lunch before dipping so much as a toe in the river.

Right now she was remembering an afternoon spent underneath the hammock in the gardens, remembering hours spent chewing blades of grass, she and Candela flattening them with their teeth and then funnelling air between their thumbs in an attempt to make the piercing whistle their father had shown them. Candela had eventually given up and fallen asleep with her long black hair unravelled and a spike of couch grass stuck with spittle to her lip. Even after all these years Con could hear the creak of the hammock and the way their mother sang the same song all afternoon in a sweetly cracked contralto. The song was a lament which the girls understood was about their mother's mother, Fernanda, who was a great beauty, and about the lost island of Cuba.

Esperanza's plait dangled over the side of the hammock. Consuela caught the feathered tip and wound the black hair around her fingers as she hummed her mother's tune. In the breathless hours after lunch when the melting streets were empty and their father was safely ensconced with his turf guide at a corner table in the Criterion Hotel, their mother retreated to her garden and wallowed in the melancholy glory of her life before she came to Australia. Consuela and Candela followed her stories, slipping effortlessly into the Spanish she had taught them all through the long afternoons since they were born and which their father had forbidden them to speak. The twins were as closely twined as plied wool, but their mother's language, an extension of Esperanza's hot sad self, drew the three of them into an intricate knot that was tied and untied endlessly in the thrumming heat of the gardens.

Their mother had never been happy in the town. From Esperanza's stories, Consuela had assembled a vision of Cuba as a fertile land dotted with sun-faded houses, a country of great beauty; Esperanza had been happy there, a *bailarina* with silver combs tucked into her long black hair. Every birthday of their childhood, when the two girls cut the cake, Consuela had squeezed her eyes shut and wished for them all to go to Cuba. Every Sunday she had snapped the stalks of roses in the gardens and carried them indoors to the plaster saints who watched over them from shadowy corners.

The saints had survived the journey from Cuba wrapped in Esperanza's dresses. They were well acquainted with the island's lush beauty and with Esperanza when she was a dancer. Surely with a little effort they could be coaxed into restoring her lost family and her happiness. Consuela had pressed rose petals to their hands and feet, their chipped smiles and vivid vacant eyes. But even as she roamed the garden — her fingers pierced by rose thorns, and the scented petals scattering as she carried them towards the house — she had known that her petitions to the saints were far too grand; they could all have been happy if only Esperanza smiled more often, but there was always some kind of trouble. Like the episode with their teacher.

Miss Blaine had called on a Friday afternoon and spent an hour in the front parlour with their mother. By the end of it, a bewildered Esperanza was wringing her hands, and their teacher, red-faced with frustration, had opened the door and called the girls, rightly suspecting they would be close by. When they appeared, Miss Blaine pounced on them with the pleading ingratiating smile she usually reserved for parents.

'Connie, Candy,' she said, 'I want one of you to explain to your mother about the school lunches.'

Esperanza waited with her hands on her hips and her toe ominously tapping out a rhythm. Consuela peered nervously at the teacher. A week earlier, Miss Blaine had threatened them with a bar of soap and said that if they insisted on jabbering in tongues she would wash out their mouths.

In the parlour, their teacher's voice was syrup-sweet. 'It's quite all right, Connie. Please go ahead and explain.'

Esperanza swiped her hand through the air in a gesture of impatience. Candela had drifted backwards towards the door with her eyes fixed on Miss Blaine's bony fingers.

Consuela coughed and glanced over her shoulder, an automatic gesture whenever she spoke Spanish. 'Miss Blaine says we have to take sandwiches for lunch. Cheese and vegemite, egg, or corned beef and pickle.'

'*Que?*'

Esperanza was under the impression the teacher had come about their schoolwork. Now she turned baffled eyes on the woman, who trembled slightly as Consuela translated the list of acceptable ingredients.

'What is wrong about their lunches?' Esperanza snapped.

Consuela translated with downcast eyes.

Miss Blaine drew a deep breath, and her long thin nose flushed. 'It's the smell,' she said. 'The classroom is very hot, and the other children complain.'

That morning they had packed thick slices of leftover *pulpeta*, Esperanza's meatloaf with boiled eggs and olives and minced garlic. Other days it might be *boliche* or the delicious *fricase de pollo*, which their mother made by soaking plump chicken legs in orange juice with chopped onion and cloves of garlic.

Esperanza rolled her eyes, and her hands darted out as if she might grab Miss Blaine by the front of her neat white

blouse and shake her. Candela ducked out into the hallway, but Consuela stepped between her mother and the
teacher, soothing, placating. 'We will make the lunches,'
she said in English. '*Australian* lunches.'

Miss Blaine smiled brightly as she edged towards the
door. 'Tell your mother I'm sorry.'

'I'll tell her,' Consuela said.

But she didn't bother translating Miss Blaine's regret. It
would do no good. Esperanza knew no other way to pre-
pare food. When she went to the shops she bought the
ingredients she recognised. Whatever she couldn't find,
she grew fresh in the gardens. Candela and Consuela were
the only children in the town who ate mangoes, who sucked
on quartered lemons without screwing up their faces. On
Saturday afternoons they peeled whole cloves of garlic to
lace the pot roast. But after Miss Blaine's visit, Consuela
rose earlier on school mornings and made two rounds of
cheese sandwiches, which she wrapped in greaseproof
paper. The sandwiches were bland, but it was better to eat
them than to cause more trouble.

On the evening of the school lunch incident, their
mother had told them she was expecting a baby.

'It will be a boy,' Esperanza had said firmly. 'And I will
call him Diego, the same as my father.'

Their father said, 'Geez, Essie, Diego-the-dago. Can't
you give him a name the other kids can pronounce?'

Esperanza pretended not to understand. When he
proposed other names, Australian names, she turned her
face and sat, stiff and silent, staring out at the garden, while
their father cursed under his breath. Two weeks before
the baby was born, and with her breasts already dripping,
Esperanza escorted her husband upstairs to their bedroom
to discuss once and for all the question of the baby's name.

Consuela knew their father would yield, and she wondered at this gift their mother had of managing his stubborn temperament. Since Esperanza refused to speak English and their father could only swear in Spanish, the two girls marvelled at the smoothness with which these treaties were negotiated and invariably ended in their mother having her way.

As Esperanza had predicted, the baby was a boy and she named him Diego. Everyone called him Dig; it was a mining town after all and boys were expected to grow up and work underground. Their father's friends had gathered at the house to drink cold beer in the kitchen. Wetting the baby's head, they called it. The celebration lasted several days, the men smoking and drinking and raising their glasses to the tiny scrap with a thatch of dark-brown hair as he dozed in Esperanza's lap. Their father's friends told jokes and reminisced; sometimes the stories made the men shout with laughter and slap their palms against their knees. Everyone laughed except Esperanza, whose smooth face remained vacant. The Cuban had a reputation in the town for silence, but her daughters knew their mother was capable of unleashing a flash flood of language, a deluge that could have swept away the whole uncomprehending population of the town.

MIRI

Miri dragged a chair onto the side verandah and settled her back against its lumpy cushions. It was quiet, with only the sparrows flitting among the leaves of the grapevine and occasionally swooping out to perch in the curls of the wrought-iron lacework. Earlier she had watched as Zett washed single grapes and squeezed the juice into Opal's mouth. Zett had offered her a bunch.

'I've hardly seen you eat a thing since you got here,' she said.

Miri had shaken her head. Every time she looked at food she was assailed by images of Alice's elbows and knees, of her sleek little head drooping on the slender stalk of her neck. Her thoughts of Alice were so sharp she could cut herself on them.

A dog barked at the back of Lois's house as Miri sat motionless, staring across the dusty green of the gardens. When she was a child here, the air had a crackle, as if the town was loaded with secret energy. Now it felt dead. She looked out over the gardens and Lois's rooftop towards the red blur of the desert. After dark she would drag out Con's hose and sprinkler and move it around the beds. Meanwhile she sat with the brown light of late afternoon falling and a mug of tea cooling beside her chair, sat until the sparrows on the electricity wires were hard to pick out in the fading light. Along the road towards the town, a yellow streetlight came on. Miri sipped cold tea and didn't notice when the first stars appeared.

On that last visit to the flat in Glebe, Alice was thinner than ever and wouldn't be coaxed out.

'I don't want to do the cafe thing,' she said. 'I'll make you a coffee here.'

The skin on Alice's face was taut as a drum across the cheekbones and the smudged eyes gave her a bruised look. She sat on one of the rumpled divan beds and picked at a hole in her fishnet tights. The Doc Martens dangling on the strings of her legs looked huge.

Miri had to exert all her willpower not to reach out and scoop Alice into her arms as she had when her daughter was small. At the same time she was seized by the desire to shake her until common sense kicked in. What stopped her was the fierce resistance this ghostly child could muster.

Alice went to the kitchen to boil water. Through the open doorway, Miri watched her reach into a cupboard for mugs and a jar of coffee, then slide four chocolate biscuits onto a plate. When the kettle had boiled, Alice lifted it with both hands while Miri rummaged in her purse until she found a tissue and surreptitiously dabbed her eyes.

'You shouldn't have gone back to drinking coffee,' Alice said as she set down the mugs. 'Caffeine can throw your heartbeat out of whack.'

A quarrelsome thread in her voice warned Miri not to argue. They sat listening to the traffic sounds with the plate of biscuits between them. Alice seemed twitchy, rising to smooth wrinkles from the throw on the divan, crossing to the window and pushing aside the net curtain to stare into the street, letting the curtain fall and returning to her chair.

'What happened with your photographs?' she said.

'The exhibition's over. People said they liked them.'

'Anyone important?'

'No, just people.'

Alice sipped hot water from her mug, then took a biscuit from the plate. 'I should've gone to see them.'

'Another time.'

As Alice brought the biscuit to her lips, Miri tried to look away but couldn't. The chocolate-covered disc was dark against her skin, and as Alice took a tiny bite her eyes drifted to the window.

'What were your pictures like?'

Her daughter's blue-black hair and porcelain skin were framed by the tall windows overlooking the street.

'They were black and white. Single pieces of fruit — pears mostly — on squares of waxed paper laid over scarred wood. I used Mum's time exposure technique; it seemed to work.'

Alice nodded. 'I'm sorry I didn't go.'

She wanted to tell Alice about the reviewer from an arts magazine who had written, 'Passmore's pears are intense, isolated objects. Imbued with some unspeakable sorrow, their mute and luminous dignity has about it the persistence of eternity.'

That would have made them both laugh, once.

Instead, she shrugged. 'You can see them at home sometime.'

The chocolate biscuit had begun to soften in Alice's hand and she slid it back onto the plate, covering the action by rising to open the window.

When Miri stood up to leave, Alice surprised her by leaning close for a kiss. She surrendered then to the need for touch, but instead of solid flesh, she found herself embracing patchouli-scented air, air that contained at its core the birdlike bones of her daughter.

The street door clicked behind her as she walked away fast, stalking past the cafe and the primary school, on and on until she arrived at a park. Homeless people lolled on the grass in the late sunshine, passing a bottle. Teenage boys were fooling around, smoking and chucking stones at a drinking fountain. Miri sank onto a bench and hugged her sides as sobs erupted, uncontrollable as hiccups. From the corner of her eye she saw the homeless people swivel their heads in her direction, but she was not one of them and after a moment they turned back to the bottle.

A week later, Laura Petit called to tell them she had persuaded Alice to check into St Vincent's Hospital. 'If she transfers to the Firth Clinic, I can monitor her more closely,' she said.

Miri opened her mouth to answer but no sound emerged. She handed the telephone to Jack, stared at him as he paced up and down the kitchen.

'Book her a private room,' Jack said.

When he put the phone down, he turned to Miri, his eyes screwed up as if squinting into the sun.

'Laura says it is best if you and I don't visit until Alice settles in and stabilises.'

She and Jack slept under a creamy drift of mosquito netting with the windows open wide. The nights were dense and airless but she pressed close to Jack's side, leaving no space for anxiety or dreams. Each night when she closed her eyes she had to quell her apprehension about Alice, but once asleep, their daughter was always well and strong. Instead, her recurring dreams were of Nell Bardot's wide-awake eyes, of Nell emerging, boneless and supple, from a sequinned sheath as she talked about her mother, the Snakebite fan. More than once, Miri dreamed of cutting into that sparkly party dress with scissors, not the great swooping slashes she would execute when conscious, but a web of neat cuts, an exercise in mindfulness.

AZIZ

The fierce light sliced the town's main street like a cleaver. It made even young girls look tough, and older than their years. He studied them from underneath his lashes, observing the parade of bare flesh with wonder. A girl strode by wearing a black skirt that frilled above the knee, shoes with tall narrow heels. Her clingy white top exposed a hand's width of midriff, and the low-slung skirt barely covered the shallow bowl of her abdomen. She looked tight and self-contained, and the sight of her made his head float free from his body. He heard his mother's voice, muffled beneath her burqa, warning his sisters of the lethal nature of white shoes.

Outside a public house he saw two women fighting, and the sight jolted through him like an electric shock. The way the women flaunted their bodies was bad behaviour, *haram*, and the way it affected him was not good, but not sinful either. Jamila had been *halal*, everything that was good. Given freedom, and time, would Jamila have come to consider this place her home? Could a place be home if no memories attached to it, if the culture swamped and endangered your own beliefs?

Surely in the heavens and earth there are signs for the believers.

Afghanistan was the perpetual landscape of his dreams. He was born there before the Russians came, in the days when his father, a scholar turned carpet merchant, covered great distances — north to Mazar-i-Sharif to buy from Uzbek villagers, west and north-west to Maimana and Herat for Beluch rugs.

The memory of the crumbling warehouse in Kabul, bright with kilim and sumak rugs and reeking of their vegetable-dyed threads and of copper sulfate or urine from the fixing baths, never failed to soothe him. He had been especially fond of the office — dim behind a pair of tall shuttered windows that opened onto the street — where his father sat to do the paperwork or to entertain certain valued customers. This was where friends came to gossip over glasses of *chay sia,* or perhaps green tea with cardamom, and it was here, on shelves carefully lined with newspaper, that his father kept his precious library of books about botany, physics, biology, chemistry, astronomy and medicine. The books Aziz loved best, though, were about carpets. He remembered the weight and texture of the carpet books in his lap, volumes so old and well used that the loosened pages had to be held in place with ribbon, or a plait of carpet threads.

Now, he squatted in a patch of shade on the main street of this unknown town and watched two young women walk side by side towards him. Both were using mobile phones; one of them was talking and the other pressed buttons with her thumbs as she stared at the screen. The women's clothing was *haram.* Some of the worst he had seen. Hunger knotted his stomach and his tired muscles ached. He glanced down at their feet as they passed — painted nails, a silver toe ring, the delicate ankle bones of fillies — and wondered whether he would ever be able to look one of these women in the eye.

As a young man, Aziz's father had left Afghanistan to study in Pakistan and India. His special interest was tribal carpets of the eighteenth and nineteenth centuries and as well as writing scholarly essays he had spent many years assembling a collection, which had become the foundation of their business.

From the age of seven, Aziz had worked with his father after school and at other odd times, running messages and packing rugs for delivery. By the time he was twelve his father had taught him to keep accounts, then, at fifteen, to sort and grade the stock. This was the part that Aziz loved best; it involved many hours of thumbing through the carpet books, or discussing with his father the fragments of pattern salvaged from rare but damaged carpets, which were stored in wide shallow drawers between sheets of tissue paper. From the beginning, Aziz had favoured the rich red Turkmen rugs and the delicately faded antique carpets, but he appreciated the simplicity and vigour of lesser rugs. There was poetry in carpets, especially the tribal designs, whose colours and patterns vibrated in harmony with some inner gland that both calmed and stimulated his senses. The work was hard, but Aziz had never minded.

His younger brother, Masir, had yearned for independence and a different career.

'Bah! It's like being buried alive,' Masir said of a day spent labouring among the whirling dust motes in the warehouse.

His mind was too agile and impatient for packing carpets, and in the end their father agreed his youngest son could study engineering. But by the time he went for the entry test, the Taliban had turned Kabul University into a religious campus.

Even before the Taliban took control of Kabul, their lives had become difficult. Kabulis were hungry and there were few buyers for the carpets. Their father had long since packed his books into crates and sunk them under the floorboards of the main warehouse, leaving on the bookshelves only a battered volume of the Qur'an The few foreigners passing through the capital were still buying rugs and carpets, but competition was fierce and, quick to recognise their advantage, the *kharagis* beat down the prices.

In the city, poor people made the rounds of the hotels, trading whatever they could lay hands on, or begging left-over food. The hotels were so empty that even scraps were scarce. Aziz had begun to fear his family would soon join these desperate souls.

On the flat roof of their house, where Masir kept his prized racing pigeons, neighbourhood boys clambered up to set traps. Every night, fewer birds returned from the evening exercise of circling, diving and tumbling above the rooftops. Lured away by hungry neighbours, Masir's birds were sold in the bazaar, or ended in pilau. Masir was outraged, but their mother, Nadira, said sharply that as they would soon have nothing to eat he had better take good care of the creatures. The only way the family had survived that last year was with the help of a business contact in Peshawar, who had sold a small number of carpets for them at a modest profit.

When he woke in the night, shaking and sweating from the terror of a recurring dream, Aziz often found himself poised at the moment where, against their father's wishes, Masir had run off to join the rebel forces in the north. Within a month their sister's husband had followed and her in-laws, blaming Masir, had thrust Amal and her five-year-old son back on the family's diminishing resources.

His father's carpet trade had survived the Russian invasion. It had even survived the civil war. But only months before the Taliban would lose control of Kabul, soldiers doused the warehouse with petrol and set it alight. His family's wealth was contained in the carpets, in yards of careful knots that took nomadic women six months or a year to make, in Turkmen wedding carpets with their pale grounds and meandering wedding caravans, in antiquarian tekemets and suzanis. Prayer rugs with the holy mihrab woven into them perished in the fire alongside carpets swarming with animals and birds, with Herati vase shapes, medallions and flowers; as the family slept, the fire transformed them into paupers.

Then, in the early hours, a car pulled up outside their house. The curfew-bound streets were empty and no-one saw who held the lighter and the tin of gasoline.

The screams of his mother and young sisters resonated on and on inside his head. In his dreams they were always running, their yards of hair and layers of clothing dripping flame. His own body carried scars from the fire, minute white arrows on his arms, chest, and the soles of his feet, but they were nothing. Nothing. His older sister, Amal, had been visiting her husband's family, hoping for her son's sake to effect a reconciliation. The visit had gone well and they had stayed the night, returning the next day to the charred ruins of the house.

Except in dreams, over which he had no control, he never allowed his thoughts to approach the night of the fire directly. It hovered near him, always. But whenever it pressed too close he pushed it firmly away, fearful that he might succumb to temptation, as others had done, and turn the gasoline and the lighter on his own clothing.

After three days of mourning, he and his father made the decision to go to Pakistan, taking with them the few carpets of value that had survived the fire: three rare blue Salor rugs, a fine nineteenth-century Tekke carpet and some antique prayer mats, which his father had never planned to part with. Amal and her small son, Yassin, accompanied them. On the journey Aziz discovered an Afghanistan he never knew existed. Stony mountain sides laced with the trails of opium smugglers; tawny plains dotted with land-mines, which fleeing refugees must skim to reach the border. In dreams his *shalwar kameez* caught on the thistles that pushed between the rocks on the roundabout route they followed to Peshawar.

Over and over he lived the moment when they reached a sprawling refugee camp across the border in Pakistan. The people there were desperate and starving, their faces and limbs disfigured by skin diseases, the children with swollen malnourished bellies. He especially remembered some little ones who had been travelling for five days and nights, mute with shock and deaf from the recent bombing raids around Kabul airport. No-one could say if their deafness would be permanent. People wrapped sheets of plastic around propped sticks to fashion tents and, during the day, the plastic intensified the heat. Children collapsed and died of heatstroke and dehydration.

A woman in the tent beside them nursed a child with meningitis. Aziz heard her sobbing to Amal that the hospital was asking one thousand rupees for an injection.

In his pocket he had more than one thousand rupees. He took out the money and looked at it, wondering if he should give some to the woman. Then his nephew, Yassin, ran to him, crying; he had cut his foot while wandering about the camp and the wound needed dressing. There was no knowing what disaster might befall them next. Aziz tied the money into his turban cloth and went to look for water. That night, when the child in the next tent died, he plugged his fingers into his ears against the screams and buried his remorse under a recitation from the Qur'an: *There is no fault in the blind, and there is no fault in the lame, and there is no fault in the sick.*

In Peshawar, his father's business contact greeted them coolly. The only shelter he could offer was a shed at the back of his house that had been used for storing wood and now sheltered two goats. It pained Aziz to see his father in these circumstances. If the old man had been stronger they might have turned back, perhaps attempted the longer crossing to Iran and from there into Turkey and on to Europe. Instead, his father, Amal and Yassin remained in the goat shed in Peshawar, while Aziz went on alone.

His impossible quest was to establish a better life for all of them but, realistically, his hopes for the future rested on Yassin. He doubted he would ever see his father again.

ZETT

Three a.m. The house was quiet but Zett felt the distant menace of the town. She had planned to be away by now, but here she was, stuck, just as her mother had been. Twenty years ago, Sadie had left the house she rented in the town and brought them to Havana Gardens, maybe even to this very room, although it would have been a tight squeeze with four children. They had stayed for three months, the first peace and quiet she could ever remember, until their mother got itchy feet and they hit the road for Sydney.

The way she had recreated her mother's life felt cyclical, predictable, almost as if numbers were involved. She eased Opal's face out of her armpit. The attic was stifling, but she was afraid to sleep with the stair door ajar. Jude was out there circling. She should have made funeral arrangements instead of escape plans, because it was only a matter of time until he found her.

A fluttering pain in her chest made her groan and she eased away from the baby, forcing her body to go limp as she concentrated on her breathing. The panic attacks had started about a year ago. Sometimes she could fend off the pain if she made her mind blank quickly enough. Having worked up the nerve to describe her symptoms to the doctor, at least she knew what it was. Supposedly, nothing to worry about.

'It feels like I'm having a bloody heart attack,' she told him.

The doctor pressed his stethoscope against her chest, and then her back. She caught the whiff of whisky on his breath as he pumped air into the pink blood pressure bandage.

'Everything all right at home?' he said.

She caught his eye and for a moment considered blurting out the truth. Other times, when she'd turned up brindled with bruises and dragging various broken bones, he had pretended to believe she'd fallen down the back steps. Once she'd invented an elaborate tale of being hit by kids playing frisbee. The doctor's red-rimmed eyes had fixed on her, inviting confession, but she'd stared back at his yellowish complexion, shrugged and started chewing on a wad of gum.

'Everything's fine.'

Her blood pressure was normal, he said.

'It's just the way my heart thumps in the middle of the night that frightens me to death.'

The doctor told her to try deep breathing, like in childbirth. Sometimes it worked. She would not die of anxiety. Not yet, anyway. If she stayed quiet it would pass. Zett tried to distract herself by skipping backwards through her life.

'Think you've got it bad now,' she whispered, 'what about the time in Sydney when Sadie went missing for three days and there was nothing in the fridge and your sisters were looking up hospitals in the phone book and ringing them one by one?'

Her mother had done that every so often: thrown a turn and done a runner. It got so they could recognise the signs. Whenever Zett opened the front door and found Sadie bleaching everything in sight — walls, floors, sink — she knew better than to ask what was up. After the second or third time, Louise and Michelle hadn't even bothered to ring the hospitals. Sadie always came back.

Zett's chest tightened. What about the time she went for the abortion, eighteen and not very cluey, in spite of her upbringing? By the time she had worked out what was wrong, she swore the baby was kicking. She went alone. The woman who did it rigged up a screen so Zett couldn't see what was going on down below. When it was over, she'd asked if it had been a boy or a girl.

The woman tapped her sharply on the knee. 'Doesn't matter now,' she said, 'you can get dressed in a minute.'

She remembered water gushing into the sink, the sucking sound as it drained and the heaviness of her limbs. She had felt too beaten to persist, but even now she still wondered.

Their mother told them once that every time she'd fallen pregnant she had thought of having them aborted or adopted. 'Poor little buggers,' she said. 'Might have been better for youse if I had.'

'Think you've got it bad now, what about the chicken farm?'

After twenty years, the memory of the farm still gave her the horrors. It was on the outskirts of Sydney, their first stop after Havana Gardens. Zett remembered the cages of neurotic pecking birds, the noise and putrid smell. Sadie's job in the mornings was to find the birds that looked sick and cut off their heads. She remembered her terror as the headless bodies thumped about the yard spurting blood. On the production line, freshly killed chickens were hung on hooks and dipped into boiling water. The smell of wet feathers made Zett puke. Louise and Michelle could pluck chickens in a flash, but it turned out Zett was allergic to feathers. There were turkeys, too, but they were plucked dry. The feathers got everywhere.

She remembered the forty-four-gallon drum of turkey innards with its constant blue-black cloud of blowflies. One day, she and her brother were standing beside it when one of the farm girls walked past and made a nasty remark. Cam reached into the drum and pulled out a length of turkey intestine. He swung it like a rope, and when it wrapped around the girl's neck she ran, screaming, with the turkey gizzard flapping behind her.

The chicken farm had been a career change for Sadie. She'd tried her best, but it hadn't worked out. They had stayed just long enough for the farm to become the bench-mark against which hard times past, present and future would be measured.

Zett rolled to the edge of the sofa to give Opal more air. As always when she paused between thoughts, an image of Jude arrived unbidden. If the two-up had started again down at George's Lane, her husband might be there in his civvies. She'd gone with him once. Never again. The front for the game was a greasy spoon cafe run by a Lebanese family. Curried sausages and steak and eggs served up at all hours. Paper plates to save on washing-up. In the back and down a step was the game. Men packed in shoulder to shoulder on pay night, and they carried on until they faded. Women were not allowed. Sometimes one would turn up and try to pull a husband out, tugging at a sleeve as he was trying to bet his way out of trouble.

A few weeks back, two blokes wearing balaclavas and waving guns had come looking for the game and knocked at the house next door by mistake. Of course, old Duff Petrie opened up, then shouted to his wife to call the police. Orla Petrie was as silly as a hen; she'd panicked and slammed the door, locking Duff out on the verandah with the gunmen. In the end, the would-be robbers jumped back in their car and drove off, but Orla had squawked to the press, and Jude had been forced to close the game. He'd told Zett how the Lebanese went scuttling like dung beetles when he turned up in their scruffy kitchen to investigate. Jude swore they knew the gunmen.

'Look, tell us who it was and you can have the game back,' he told them.

But the Lebs had more sense; the balaclavas might sober up. Rather than dob them in, they had shoved the curried sausages and steaks into the freezer. The minute Jude hinted that he might let them have the game back, the Lebs defrosted. This freeze and defrost routine went on until the sausages would have killed anyone who touched them. Zett wondered if the Lebanese had finally ditched the meat, or if they were hanging on in hope.

It was these moments of insanity that had entertained her as she nursed her injuries. In five years of marriage there had been a constant stream of cracked ribs, sprained wrists, bruises spreading beneath her clothing or the camouflage of her hair. This was how it was in the town, men and women slogging it out in small tin houses, with the occasional shooting or show-stopper, like the silly bastards who had tried to rob the game.

Zett wedged Opal against the back of the sofa and slithered onto the floor. She fumbled for her cigarettes; a snake would calm her nerves. She found the packet beside the ashtray, eased one out and propped her buttocks on the broad arm of the sofa as she lit up. The square of black window was sprinkled with stars; out on the river flats a bonfire flickered. Zett looked at it and shivered. It would only take a few wrong moves to end up out there, grubbing in the dirt, struggling to raise Opal among druggies and glue-sniffers. She had to keep a grip, whatever happened.

She watched a police vehicle cruise along the back road; it was heading towards the flats with its blue light flashing. For as long as she could remember, the black settlement had existed as an invisible satellite to the town. In the last few years, with the government housing scheme, the settlement across the river had become more solid-looking, even though the builders had walked off and left the job half done. Some houses were not much more than concrete slabs with wooden studwork, over which people tacked hessian sacks, sheets of plastic and pieces of old carpet. She'd heard the community centre was finished, but water and electricity had never been connected. At night the sounds of shouting and fighting and singing drifted in from this blacked-out town and gangs of Aboriginal kids crossed the river and roamed around looking for trouble. Whatever went wrong, they copped the blame, and as Jude said, they probably deserved it.

The sudden whine of a siren made her shake, and she ducked below the sill. No-one could see her, but still, Jude was on the prowl. Perhaps he was searching for her among the lost souls on the flats. He'd never let her get away, that was for sure.

It was bad luck that she'd seen anything. Those stupid lunches. Jude had gone on a diet — probably after screwing some woman who'd remarked on his paunch — and laid down the law about what he'd eat and what he wouldn't.

Grilled chicken breasts, boiled eggs and lettuce, mainly. Zett was to cook fresh chicken each day and bring it down to the station. She'd done it for two weeks, and he'd lost a couple of kilos. Big deal.

The last time she saw Jude she'd arrived with the plastic containers and there was no-one in the office, so she dropped the lunch on his desk and wandered through to the lockup. Jude and a buddy were busy beating the daylights out of young Billy Martin. They had their backs to her, putting the boot in while Billy squirmed on the concrete floor. There was blood on the walls and Billy's chest was smeared with it. She saw Jude crouched beside him, the full width of his shoulders facing her; the other cop just drawing back his boot; Billy's young body, surprisingly wasted, with blood trickling in a thin sticky line from one of his ears.

She'd eased out quick and gone straight home. Her husband kept a stash of firearms in a locked box in the wardrobe and she'd picked out a handgun, slipped it into Opal's nappy bag, then bolted. Having the gun helped on these nights when she woke, jittery with panic, although she had no illusions it would save her.

On the radio it said that Billy Martin had died in his cell a few hours after she'd seen him. He was supposed to have hung himself with strips ripped off his T-shirt, but that was bullshit. All he'd been wearing was a filthy pair of boxer shorts. Billy was the third brother from the same family to die in custody. Zett knew his mother, Flo — a half-caste with numerous kids, some of whom were as good as white. Flo had gone boonta a couple of years back after the first boy died, walking through town on paydays singing and shouting, rolling her big sad eyes and scaring people. In her wreck of a house out on the flats a transistor radio blared night and day, as if Flo couldn't bear to be alone with her thoughts. Jude had pulled her in for questioning a few times and, from the smug expression on his face when he talked about it, Zett wondered what else he'd done with her — anything was possible with people from the no-man's-land of the river flats.

Zett squashed out the cigarette and reached for another. Miri's escapee had probably gravitated there. With his colour and his potential to bring trouble, he belonged out with Flo and rest of them. Selfish bitch that she was, she hoped the cops were taken up with sniffing after him, because a stink was brewing over Billy Martin. When he'd found his lunch, Jude must have known she'd seen Billy on the floor. No, he'd never let her leave the town.

AZIZ

However far he travelled, in any direction, he was searching for a way back. Always back. Days when his eyes had streamed, when the salty flow of tears distorted his vision and he had lurched, step to step, field to field, town to town, carrying no memory of his passage, on those days and on all others he had been searching every moment for a way back.

What kind of person chose exile? Did anyone ever choose? Officially, he did not exist. He had no travel documents, no papers, nothing to stake his claim on the earth which his great-grandfathers once hunted with eagles and which, as far as he could tell, was governed now by guns and moneylenders. Absence defined him. It was the biggest part of him, just as the emptiness of the sky was always bigger than the land. And within this vast absence he felt himself to be a series of disconnected episodes, gestures and reactions, stung into action and lumpily strung together by memory.

Memory was the adhesive that bound the universe. If he existed at all it was in the collective memory of his far-flung family, while they depended for existence upon his fixing them in the beam of his thoughts. Each morning when he woke he counted the people, still living, who remembered him. He feared them diminishing and wondered if the weakness that sprang at him out of nowhere was a sign that one of his memory-holders had died. He wondered, too, what would happen when there was no longer anyone alive who remembered him; would he finally become invisible? Still, at times, the presence of his family was as solid as the road. He heard their voices, quarrels, laughter, prayers, urging him on. But oh, how difficult it was to hold absent people and places steady. Distance had a power, verging on divine, to erase households, towns, cities, whole continents, all the complex lives, both known and unknown. Distance rearranged possibilities, luck, coincidence. It destroyed personal history. As he travelled, his world was erased behind him, absorbed into the void that extended to infinity from the spot where he stood at this moment, feverish and stranded.

He stood with his back to the sun, wiped the sweat from his eyelids and told himself not to be so stupid. The road still stretched before him, one thousand miles, or maybe two. Faced with the impossible, the Qur'an guided and comforted him.

This is My Straight Road, so follow it . . .

Sometimes he resorted to the poet Rūmī. Rūmī was a friend to walk with, but, above all, he walked with Allah. The food the woman had given him was an unaccustomed weight in his stomach. It slowed his legs. Sweat slid from his underarms across his belly as he wandered the fringes of the town in search of a shady spot to rest.

Viewed from back lanes the town was a patchwork of corrugated iron, a land of fragments, where black plastic bin bags blossomed among the dismembered carcasses of cars, where broken parts of brightly coloured toys were scattered among discarded household appliances. He shook his head at the evidence of waste, at a culture so acquisitive that no time was set aside to mend. Small in scale, the town still reminded him of the ugly underside of cities he had seen from trains, of rubbish tumbling over rubbish along the embankments, higgledy houses, beaten streets. The emptiness of Afghanistan had modelled his senses. Its landscapes bathed in saffron light. Its bare-walled houses. By comparison, the town was cluttered and ugly.

Dogs leapt at the fences, barking. His head began to ache. By its isolation, the town had become another kind of prison from which he must escape. In the distance, the span of an iron bridge loomed battleship grey. He walked towards it and came upon the river, sluggish water over-hung with willows. When he had crossed to the other side he turned and looked back at the town, dazzled by the undulating shimmer of its rooftops.

Behind him, half-a-dozen trees rippled above the liquid plain, an oasis, inhabited by *jinn.* He shuffled across the baked ground until the trees solidified. Here, around a grid of unsealed streets, were houses missing roofs and walls. On the outskirts, an old man stretched on a blanket, smoking. A woman pegged washing. There was radio noise. When the woman turned, her face was immobile, a mask with two red holes for the eyes. She floated towards him, the shape of her mouth distorted by suffering. Her sorrow hit him like a hammer.

Bismillah ir Rahman ir Rahim . . . the opening of the Qur'an came unbidden as his gaze fastened with recognition on another lost soul. He stumbled towards her.

Over every soul there is a watcher.

He said it before he fell, before the air thickened and his ears began to roar. He felt nothing as the ground hit him.

Over every soul there is a watcher.

MIRI

She squatted on the bedroom floor in front of her suitcase, tugged out the tangled contents and began to fold them into piles. There were pieces of clothing she would have no use for: wispy dresses, a beaded jacket. It was clear she'd been on autopilot when she packed. Even now she could not think straight. It was as if every thought set up a heat in her head. She dreaded waking each day, dreaded her dreams, and sometimes, when the heat was too much, she panted softly like a dog to disperse it.

A white silk blouse was crushed between two odd shoes. Strange how expensive clothing weighed almost nothing; either that or it was heavier than the fibres of cheaper fabrics. She smoothed out the silk and folded it. In the bottom of the case was another blouse, wine-red with panels of embroidery. Miri sat back on her heels, remembering how and where she'd found it.

It had been a Friday afternoon. She'd been working, shooting a commercial at a beach south of the city, and after two days had been glad to wave goodbye to the crew and head for Sydney. Gerroa, Werri Beach, Dapto, Wollongong West. Skimming up the battered sweep of Broadway three hours later on a sudden wave of optimism, she was humming under her breath. By the time she dropped the suitcase in the bedroom she felt so light she was almost gliding. The mile of bleached sand with its gaudy props and jaded crew receded. She was home again, and Alice was getting better, she was going to be all right.

Outside the bedroom window the evening sky was luminous, and when she hooked back the curtains the walls were stippled rose and mauve. The first gulp of gin and tonic in the kitchen sent a shiver up her bare arms. She was just starting on the second as she emptied her suitcase and waited for the shower to run hot.

And then the electrifying discovery of strange garments nestled among her dresses in the wardrobe, a moment of stunned silence before Miri plunged in with both hands. Coat-hangers screeched and scraped as she tore a space around the unfamiliar clothing. The clues had been cleverly planted. A slender black dress, a blouse with panels of gypsy embroidery; they were things she might have worn herself. Jack could have checked the wardrobe and never noticed, but the dress and the gypsy blouse definitely didn't belong.

Gravity had doubled as she stared at the blouse. It dragged at her with the weight of nineteen years of marriage, and then, inside her head, something began to pump until it threatened to explode. Once, the resilience of her body would have been enough to put even the tug of the planet in its place. But that was then.

Now, in her mother's bedroom, Miri took the blouse from the suitcase and slipped it onto a hanger. She was sliding it into the wardrobe when Zett appeared in the doorway with a loaf of bread in her hand and Opal balanced on a hip.

She jerked her head in the direction of the kitchen. 'Well, I said he'd turn up again and he sure enough has.'

'What?'

'Dumped on the back step like an abandoned baby and about as helpless.'

Miri followed Zett down to the kitchen.

'I was heating Opal's dinner when Flo Martin tapped at the window and scared the shit out of me.'

Miri remembered Flo Martin. Flo had been a stunner in her day, the sort of woman men turned to look at in the street. But once they realised she was from the river flats they'd mutter things or crack filthy jokes.

Zett mimicked perfectly the Aboriginal woman's gruff dry voice. ' "This fella's gunna bring trouble and rather you get it than poor Flo," is what she said. Then she took off.'

He lay on the verandah with his arm shielding his eyes. When Miri leaned over him he looked up once under his hand, before his eyes rolled back in his head and he began to shiver.

'See what I mean?'

Miri sighed. 'We'll have to bring him inside,' she said.

AZIZ

When he had woken the first time it was with the sun in his eyes and someone pulling at his arms. Then an elbow in his ribs and the whiff of cigarette smoke as a radio beat out senseless conversation. A woman's smoky voice said something sharp, something directed at him. He understood by the tone of it and by the way she jerked his arms about that she wanted him to get up, but he could not do as she asked. His leg throbbed, and his body was bathed in sweat. After a while the woman gave up, and some time later he felt a bottle tilted to his lips. Tepid water trickled down his neck and soaked his shirt. The shadows of the figures standing over him stretched long and thin in the syrupy sunlight. It was afternoon then, and he guessed he was among the *jinn*, might have been there for days, or even weeks.

After sipping water, he plummeted from consciousness into dream landscapes, harsh black hills, snowy wastelands, rutted roads, and himself bouncing in the back of a white open-backed truck with the wind and sand stinging his eyes. Pakistani voices mocked him as he dropped into a sweatshop where racketing machinery stamped metal shapes and took off the fingers of the slowest.

He woke whimpering and squeezing his fingers into fists. A dog with orange eyes and fur sniffed at the cuff of his shirt. A child with a runny nose and scabby knees stood to one side, sucking its thumb and staring. Close by, he could hear someone struggling for breath. He rolled his head and saw a woman sucking an inhaler. He'd seen people use them before. A cigarette dangled from her left hand, and the blue smoke spiralled into the sun. The woman's hair and skin were tawny, her bare arms mottled with bruises. An old black man with greying whiskers and pouched eyes stood beside her shaking his head.

Aziz had no idea what the man was saying in his gruff voice, but he picked up the word *police*. He closed his eyes, and almost at once he was back in the detention camp, barefoot on the baked ground of the compound and waiting his turn for the shower. From the women's block came the sound of crying. He heard the guard's voice, strong and teasing, and then an Iranian voice, female, not so young. She was trying to speak calmly.

'Soap,' the woman said in English, a strange blunt sound, followed by a storm of pleading and apology in Farsi. There was a pause and then the woman's voice quavered as she said again, 'Soap.'

Aziz gathered from her rapid Farsi that the woman had learned this word by heart. Someone had told her it was the right word, but it would not work for her.

'Say please!' shouted the guard. 'Where's your manners?'

He understood this from the English classes. It was a favourite rebuke in the camp, as if detainees were automatically less courteous than guards because they spoke a different language.

'Soap.' The woman said it quietly, but her voice was tight and anxious and Aziz could tell she was growing less sure about the rightness of the word. In Farsi, she begged the guard's forgiveness. Aziz guessed the soap was being held just out of reach. He had seen guards do that with sanitary pads and toilet paper. The women cringed and scuttled away rather than reach for what they needed in public, in front of men.

The guard roared, 'Not until you say please,' and a door slammed.

Please. Please. It was the first English word they learned, in an effort to placate their captors, but this woman had just arrived. He heard a long low moan on the other side of the wall; the Iranian woman had given up.

Water trickled in the drain beside him. His turn came and he stepped onto the wet concrete of the shower room. The hiss of the water overwhelmed the sound of the woman weeping, and when he emerged it was to silence, broken only by the harsh cries of the large black birds that swooped in out of the desert and perched on the roof of the accommodation block.

When he opened his eyes again it was dusk. A fire smoked in the open, and the tawny-haired woman was cooking something in a pan that sizzled and spat. He could smell the greasy food but did not feel hungry. He wondered when he had last eaten. From where he lay he could see a row of wooden houses. It seemed as if he was stretched in the middle of a street, and when he looked closely he saw that there was a house, or the beginnings of one, not far from where the woman hunched over the fire. The other houses had walls but no windows. A few had slanting tin roofs.

The woman waved her arm in his direction, then said something to the old man, who limped away towards one of the houses. Aziz slid a hand down his leg. The limb felt enormous, like the trunk of a fallen tree. The throbbing had shifted from his leg to his head and he began to shiver. When he tried to move his foot there was resistance, as if he'd been hobbled. He had once seen a group of men killing a cow, tying its legs and weighing it down with their bodies while one of them worked at its throat with the knife. The cow had kept struggling, fountaining blood, until finally the head was severed.

He felt himself lifted, and a surge of apprehension gave him the strength to raise his head. He was being carried away from the fire towards a square of light. His armpits were locked over the bony shoulders of the men carrying him, and he screamed as his leg dragged and bumped over the rough ground. The square of light became a window. The walking ceased, and he woke on dry wooden boards. And then the door opened and the woman bent over him. Her hair flapped like the wings of a black bird. Her eyes were soft and sad. He spoke to her in Dari, a torrent of explanation and apology for his obvious state of need.

The woman seemed to listen, then shook her head.

Although some part of his brain knew it was inevitable, when she spoke he almost shrieked out loud his grief and disappointment that she did not answer in his own language.

MIRI

They lifted him under his arms to drag him inside and stretch him on the kitchen floor. Zett hovered over him with her hands on her hips, while Miri locked the back door and drew the roller blind.

'He's so out of it,' Zett said. 'Looks to me like he needs proper doctoring.'

'If we do that, maybe . . .'

'Yeah, he'll be in the lockup faster than you can say escapee.'

'You think that's what he is?'

'Don't you?'

Miri shrugged. A crust of blood rimmed his lower lip, and his breathing was heavy. Her mouth hardened as she thought of the bus driver with his meaty fists and the bullet-headed policemen who had come barging into the house.

Zett pushed her fringe out of her eyes. 'I think he's coming round a bit. Maybe he's just dehydrated.'

A pulse beat softly at the base of his throat. Miri lifted his hand; the skin was hot and dry. He was conscious and not so ill that he needed an ambulance. There would be doctors in the phone book. Or they could get him into the car and she could drive to the hospital. But at the hospital there would be questions.

His fingers pressed her wrist as she looked into his exhausted eyes. 'I'll talk to Lois,' she said.

The sprinklers Miri had set out earlier hissed unseen as she hurried along the path towards Lois's house. The scent of the watered gardens jerked her back to the time, right after her mother died, when Con had become fierce and silent, absorbed with dogs and horses and gardening, forgetful of mealtimes, of Miri's bedtime, of the need to load the washing machine. The house was never empty, yet with her mother gone it had felt abandoned and desolate. After a while Miri had drifted in Lois's direction. Unlike Con, Lois often talked about Candela, and Miri grew skilled at prompting her. And if there was a problem, as there often was with a household full of strangers, Lois was never stuck for an idea about what to do. She would know what to do now.

The damp fronds of tree ferns brushed her cheeks as she pushed past them to a gate with a radiant sun embedded in its iron spokes. The gate stood open, and as she emerged onto the footpath, she spotted the glow of a cigarette on Lois's verandah.

Her aunt's breathy voice floated towards her. 'How're you doin', doll?'

Up close, she could see Lois was wearing shortie pyjamas and mules with a fluff of marabou feathers.

'Listen, Lo, who's the backyard quack these days?'

'Someone pregnant?'

Miri shook her head. 'Not pregnant, sick.'

'To tell you the truth I thought you were looking real off-colour when you got here, hon.'

Miri climbed up onto the slab of concrete and squatted beside Lois's chair.

'Not me, Lo. It's someone at the house.'

'Where from?'

'Who knows? Flo's lot just dumped him on the back step.'

'Blackfella?'

'No. Foreign, though. Doesn't speak much English.'

Lois ground out the cigarette on the cement and squinted at Miri. 'You sure he's not dangerous?'

'Don't think so, just sick.'

'Artie Rose's your best bet. He doctors dogs and horses better than that useless Stan Priddle, the vet. Sewed Tania back together after two Alsatians chewed her up. Dig swears by him.'

'He's safe with people, is he?'

Lois laughed. 'Course he is. You remember Artie, he was a proper doctor till he got in a row with one of the bosses up the mines.' She pointed to the path that led from the sun gate towards the western side of the gardens. 'There, behind the blue fence. Tell him you're Candy's daughter. He was sweet on your mother.'

'You mean the Polish bloke, Arthur Rosenberg?'

'That's right.'

As a child, Miri had watched him from the upstairs balcony as he pegged washing in his front yard. A lanky figure in singlet and shorts, his arms and legs glowed like white neon on washdays.

'I thought Con told me he'd died,' she said.

Lois shook her head. 'He had a breakdown and went away for a couple years. People say things, but take my word for it, there's nothing wrong with Artie.'

As Miri walked towards his house, she reflected that, in time, people might say the same about her.

Artie Rose's house was wooden, painted turquoise with pink trim. In the front yard rosemary bushes had been clipped into lumpy mounds, and the light bulb on the verandah wore a halo of moths and mosquitoes. Between the bushes, tin shapes balanced on spikes of varying heights or leaned at odd angles as if drunk. Sunflower faces, butterflies, ladybugs, an angel that was a twin for the weathervane on the roof of Havana Gardens. Scattered here and there were figurines, women in flowing plaster robes, cherubs with chubby hands clasping birdbaths and bowls of striped petunias. The effect of the tin cut-outs was childlike and jolly, and the statues reminded Miri of the shabby saints inside Havana Gardens. At the side of the house, an ancient flatbed truck stood under a pergola with its rear end jacked up.

The front door was open, and Miri peered along a passage towards a rectangle of fluorescent light.

'Anyone home?'

Shadows on the concrete steps made the shapes of hands, and from the back of the house came the whirr of machinery.

'Hello?' Miri edged into the passage and tripped over a car battery and a knee-high stack of *National Geographic* magazines. The hall carpet was dingy, its pile flattened. The walls had been papered with colour pictures torn from magazines, misty European cities pasted beside Amazonian tribes and Arctic snow. An odour of cigarettes and beer wafted from a room where the innards of an ancient wireless were laid out in neat lines on the carpet.

Artie Rose was in his kitchen, bent over an electric coffee grinder. He straightened as she appeared in the doorway, turned off the machine and stared at her in silence.

'The door was open,' she said.

He wiped his hands on a corner of the tablecloth. 'So, it is the niece of Connie Kissack,' he said. 'How is Connie going in the hospital?'

His heavily accented English struck her as familiar and pleasing, like voices overheard in corner shops and in the shabby hallways of rooming houses during her early days in Sydney.

'Finding the boredom harder to bear than the broken hip. I'm Miriam, but you worked that out pretty quick.'

He smiled as he measured ground coffee into a percolator and set it on the gas stove. 'A blind man could spot a Kissack woman a mile off. You are all like Essie, even though she refused to be a Kissack until the day she died, when they did carve it on her headstone anyway.'

The sleeves of his navy blue shirt were rolled up over forearms the colour of a well-done roast. A slice of white glimmered below the triangle of tanned skin at his neck and round steel-rimmed glasses appeared embedded in the sockets of his deep-set eyes. He was the same as Miri remembered, but older, somewhere in his seventies she guessed. His kitchen was a jumble of worn and cracked surfaces, of curling lino, scratched laminex. On the back wall, cooking utensils dangled on nails and missing shapes were outlined in felt pen, as if his spatula, rolling pin and wooden spoon were carpenter's tools.

Above the table, photographs were thumbtacked to the plasterboard, people in heavy coats and old-fashioned hats, their faces the colour of blanched almonds, their smiles tentative; in the eyes and mouths and hands she saw echoes of Artie Rose. Then, pinned in the centre, was a photograph she had seen before of a woman and a child walking beside a river in summer clothing. The figures were caught mid-stride and the woman's black hair billowed in an invisible breeze as she turned to call to someone outside the picture frame. The woman looked like her mother, or maybe Con. The child, she was certain, was herself. Miri turned to ask Artie about it, but his penetrating gaze was fixed upon her.

'I do not get many visitors,' he said. 'Usually there is a reason.'

The percolator puffed steam, and she watched him pick it up and pour coffee into a thick white cup. He handed it to her and found a clean cup for himself.

'Someone's sick and Lois says you're the best person to look him over.'

'You would like milk or sugar?'

'Black is fine.'

Artie Rose blew across the surface of the coffee and took a sip. 'Ah, sickness,' he said. 'And so you come to my house. That means a gunshot wound or a knife in the gut perhaps?'

'Nothing like that. He's got a temperature. He looks bad, but I don't think he's going to die.' She took a sip of coffee. 'I don't know exactly what's wrong; I'm not a doctor.'

The bluish light passed over Artie's thinning hair, draining colour from his skin and defining grooves that ran from nose to chin on either side of his long sad face. Beneath the scent of coffee, a whiff of cat litter drifted in from the back porch. Somewhere a dog whined, and paws scrabbled against wood.

'According to the official wisdom of this town, neither am I.'

'Lois says you heal more animals than the vet.'

'Oh,' he waved dismissively, 'that is not difficult. Did you know that people have their dogs put down before they go on holiday because the kennel fees got too expensive? Stan Priddle is happy to oblige.' He nodded towards the noise out back. 'A dingo pup I found limping around full of air gun pellets. That is the kind of patch-up job I do these days. It has been a while since I have been asked to mend a human.' Behind the glasses, Artie's eyes were the colour of blue slate. He set down his cup and winked at her. 'But no harm is there in looking. So, let us inspect your sick human and no questions will I ask.'

Zett had disappeared upstairs, but the man was still stretched out on the lino where she had left him, his black hair slick with sweat. When Artie Rose knelt beside him, he tried to lift his head.

'Be still, my friend.' Artie laid a hand on his forehead. 'Ah, you were quite right about the temperature!'

From a battered brown case, he produced a stethoscope and a thermometer. Miri pulled out a chair and sat at the table, while Artie pressed the stethoscope to the patient's chest. It was almost eight o'clock, and from the direction of the town came the sudden whoop of a siren; she hoped the police would not choose this moment to make another house call. Miri watched Artie gently run his hands down the man's body. When he touched the right leg there was a sharp yelp, and the foot jerked.

'We must remove this shoe.'

The man wore grey trainers that might once have been white. The sides were cracked and the sole flapped free on the left foot. Artie poked at the flap of rubber and began to ease the shoe from the foot, until the man gave a hoarse cry.

'You have some scissors?'

She found a pair of sewing scissors in the cutlery drawer, and together they cut the shoe along the frayed side seam, peeling it away to reveal a filthy sock stained with dried blood. The man rolled and muttered as Artie slit the thin cotton.

There was a wound at the base of the big toe, and his foot had lost its shape in the swelling.

Artie shook his head over it, and said in his formal, slightly back-to-front English, 'Your friend did get his foot infected. Also there is a foreign object embedded. Brown glass. A shard from a beer bottle would be my guess.'

'Can you do anything?'

Artie sat back on his heels. 'The infection could be dangerous.' He looked around the kitchen as if assessing it, then back at Miri. 'We must operate to remove the glass,' he said. 'Are you the squeamish sort?'

'I might be.'

She stood up and moved aimlessly towards the cutlery drawer, opened it, closed it again, then leaned against the sink and looked back at the man's thin arms jutting from the sleeves of his T-shirt, his black hair against the yellow lino.

'What do I have to do?'

Artie opened his case and picked through the instruments inside. 'Please do like in the films. Boil up water.'

In the end she went for Dig, who helped them carry the patient to the long table in the dining room. Miri had cleared it of old newspapers and racing guides and covered it with a clean sheet. Dig found a 100-watt light bulb for the overhead socket and climbed up on a chair to fit it, while Artie sterilised instruments in Con's preserving pan. With everything ready, they began.

'If you would be so kind as to cut away the trouser leg?' Artie handed Miri the scissors.

The felted cloth divided easily as she worked her way down the seam. The man turned his head and moaned softly when Artie fumbled in his case and produced a disposable syringe.

'Ketamine can be kind to humans as well as to horses,' he said, easing the needle into the man's thigh. 'It will all be over in the blink of an eye, my friend.'

Once the injection had taken effect, Dig held the foot steady while Artie probed the wound. Miri retreated to the bay window. She was dying for a cigarette, but it seemed callous to light one. Artie worked in silence until the pain breached the threshold of the drug, and the patient yelled. The man's groping hands found the table edges, and he tried to pull himself up, but Dig's big square palm on his chest flattened him against the table.

'Orright, mate, just hold still a minute,' he said.

Artie hunched over the foot, light winking on the round lenses of his glasses and his long serious face creased in concentration. When the patient strained to withdraw his foot from Dig's grip, Artie muttered soothing noises, while his fingers tightened on the tweezers. In another minute he grunted with satisfaction, and drew an inch-long shard of brown glass from the pulpy wound. The patient's hoarse cry as Artie swabbed the foot with disinfectant made Miri flinch. She peered over Dig's shoulder, expecting to have to help subdue the struggling figure on the table, but the man suddenly passed out. In another moment Artie was drawing the wound together with a row of neat black stitches. Afterwards he soaked a wad of sterile dressing in honey.

'Same's when Artie fixed my racing dog after she jumped a barbed wire fence last year,' Dig said as Miri eyed the honey jar.

'Honey is nature's healer. In a week, I promise you, that foot will be pink, like the foot of a newborn.'

Her uncle flashed a grin. 'Lucky Tikki romped home ten lengths ahead of the field on her next race. The bookies wept for a week.'

Artie wound a crepe bandage around the dressing. 'A spectacular win,' he said. 'But more to do with the caffeine you dosed her with than the honey I put on her wounds.'

Dig shook his head. 'That bloody dog was lazy. Could've won under her own steam if she'd wanted to, but the caffeine lit her fuse all right. Now she's got the right idea she places at every start.'

Artie pinned the tail of the bandage with a safety pin, then slid his fingers around the patient's wrist, taking his pulse. They waited while he counted the beats and nodded his satisfaction.

'Our friend here must rest while the wound heals. You have spare bedrooms upstairs?'

As Miri watched the man on the table, his hollow cheeks with the long lashes fanned against the sallow skin, a warning buzzed behind her breastbone: once installed, he would have to be nursed for a week, or maybe longer. If the police came back he would be difficult to hide. Yet his black hair and reed-thin body so reminded her of Alice that she found herself climbing the stairs, pushing open bedroom doors without reluctance.

The door of the blue room opened off a larger bedroom at the back of the house, a narrow space that had once been her mother's workroom. Here, Candela had hand-tinted studio portraits, working roses into children's lips and cheeks, colouring the endless photographs of dogs and horses winning and losing races that had given her a steady income. There had been a table under the window where she laid out the lists of jockeys' racing silks. Now the room was bare, but dull carmine and ochre smudges stained the pale blue plaster of the back wall and a dribble of ultramarine paint meandered across the floorboards from the door to the place where the work table had once stood. The arrangement was not perfect, but with Zett and Opal in the attic it was the best she could do.

Dig helped her drag in a mattress from the outer bedroom and push it into the corner. In Con's linen press she found stacks of worn cotton sheets. After she had made up the bed, Dig and Artie bundled the patient into a clean sheet and carried him upstairs. Miri had found a sheepskin rug to soften the mattress and spread it under his shoulders as they laid him on the bed.

'One red capsule, three times a day.' Artie handed Miri a bottle. 'And the white ones for the pain – give two when necessary. He will be thirsty when he wakes.'

The bottle of antibiotics bore a veterinary label and instructions for dosing a dog. Miri shrugged; Artie Rose seemed to know what he was doing.

After Artie and Dig had left, she carried a bowl of warm water, soap, a sponge and a fresh towel to the blue room and, after only the smallest hesitation, eased the soiled T-shirt over his arms and head and stripped away the remains of his trousers. He wore no underwear. With the sheet peeled back, his navel was a shadowy indentation in the hollow abdomen, and his penis, softly curled in a nest of pubic hair, looked so vulnerable, so private, that she quickly tucked the sheet around his body.

He stirred and opened his eyes as if he had felt her gaze.

'How are you feeling?' she said.

His puzzled eyes drifted from her face to the window, then closed again, and she wondered whether the horse tranquilliser was keeping him from consciousness, or if he was just reluctant to wake.

From long habit, she inspected the labels as she folded his clothes. The T-shirt was a chain-store brand, pure cotton that had lost its shape over many washes. The trousers, as she had suspected, were the bottom half of a woollen suit that had been a quality item in its day, stiff now with dust and with a strong odour of livestock clinging to the fabric. A stone rolled from a pocket and bounced across the floor; it was the size of a small pear and roughly the same shape, soft yellow with rust-coloured flecks. Miri felt the weight of it in her palm, squeezed it once and set it on the windowsill.

Although he no longer felt like a complete stranger, it was odd to be alone with a man in this room where she had once sharpened coloured pencils for her mother. She let the warm soapy water trickle from the sponge and thought of Con's omens for good and evil as she pressed it against his cheek. She had shared the last of her water with him in the desert, had twice rescued and once cooked breakfast for him, she had watched him faint with pain during the operation on his foot, and now, undressing his limp body, had learned that he carried a pear-shaped stone in his pocket. She and Jack had been married for almost twenty years, and yet Miri could not say for sure what she would find if she were to empty his pockets.

She washed his face, relieved to have something definite to do. His chest was soft, smooth as warm marble. Turning over his hands one at a time, she passed the sponge over calluses at the backs of the finger joints and across the tops of the palms. His hands were used to heavy work, but she could have looped her fingers around his narrow wrists.

For an hour or more she sat beside him while he slept, following the rhythm of his breathing, letting time slide over her as she gazed at the rectangle of sky framed in the window.

The clinic where Alice had become a patient was a rambling stone house near Centennial Park, set back from the street in a garden of painfully bright flowers. Inside, the wooden floors and bare walls conjured a monastic calm. A receptionist checked Alice's details on a concealed computer screen. Tap tap tap. She looked up and smiled at Miri as if this was any normal day, any normal hospital.

'Mrs Passmore,' she said, 'morning meditation is just about to finish, and then you will be able to see your daughter in the day lounge.'

'Does she know I'm coming?'

The receptionist's coral-coloured smile was pasted to her smooth face. 'Oh, yes,' she said, and nodded as if everything would be fine.

From the waiting room she stared into a courtyard rimmed by red hibiscus. With their thrusting stamens and petals wide open to the sun, the flowers looked so optimistic that the sight of them made her want to cry. Her daughter had been here a fortnight and this was Miri's first visit.

A middle-aged couple came in and sat with their backs to the windows. The woman wore white, and gold chains gleamed against her heavily tanned skin. They didn't look at her, or each other.

'Miri!' Laura Petit hurried towards her on caramel leather heels. Her hair was loose, straight and fine and white as a veil. 'How're you doing?'

Miri grasped Laura's hand. 'Is she any better?'

Across the room, the woman in white inclined her head to catch the answer.

Laura's smile was cautious. 'It's early days yet.' She led the way along a wide corridor to a terrace beside the day lounge.

Alice was so still that at first Miri didn't see her. Then she turned her head, and sunlight struck magenta highlights in her hair with the ferocity of clashing cymbals.

'Hello,' Alice said.

Her voice was listless and through the translucent sleeves of her blouse the knobs of her elbows looked swollen against her withered arms. Miri felt swamped, as if the terrace had been transformed suddenly into a pool of liquid light, and she must breast-stroke to reach her daughter.

Laura's heels tip-tapped away into the shadowed interior of the day lounge.

'There are seats at the end,' Alice said, her eyes enormous. She wasn't wearing any make-up, just a rim of black kohl around her eyes.

They moved towards a picnic table and wooden chairs set in latticed shade. Miri slid a carrier bag onto the table. It contained a rug made of knitted squares that Alice had kept on a chest in her bedroom since she was small, a comfort blanket of many colours.

'I didn't know what to bring, so . . .'

Alice slipped a hand inside the bag and squeezed the wool.

'Thanks.'

'You went to meditation?'

'Every morning. There's no choice.' She screwed up her mouth into a disparaging shape that was so like Jack. 'But it's okay.'

'I wanted to come before.'

'I know. Laura's rules.'

'So how do you pass the days, apart from meditation?'

Alice pulled another face. 'I have to write a diary. Laura says it will help me to express my thoughts.'

'And does it?'

Alice picked at the stitching on her black skirt. 'Maybe.'

'You father will call by tomorrow afternoon.'

Alice turned her head towards the day lounge, and Miri followed her gaze to where the woman in white bent over an emaciated young man in a wheelchair. The patient was about twenty-five, with a shaved head and wire-rimmed glasses. Alice hugged her chest as if it ached and began to make small rhythmic movements, back and forth on the chair.

'Tell him not to come,' she said.

Miri stared at her in silence.

'Seriously, I don't want to see him,' she said. 'If he comes I'll tell Laura not to let him in.'

The sun shining through the lattice swept squares of light across Alice's face.

'But—'

'I *saw* him.' Alice's voice was low and grainy, as if she might scream suddenly, or burst into tears, but she swallowed instead. 'Him and that slut he's been shagging.'

Miri closed her eyes. Parts of her felt frozen and other parts began to melt as she waited for Alice to compose herself. The two of them stared across at the day lounge as the woman in white dropped to her knees beside the young man in the wheelchair. She had hold of his hand but he pulled it away, removed his glasses and started to clean them, polishing and polishing, while the woman knelt beside him, weeping.

An incoherent shriek erupted from an open window above their heads and Miri's head jerked towards the sound. Alice ignored it. When she spoke, her voice was flat.

'He thought I was out,' she said, 'but I was in my room, bumming off a lecture. They were in the spa. She was all over him.'

Miri pressed her palms together between her knees and swallowed. She saw it as clearly as if on a cinema screen, brief moments of steamy sex that would be edited out of the finished cut. She guessed the female lead was Nell.

How to explain to Alice that Jack's infidelities were a part of him that she couldn't change, that he worked with women, often intimately, and sometimes he became obsessed with them, or they with him.

Finally Miri said, 'Just because he's cheated on me doesn't mean he doesn't care about you.'

'Bullshit!'

'Your father loves you.'

'He loves himself, is what he loves. What I saw them doing . . .' She closed her eyes and swallowed, unable to go on.

Alice's hands were cold, despite the summer heat. Miri had covered them with her own. 'Sweetheart . . .'

Jack would not knowingly have hurt Alice, but careless-ness could wreak as much harm as a premeditated act. Damage was damage, and although Miri would come to see the anorexia as a strange, complex state of being, almost like a malign spirit that inhabited Alice rather than an illness caused by any single moment or experience, damage was damage, a crack through which such a spirit could enter and take up residence.

Her daughter's eyes opened wide. 'It's not even like it was the first time, Mum. You should leave. I said so years ago, but you wouldn't.'

Miri stared uncertainly at Alice. She and Jack were so entwined with money and work it was impossible to simply cut a thread. Any change meant unravelling the entire piece, creating a whole new life.

'It's not that easy,' she said.

Alice shrugged. 'Isn't it?'

Looking at her defiant face, Miri remembered a morning when Alice was around five and had tugged at her hand as if trying to drag her into another room.

'Let's go live on our own,' she said.

Miri had laughed. 'Why?'

'Because we are nicer than Daddy.'

When the visiting hour was over Miri kissed Alice lightly on both cheeks and walked to her car. She didn't remember driving home, but somehow she found herself standing on the upstairs landing at the window overlooking the street. All afternoon she stood and watched the shadows stretch and the traffic thicken, watched the triangle of grey pavement, the blue plumbago flowers frothing over the path.

Jack's first infidelity had shocked her hollow. The woman, Keiko, was Japanese and older, although her face and body were remarkably ageless in Jack's photographs. Alice was small then, a toddler waiting to bounce from behind the door when her father came home from work. Small enough, Miri hoped, not to notice the furious white-lipped silences between them, the late-night tears and accusations. Jack was obsessed with Keiko. And then, as suddenly as it had begun, it was over. His interest evaporated, and he was sorry. They took Alice on a holiday to Queensland, pointed out coloured fish, performing dolphins, glowing gardens of coral, in strong bright voices. In a cabin in the rainforest they darned the tear in their marriage. But back in Sydney, she would glance out of the window and see Keiko in the street. The woman stood motionless under one of the plane trees that grew up out of the pavement, a stiff figure with a scarlet mouth and hair as sharp as a blade against her cheek. The sight of Keiko standing there like a life-size statue made her almost faint with terror. She never told Jack for fear of rekindling the affair, just closed the blinds and called Alice into another room. Eventually Keiko disappeared. It was years before she heard of stalkers, years before she realised the woman could have been a danger to her or to Alice. At the time she hadn't known that the greatest danger lay in her own self-doubt, the suspicion that somehow Jack's lack of loyalty was all she deserved.

After Keiko there were others, but the shock was never as great as the first time. By then, all the couples they knew lived the same way; either the husband was cheating, or the wife, or both. Miri withdrew. She created a separate life for herself and Alice, a quiet island where Alice busily dug for treasure, built sandcastles, collected seashells. Sometimes Jack joined them on the island and then the days and nights sparkled with greater brilliance; they rode the ferries back and forth across the harbour, they ate ice-cream and rode the ghost train at Luna Park, laughing and screaming and pulling silly faces for Jack's camera.

She was still waiting on the stairs when Jack came home. She watched him park the car, answer a call on his mobile phone and then reach into the back seat to collect his briefcase. When he straightened, he looked strong and happy. How could Jack be happy? Then, as he slipped the phone into his pocket his face changed, and she understood that happiness was something Jack put on and took off like clothes. Her husband had a happy shirt, given to him by someone else, and when he was at home he took it off.

Miri leaned against the windowsill for support. Their marriage had been a mess for so long that she had lost the shape of it. He came through the front door whistling, oblivious as a Sunday driver in the seconds before a head-on collision.

When he saw her on the landing, his body stiffened. 'What's happened?' he said.

She watched Jack's mouth, the way his lips narrowed when he asked questions. His eyes were a clear saltwater blue. She used to love the way his eyes roamed over her body, but now his gaze made her uncomfortable. She knew her white linen shirt was wrinkled, that fine lines radiated from the corners of her eyes. Jack noticed everything. She turned towards the open window and the street, where a young couple walked with their arms entwined.

'I went to the clinic this morning,' she said.

'How is she?'

Reluctantly, she turned back to him. 'Alice doesn't want to see you.'

He stood very still. From this angle she could see the bowl of his skull with its dense crop of curls. She knew the weight and texture of it in the angle of her neck and shoulder, between her breasts, on the soft shallow mound of her belly. Laughter drifted in from the street.

'I'll leave it a day or two,' he said. His voice was tentative. 'Alice will start feeling better and—'

'No, she won't.'

'Look, Laura says—'

'Alice saw you with Nell Bardot.' Miri's voice thickened. 'You were . . . here.'

Jack cleared his throat.

Suddenly, Miri could not stomach any more deceit. She wanted to rip their marriage open, to tear Jack the way she had been torn.

Her mouth twisted, making what she knew was a savage, ugly shape. 'She was here when you were fucking. She saw you in the bathroom and little Nell had your dick in her mouth. How could you let that happen to Alice, what were you thinking? Are you surprised that she can't eat?'

Jack took half a step backwards. He opened his hands in a gesture of regret. But Miri was down the stairs before he could defend himself, ripping at the open neck of his shirt, her nails shredding the thin cotton, scraping skin. Buttons popped and spun on the wooden floor. He didn't fight, or even strongly resist, just backed through the front door and somehow dematerialised. She heard the street door slam. A minute later his car started up and he drove away.

In the dining room, sunlight streamed through a chink in the curtains and struck the chandelier, projecting beads of light around the walls. Light spots struck the mirror above the sideboard and refracted sideways, roaming the table and Miri's hands as she hunched on one of Con's padded dining chairs. With her chin resting on her knees, Miri gazed at the dozens of photographs dealt out in rows on the table in front of her. Here was Alice's first gummy smile; Alice on her fifth birthday blowing out the candles on a cake; a soft-focus snap of a school nativity scene the year Alice was picked to play Mary and held the Jesus doll so tenderly all through the tea party afterwards. As far as Miri could tell, all the pictures she had ever sent from Sydney were there, as well as a few taken when she and Alice had visited Havana Gardens.

Her favourite photograph showed Alice in a close-fitting summer dress, white with a pattern of red hibiscus. It was early evening and Alice and Jack sat together on a balcony at a table set for dinner. Alice held a seashell in one hand and a glass in the other; it was a glass of champagne poured to celebrate her birthday. In the background, water shimmered. Miri turned the picture over and rubbed her thumb across the back where she had written *Alice's sixteenth birthday*.

They had rented a house at Church Point for the holidays, a place where wooden landings jutted like runs of words in a crossword puzzle into a saltwater inlet of Pittwater. Miri remembered taking the photograph, remembered the blueness of the sea and sky and how she had drawn the wobbly pastel air deep into her lungs and held it, so as not to shake the camera; if she had stuck out her tongue at that moment, it might have been blue.

As the shutter clicked, two young boys were walking up the road swinging a plastic bucket between them, juggling fishing rods and tackle boxes. The boys were just visible in the background over Alice's shoulder. Lights sparkled in pockets of shadow on the far shore. In the photograph, their daughter looked like a shrub in full flower, a young woman whose wild beauty would deepen with maturity. This captured moment overflowed with promise: the Alice on this balcony would become an accomplished musician, a luminous bride, an adoring mother. And yet the moment lied: even then there must have been a sign that Alice would never become any of these things.

Miri wondered if the boys with the rods and plastic bucket still fished around Church Point, wondered if the sea and sky still melted to a puddle of pastel pinks and blues on summer evenings.

With Alice gone, it seemed hardly possible. But she had known it before, after Candela died, this same blind cruelty of life rolling on, of objects persisting in their insentient existence after their owner had vanished. That shell was somewhere now, whereas Alice was only space.

It was like those times she and Jack had travelled to America, on a plane for so long that she had begun to wonder if they would ever arrive, ever get back. High above the Pacific, unable to sleep, Miri had visualised the empty rooms they'd left, the walls of unseen pictures and their belongings still in place. Thinking of it was spooky, almost as if they might be dead.

Now, she stared at the photograph of Alice and wondered if Jack remembered the white dress with the red flowers, the table set for dinner, the boys with their fishing rods. If Jack had no memory of this day then there was only her word for it. Her word and the photograph. And if she was not there to interpret, how was anyone ever to know that this was Alice Passmore on her sixteenth birthday?

Miri sighed and laid her head on the table. The photograph was a two-dimensional image that would eventually disintegrate.

AZIZ

He hates dead people for the influence they exert upon the living, for the ongoing reproach of their absence. Most of all he hates them for having moved beyond the reach of argument. Now there would never be a morning when his younger sisters' chattering requests made his muscles flex with resistance, never an afternoon when his mother would shake her finger in front of his nose on account of some misdemeanour that had roused her displeasure.

On the telephone from Peshawar, his father had screamed that the boat journey to Australia was an act of madness, that he had heard terrible stories of refugees perishing, or, if they survived the journey, being put in prison. It would be less dangerous to return to Afghanistan, he said – but they both knew Australia was the only hope. There was nothing for them in Kabul. The dispute had raged until Aziz's phone card expired and he walked away from the phone box determined to succeed. Their conversation had put fire in his blood. It let him know that, despite their separation, his father loved him, unlike the one-sided talks he now had with his mother. The problem with the dead was that they never disagreed.

In Indonesia, he had waited two weeks in a broken-down hotel room, watching rats scurry in the wet alleyway below his window. He had been afraid to go out for more than a few minutes at a time for fear of missing the contact who would guide him to the boat, so he had slept a lot and eaten little.

Of the sea voyage, the early part of it, Aziz retained only the haziest impression. The limitless glittering ocean, its restless, ever-changing surface and his dread of its unimaginable depth had stuck with him, but the discomfort of the overcrowded fishing boat, the lack of food and fresh drinking water, had not locked into his memory in the way of other experiences. He was proud of how thoroughly he had erased it from his mind; thirteen days cast adrift in a hellish realm and he could look back on it almost without a murmur.

But the last part he remembered in a way he knew would torment him for years. It started on the fourteenth day, when the boat began to seem less purposeful. Instead of nosing into the waves it slewed around and begun to shudder and rock uncomfortably. Some people were sick and the stink of vomit set off others. The boat was low in the water. People began to sob and scream. The surface of the sea was glassy with lacy foam patches, and the sun bore down on them with sudden menacing weight. And then the boat had groaned and died beneath them, sucked down and away with a devouring, terrifying sound. He was in churning water with other bodies squirming and thrashing around him.

Children floated with their skinny arms and legs extended like starfish. Others sank and disappeared. Aziz was buffeted by debris and still not convinced the boat had sunk. He had twisted and turned, frantic to find something solid, but wherever he looked the sea was empty to the horizon. A breeze sprang up and ruffled the surface with little ridges, like an iced cake finished with a palette knife. The horror of that moment, the hopelessness of it, still made him gasp.

It seemed as if he was waterlogged for days before the yacht appeared and its lifeboat began to circle. Strong arms lifted him from the sea. Others had already been picked up. On board, they blurted out their terror and relief, but when they arrived in Cairns, Australian immigration officials greeted them with tight closed faces and police officers waited at the bottom of the gangway.

A translator was found for them, a tiny frizz-haired woman with thick glasses, who listened carefully and related their stories in choppy English.

'Three women were in labour when the boat began to sink,' the translator said.

Aziz leaned towards the table where she sat. Yes, yes. When they heard the truth these stony hearts would soften.

'Two were left behind when the refugees abandoned ship, but the third was seen floating away. She was floating on the surface of the ocean with her baby still attached by the umbilical cord.'

One bottomless afternoon in camp with their eyeballs aching from the glare, he told Jamila about the dead baby. Later, he wished that he had kept it to himself. Jamila had her own problems with the dead.

'I myself am next to dead,' she told him. 'Nothing tethers me. I belong nowhere. When I think about my family, my mind is empty. It is empty when I think about the future.'

Aziz understood. Emptiness and despair were natural states for souls who lived in limbo. Jamila had lost every member of her close family. There was no-one left to arrange her marriage, so to raise her spirits he decided to arrange it himself.

'Listen,' he said, 'when we get out of here, you and I will stick together. We will marry. Create a solid family. Our children will fill the blank spaces. In Australia, we will work hard. Time will pass and the pain will ease.'

Jamila fixed him with her bronze eyes. 'But will it ever vanish?' she asked.

A single fine dark hair had escaped the boundary of her headscarf and waved on a draught of bone-dry air. He watched it graze her cheekbone and curl towards the tiny mole beside her top lip.

He didn't know the answer, but he wished to soothe her. 'It will,' he said.

She knew he was lying. Still, the image he had conjured of a life lived in a flurry of children, of days spent building a home, pebble by pebble, stone by stone, softened her mouth.

When she glanced sideways her eyes reflected the shifting clouds. 'If the first child is a boy I like the name Massoud,' she said, 'and if it is a girl . . .' Jamila put a fingertip to her lips and her eyes lost focus while she searched.

It was around the time of that conversation that Jamila became sensitive to specks of dust, to stray hairs and flakes of skin shed by other inmates, particles so minute they were all but invisible. She could not sit without first stroking again and again at the seat, could not find peace in any corner of the compound.

'The women and children,' she told him, 'have lost the way of smiling with their eyes.' Her head and shoulders drooped as if the collective sorrow of the compound was pressing her into the ground.

He observed her setting up small routines; repetitive words and phrases peppered her conversation. She sat for hours rocking. She told him she had lost some feeling in her fingers: her body was stiffening, shutting down in response to her anguish.

He remembered this numbness with gratitude, praying that when the moment came, Jamila had felt nothing. But it ate away at him, too, the realisation that the dream he had offered was not enough. The knowledge circulated in his bloodstream like a toxin. Worse still, Jamila's eyes were everywhere. He saw them in the restless clouds, in the pure lapis lazuli sky. And each time he saw Jamila's eyes he mourned the loss of their children: the boy, Massoud, and the girl child whose name he did not know.

MIRI

Miri took the roll of film from her mother's camera into Photokwik and then, to pass the hour until it was developed, wandered along the main street to the town library. The sweaty smell of old books circulated in the air conditioning as the librarian filled out a borrower's ticket without asking for ID.

'Looking for anything in particular?'

Miri wondered if she could summon the concentration to read a whole book; the story would have to be gripping. 'Something engrossing,' she said.

The nearest shelves held historical romances and thrillers. Further along, the non-fiction books were big and heavy, and she edged past them to a row of hardbacks with faded spines that looked like they had not been opened in years. She tipped her head sideways to read the titles. They were all by dead French authors. France was a dizzying distance from the town, as far away as it was possible to get. She filled a string bag with novels and took it to the desk.

The librarian adjusted her glasses with a forefinger. 'I wouldn't have thought Balzac or Zola were that engrossing,' she said.

Miri avoided the woman's eyes as she picked up the print-out of due dates and put the books back into the bag.

At Photokwik a gaudy envelope with her name on it was propped on a rack behind the counter. The shop assistant peeled off white cotton gloves to take the money and Miri slipped the photographs into the bag alongside the books.

At the hospital, she slid from her purse a copy of the snapshot she'd seen in Artie's kitchen and held it up for Con to see. She had found it in a bundle of prints in her mother's wardrobe. Con looked at it thoughtfully, running her thumb along the bleached surface of the river that ran out of the right-hand edge of the photograph.

'I don't know,' she said. 'It could be either one of us.'

Miri didn't believe her. Although Con and Candela had looked identical to the outside world, there were tiny personal differences; Con would recognise the scattering of moles on her sister's olive skin, or the way she had parted her hair.

'Do you remember this shirt?' Miri asked. For some reason she couldn't fathom, her aunt was pretending vagueness, but the more evasive she became, the more certain Miri grew that the woman was her mother. Why, she wondered, did Artie Rose keep her mother's picture on the wall among ancient pictures of his family? She persisted, but in the end Con put the print down and asked Miri to fill her water jug. When she returned, her aunt was asleep.

All the way home, she thought about the photograph. The woman and child had once existed. They had been as real as the river beside them at the moment when the shutter clicked. But if the woman was Candela, she had hardly grown any older, while the child had aged to look like the mother. Miri wished she could understand all that the image contained. That moment when the woman turned with quiet pleasure towards an invisible companion fanned out in all directions. It almost still existed, or the sense of it was there, if only she could decipher the photograph's secret language of shadow and gesture, of surface and soft grainy light.

Back at the house, she stuck her head into the blue room and saw that the breakfast tray with its mug of tea and triangles of toast had not been touched. When she stooped and laid her hand across the man's brow, he rolled towards her. His skin was hot and damp. She went to the bathroom for a basin of cold water, wrung out a cloth and pressed it to his forehead. His eyelids, netted with fine veins, quivered as she bathed his cheeks. As she soaked the cloth again and spread it across his chest, she wondered whether Artie Rose should take another look at him. After a couple of minutes, when his breathing was less laboured and he had drifted into a calmer sleep, she decided to wait and see.

With her back braced against the wall and the books in a stack beside her, Miri eased open the envelope of photographs. The prints were black and white and on top was one she had taken in the garden, white roses clambering through the branches of a silver birch. Next was the dry stone fountain with its statue of a leaping fish. In the background was a peach tree, its thin curling leaves shielding the fruit. The grainy prints made the garden look as it had when she was a child: lush, weedy and deserted. She turned up the picture she had snapped without thinking, the figure curved in the roots of a Moreton Bay fig. His wide-awake eyes were watchful, though remarkably unsuspicious, as he gazed up and out of the picture. Shadows pooled in the hollows beneath his eyes and in his cheeks.

Asleep, he looked about the same. She guessed that he was in his early thirties, although his face was so exhausted it was difficult to be sure.

Behind his picture was the first of her mother's photographs, a study of teacups on the kitchen table, random patterns of tea-leaves clinging to their insides as if awaiting the entrance of a fortune teller. To the right of the table, a blurred figure crossed to the sink.

Miri felt herself falling backwards into a day when her mother was still alive, still vivid and busy, passionate about photography. She passed a fingertip across the smoke-like figure, willing this ghost to reveal itself. The photograph looked like one of her mother's experiments with time exposure. Candela had been obsessed with creating images in that way, setting the camera on a tripod and keeping the shutter open in different rooms of the house to give a long exposure of the film to light. Sometimes she herself moved into the frame, dancing or simply walking across the room; sometimes it was Miri or a stray guest who accidentally appeared as a disturbance on the surface of the finished print.

Six of Candela's time exposures, enlarged and framed, still hung above the sideboard in the dining room, studies of cherries, photographed in colour and so cunningly composed that the chipped white bowl, the background of buff linen, lured every drop of colour to the burnished surface of the fruit.

The first time Jack saw her mother's cherry pictures he had studied them for a long time. 'Just makes you ache to eat cherries,' he'd said finally.

Miri turned to the next photograph, white camellias held above dark leaves in a pewter bowl, the creamy curling petals as rounded and smooth as a woman's shoulders rising from a strapless ball gown.

'You never told me she was an artist,' Jack had said.

Miri had felt secretly pleased, amazed at this evidence of a talent so special it could impress a city photographer. Looking at her mother's prints with Jack, she had suddenly seen everyday objects in a different light. They might almost have souls.

As a child, Miri had not understood that her mother had a gift, although she knew Candela was different. While other mothers got drunk in the pub or prepared backyard barbecues, her own had photographed the stars. Some weekends she would put their pillows and blankets in the car and drive out of town just before sunset. On the hot flat plains to the north she would pull off the road, set up her tripod and aim her camera lens at the sky. While they slept, the open eye of the camera recorded the expanding universe in scribbles of light. Once, she had climbed up to the concrete platform of a water tower overlooking the town and recorded the graffiti scrawl of night traffic; Miri remembered the finished picture as a ball of coloured threads centred in the dense black bowl of the surrounding desert. It was a kind of magic that Candela performed with her camera.

On one of those long hot nights stretched on the car seats, her mother explained how the distance between stars was calculated; she knew the sum for working out the vast unimaginable distance light travelled in a single year.

'And when we see the sun, what we really see is how the sun was eight minutes ago,' she said. 'What we see can never be *identical* to the sun. If the sun exploded, if it ceased to exist, we would still see it as it was. Because light carries the image.'

On the floor in the blue room, Miri thought about this sum in relation to her mother, to Jack and Alice. Nothing was ever lost, her mother had insisted. The information, flying away at speed, travelled to infinity as part of the memory of light. Everything they had ever done, every moment of their lives, was trapped in light.

At the Firth Clinic, in a room with cool lime-washed walls, she spooned strawberries and ice-cream into Alice's mouth. When the spoon came out clean, she cupped a hand over her daughter's lips until she felt her swallow. Sometimes this took five minutes, sometimes longer. They sat quietly together, Alice with her eyes closed and hands folded in her lap, while Miri looked away to where birds soared above the treetops on the boundary of the garden.

They repeated this routine every day, and by the end of the second week Alice finished the strawberries and ice-cream for the first time without help. A fortified milk-shake followed the fruit and, with the threat of a nasal tube if she refused, Alice was quiescent.

'It's hard to explain,' she said, 'but nothing tastes the way it used to. Sometimes my mouth feels full of feathers, or grit.'

Watching her, Miri's mouth was dry; she, too, found it hard to swallow.

Every morning a nurse arrived with scales and noted her daughter's weight, temperature, blood pressure and mood. Miri's facial muscles were frozen into a permanent half smile. She never allowed her eyes to dwell on the light fitting covered with a metal grille, or the windows sealed with decorative iron scrollwork. She turned away from the sight of Alice's pipe-cleaner limbs as her daughter slipped from the bed and shuffled towards the scales.

'I feel so heavy.' Alice lifted each foot, heel first, as though extracting it from quicksand.

The nurse nodded and smiled. 'Another 200 grams.'

The weight was creeping upwards in minuscule increments.

At home, Miri avoided the bathroom scales and felt the flesh melting from her own body, as she witnessed Alice's struggle. To disguise this loss from her daughter she wore soft jackets and floppy trousers, and they battled forward, one spoonful at a time.

Despite the humid weather, Alice's hands and feet were always cold, and she drew the old knitted blanket about her shoulders at meal times. Miri's eyes slid over her daughter's paper-white skin, the powdery wrapping that held her frail body together. Sometimes they took so long over lunch that the ice-cream melted to a milky pool in the bowl, but Alice was calm. She was doing her best to get well, and the nurse whispered to Miri that this was more than half the battle.

'I feel better today.' A smile warmed Alice's face. 'Laura says another kilo and I can be an outpatient.'

Miri was afraid of what would happen once the outside world replaced the sheltering regime of the clinic, but she beat off panic by visualising Alice as a grown woman, striding towards her in spring sunshine, or poised at a table overlooking water, red hibiscus patterning her dress with splashes of optimism.

Waiting for Alice to swallow, Miri cleared her throat and said quietly, 'Your father's moved out.'

In the palm of her hand, she felt the sudden jerk in Alice's throat.

'What do you mean?'

Miri lowered her hand. 'I mean I haven't seen him.'

'Since when?'

'Since I told him what you saw.'

Alice picked up the spoon and tapped it against the lip of the bowl, making small repetitive chiming sounds. 'But you know where he is, right?'

Miri turned from the bed towards the windows. 'I can guess.'

'Where then?'

'You know.'

Alice stopped tapping and pulled the blanket close around her shoulders. 'Say it! You can't solve a problem until you can say it out loud.'

'Is that what Laura teaches?'

Alice nodded.

Miri glanced at her daughter's pale earnest face. 'Then listen. I say your father is sleeping with someone. I say her name is Nell. She's about twelve. Now it's your turn, Alice.'

Alice waved her hand, an evasive gesture. 'Look, I hear a lot of stuff in here. Advice, strategies, you know? Sometimes it works and the sick people get better. Sometimes it doesn't work and then the sick people die. I'm getting better, but the sad thing is *you* don't even know you're sick.'

'I don't know what you're talking about, Alice.'

'No shit!'

Miri said, 'I'm not the one here that's sick.'

'Always running away from yourself is sick. Being someone else because it's more comfortable than who you are is sick.'

'I'm an actor. That's my work.'

'It's not your work, it's how you live. You've been doing it for so long, you just don't notice anymore.'

Miri picked up the spoon. Something had shifted, some finely balanced series of weights that held both her and Alice in place. She felt as if she might pitch forward off the chair, collapse messily on the carpet.

What Alice said was true; she had always been overwhelmed by the beauty, brains, talent, of other people: people who'd grown up surrounded by water, who'd been to university and read *War and Peace* and Proust; people whose parents drank wine with dinner; people whose mothers hadn't died yet. The moment she'd arrived in Sydney she had seen how uncouth she was, how inadequate. Drama lessons taught her to play up the natural gravity of her colouring, to keep her hands still and her mouth shut unless she had a line to say. She had sunk with gratitude into the characters she played, thankful for definite instructions, and as her skill grew people took her seriously. The outer gloss kept them distracted, but underneath she was plain Miriam Kissack: one part Cuban, one part Celt, one part nobody knew what. Because of how she looked, people believed in her, but she might have known that Alice, with her penetrating gaze, would find out how unfinished she was inside.

Miri had looked across at Alice's fragile shoulders under the blanket. Her daughter's sudden fierceness had thrown her off balance, but at the same time it gave her hope. It had shown her Alice the survivor, a vision to hold onto as she loaded the spoon with the last heart-shaped strawberry.

'Jesus, you sure he's still alive?' Zett's voice cracked the silence, making Miri jump.

'What?'

Zett jerked her head towards the man on the mattress, and Miri surfaced from the trance-like state she had floated in all the afternoon. His cheeks were drained of colour. She touched his hand: cold. His lips had a lavender tint and he was motionless under the sheet. The light in the room was dull and heavy; it would soon be dark.

'He hasn't touched the food?' Zett said.

'A few spoonfuls of broth last night.'

'Shit, that was almost twenty-four hours ago. Maybe get Artie, hey?'

While Artie was upstairs with the patient, Miri sat in the kitchen with her hands wrapped around a cup of tea. Zett buttered slices of bread, cut cheese and flipped the sandwiches together while Opal wriggled on a blanket on the floor.

'Artie's a good bloke,' Zett said. 'He'll keep quiet about me and Opal being here.'

Miri's shoulders slumped. 'I'm sorry I didn't go for him this morning.'

Zett poured boiling water into a coffee mug. 'Yeah, well, you have stuff on your mind.'

Miri set the teacup in the saucer with a clatter. Watching Opal, she'd been thinking about breaking the news of Alice's death to Dig and Lois; the thought made her feel faint. Once they knew, it would be harder to stay calm. There would be questions. Tears. And because she hadn't told them straight away, the questions and tears would be worse. She was so far ahead of them in grief she could not contemplate returning to the beginning, waiting with them while it sank in.

'Know what seems odd?' Zett said. 'You coming back. I mean, if I'd escaped from here you wouldn't see me for dust.'

The overhead light, with its yellow conical shade, made both of them and the baby look jaundiced.

'It must seem that way.'

'So how come?'

Miri folded her hands on the table and stared at them in silence.

'I mean, here's me, desperate to escape,' Zett said, 'and here's you leaving the city for this poxy town. It doesn't make sense.'

Miri clenched her hands into fists. 'I had to get away,' she said. Then, as Zett was still watching her curiously, 'I left because I lost someone.'

Zett moved towards the table. 'I didn't mean to get you upset,' she said.

Miri cupped her hands over her mouth. *You can't solve a problem until you can say it out loud.*

Her breath was warm against her palms, her voice muffled. 'Imagine if you'd lost Opal.'

Zett swivelled towards the baby and scooped her up. 'Jeez, I'm sorry,' she said. 'I had no idea.'

Miri watched the way Zett's hands tightened around Opal's chest.

Artie came into the kitchen with his brown suitcase under his arm.

'I have given him a jab,' he said. 'He could do with a saline drip, but that we haven't got. It is important to put fluids into him. Have you a large jug for water?'

Miri found a glass jug in the pantry and watched as Artie measured a level teaspoon of salt, eight of sugar, then stirred in a little warm water until the sugar dissolved.

'One litre of water to top this up.' Behind his glasses, Artie's eyes were solemn. 'You will be making him take the water every half-hour, which I would say is a pity, since you look like you are needing to sleep.'

On the floor of the blue room, Miri took a book from

the top of the stack, opened it, and immediately entered the arcade of the Pont Neuf. It was a relief to flit invisibly along this passageway between the rue Mazarine and the rue de Seine and she was soon adrift in Zola's gruesome tale of Laurent, Camille and Therese Raquin, surfacing every half-hour at the buzz of Con's eggtimer to sponge her patient's face and drip cold water into his mouth.

AZIZ

He was lost in fog, a polluted swirling substance as abrasive as crushed eggshells that set his nerves tingling from his scalp to the pain at his feet. Fog clogged his nostrils, and he coughed and shuddered as his lungs filled. The sensation of choking placed him in a whirl of mealy fibres in the carpet warehouse. He was selecting rugs for a dealer who was coming to barter with his father, and as he pulled the tufted edge of a carpet towards him the great stacks of stored rugs toppled. He lost his footing and staggered as carpets slithered and fell, as they cascaded in iridescent waves from high up in the rafters. The tough knotted surface of a kilim curled around his body, and for a moment he surfed the rolling colours before he was sucked down by the undertow. He could see nothing. Folded carpets thudded onto his arms and chest, and he gasped for Masir to pull him out before he suffocated.

Suddenly, water trickled into his mouth from somewhere, and he let it glide down his throat. Sounds came from a great distance, muffled, as if he was underground. He sank into the soft pile of the rugs, muttering his gratitude for the water which had cleared his throat of the thready carpet dust.

Sometime later he felt the woman's hands move over his body, easing away the clothing. The air was cooler now, and her warmth seeped into him when she pressed his palms or drew the sheet over his bare shoulders. She had brought a damp cloth. He heard the faint plash as she wrung it out in a bowl of water. The moist cloth pressed against his overheated skin was unbearable, and yet, once the heat was subdued, he felt the pain recede. When he opened his eyes, everything wobbled and doubled. Solids appeared fluid. The cold cloth was wrapped around his forehead like a turban. Tears of gratitude slid over his cheeks, and as the woman left the room he prayed she did not think him weak.

When she came to him again out of an eternity of silence he clung to her hand and cried out.

'Sh, sh, sh,' she whispered.

The soothing noises transcended the need for language. He moaned and gripped the woman's fingers, stretching the moment before she folded the cloth into the bowl and walked from the room.

He woke again, and the scent of vanilla alerted him to her presence. This perfume drifted from her hair, which was long and straight and brushed her shoulders when loose. He imagined it washing over him in waves, its cleanliness a balm to his wounds. Once, in the night, he groped for her with his hand, but the space beside him was empty. Still later, he heard the rustle of her clothing. His eyes and lips stung; his teeth and tongue were coated and slick. Tufts of some soft-piled material cushioned his back and shoulders.

The touch of it set him thinking of the rough coats of animals, of the sad shapes of the creatures trapped in Kabul's zoo. He saw the gruff enduring face of Marjan the lion, blinded by a Taliban bayonet, starved and battered yet exuding quiet dignity. He rolled his head on the tufted fabric, closed his eyes. Perhaps he was Marjan, or another animal.

He opened his eyes and glimpsed the woman as she leaned over him: dark hair, dark eyes, a flash of sky blue. She looked Afghan, and the thought brought a warm sensation to his chest. She had raised her burqa to tend him, and he was careful not to look at the face framed by the washed-out blue cloth. But when the delirium dumped him, exhausted and conscious, he opened his eyes to the scratched blue wall and a tiny window set so high that all it framed was sky. This was the woman's burqa, a cobalt halo that shimmered above her head as she knelt beside him. Blue, the colour of paradise, *behesht*. He recognised the woman who had picked him up on the roadside. Her head was bowed as she turned the pages of a book. She still looked sad and tired.

'Thank you,' he said quietly, surprised and pleased at how easily the English he had learned in detention slid from his tongue. Those classes, the airless room with Jamila nodding beside him on a red plastic chair, seemed several lifetimes ago. 'Thank you,' he said again.

The woman looked up and the book fell closed in her lap.

'I am Aziz,' he said. His own voice sounded strange to him, tremulous and rusty with disuse, and already he was drifting backwards into sleep.

When he woke again she was shaking him gently by the shoulder. A bowl of soup steamed on a tray beside the mattress. The room was as bare as any he had ever occupied, just the weathered plasterwork with a narrow painted-over pipe following the skirting. Bare boards supported the lumpy mattress, on which someone had placed a sheepskin.

Outside the window, birds coasted on draughts of air. He imagined the ecstasy of soaring in that enormous sky, twisting, swooping and diving without restraint. He had stumbled through his life like a man with his hands tied. Now, sickness held him prisoner.

He swallowed a spoonful of soup, and its warmth and flavour infused him with hope. Perhaps this woman had been sent to help him scramble free.

MIRI

When Miri returned from shopping, a red four-wheel drive was parked outside Havana Gardens. She pulled in behind it, switched off the Ford's engine and reached into the back seat for the supermarket bags, their contents clinking as she lifted them. She closed the car door quietly, scanning the gardens. Nobody was in sight. As she approached the front gate a figure loomed from the deep shade of the verandah. He was tall, his long face shadowed by a wide-brimmed Akubra, and as soon as she saw the red checked shirt straining across his bulky shoulders she guessed it was Jude Moran.

He leaned over the verandah rail, looking down at her.

'Hot day for walking round the shops,' he said.

He had a narrow clean-shaven face that could have been handsome, except that the distance between eyes and chin was a little too long and the jaw had a stubborn jut. Sunlight glanced off the silver belt buckle at his waist. He was broad and muscled and if there was any softness in him it had collected under that outsized buckle in an inch or two of beer fat. Miri glanced quickly at his feet. He wore elastic-sided riding boots, worn but polished.

She was acutely aware that her canvas shoulder bag contained baby wipes, little jars of chicken with noodles and a tube of Bonjela for Opal's gums.

'Were you looking for someone?'

He smiled. 'I might be. Here, let me take that.'

Before she could protest, he hooked the carrier from her fingers, swung it in his huge hand and waited for her to step up onto the verandah. Miri kept a grip on her shoulder bag, praying silently as she fumbled for the key that Zett had not chosen this moment to pitch camp in the kitchen. The front door opened straight into the hall; he would be bound to spot his wife if she came from the kitchen, or down the stairs.

'I'll take the shopping around the back,' she said, moving towards the side path, wondering how to retrieve the shopping bags from him without letting him into the house.

When they reached the back door she gave the flyscreen a loud warning bang, before slotting the key into the lock. With any luck Opal would be having an afternoon sleep.

The kitchen was empty.

Miri held in a sigh of relief, turned in the doorway and reached for the shopping bag. 'I can manage.'

He held onto it. On the threshold of the kitchen, he stood very close to her and grinned. 'Do you always invite strange men into the house without asking who they are?'

'No, never,' she said.

'So you know who I am?'

'I think I remember you from school, and I haven't invited you in.'

He grinned. 'What year?'

Miri looked blank.

'At school,' he prompted.

'Oh,' she shrugged, 'it was a long time ago.'

'A good-looking sort like you, I'd have remembered if you were in my class.' He lifted the bag. 'Here, let me put this on the table.'

She stepped backwards, and he followed her in. When he had set the shopping on the table, he pulled out a chair. She guessed he was in his early thirties, too young to have shared a classroom with her, but somehow he'd got her locked into the lie about how she knew him.

'You look familiar, that's all,' she said, feeling stubborn and stupid for persisting.

He was pleased with himself and appeared not to notice her unease. 'Jude Moran, Detective Inspector, New South Wales Police,' he said.

'I think I heard you'd gone into the police.'

'Who from?'

'My aunt.'

He looked pointedly towards the jar of Nescafé on the draining-board. 'I could fancy a cuppa, if you're putting the kettle on.'

Miri still held the canvas bag over her shoulder, afraid to set it down in case a jar of baby food rolled out at his feet.

'Put the kettle on yourself, I'll be back in a minute.'

She slipped along the hall, slung the shoulder bag over a coat hook and pushed it behind her aunt's outdoor jackets and a couple of rotting umbrellas.

'So what breeze blew you into town?' Jude said as she came back into the kitchen.

The electric kettle rumbled, and he had spooned coffee into two mugs on the draining-board.

'My aunt had an accident.'

'Fell off her horse, didn't she? Must be a game old girl.'

'Yes.' She suddenly remembered Opal's bottle tucked into the side door of the fridge. As the kettle came to the boil she lifted it, filled a mug and pushed it across the counter. 'I don't keep milk.'

'Black is fine.'

'You're looking for someone?'

'You ever come across my missus?'

'Should I have?'

Jude smiled, but he watched her closely. 'Maybe not. Zett's a few years younger and she never spent that much time at school.'

'Then why ask me?'

'She visited Con sometimes.'

'My aunt has been in hospital almost two weeks.'

Jude raised the coffee to his lips and his forehead creased. 'That's tough luck,' he said.

Miri strained to detect any sound from the upper floor, masking her impatience by forcing her body to stillness.

'You'd remember Zett,' Jude said. 'Looks like the red-head on the matchbox.' He reached into his back pocket, removed a sheet of paper and spread it on the table. 'She's got our five-month-old daughter Opal with her and this,' he jabbed a finger at the paper, 'is a court order.' He nudged the paper towards Miri. 'I'm going for custody of Opal.'

Miri stared at the government crest and the faintly blurred paragraphs of typescript on the page, at Jude's thumb and fingers, which were the size and shape of the bruise on Opal's torso.

'Does your wife know you're going for custody?'

'She ticked off before I could tell her.'

'Perhaps she's already left town.'

Jude shook his head. 'She could have, but I've an idea she's still around.'

'Well, if I bump into her, I'll tell her.'

He leaned towards her, and his eyes were a cold deep blue. 'Don't tell Zett anything,' he said. 'Call me. Here.' He flipped a card from the top pocket of his shirt and pushed it across the table.

She nodded, picked up her coffee mug and moved towards the sink. His eyes were on her back as she rinsed the mug and up-ended it on the draining-board. When she turned around he was looking at her.

'You ever go out in the evenings for a drink?'

She reached for a tea towel, was opening her mouth to snap out a reply when she realised he was asking her out.

'No.'

'The Five Mile Creek Hotel's got a ladies' bar. It's a nice place to sink a few cold beers and watch the sun set over the desert. I could drive you out sometime.'

She rubbed the tea towel over the rim of her coffee mug. Her wedding ring had been left behind in Sydney, and she couldn't bring herself to fend him off by mentioning Jack. 'I'm not very social,' she said.

Jude unfolded from the chair, plucked his hat from the table and moved beside her to put his empty mug in the sink. His bulk seemed to compress the air in the kitchen and create a sudden shortage of oxygen. She had to resist the impulse to step beyond his reach.

He opened the back door. 'I'll drop by some evening and pick you up,' he said, and winked as if she'd agreed to go.

Miri rushed to the dining room window, reassured by

the red blur of his shirt moving towards the car. She watched him open the door and swing up into the driver's seat, kept watch from behind the curtain as the car pulled away and disappeared along the road. In the wake of Jude Moran's visit, the house no longer felt safe. She glanced over her shoulder as if expecting some hostile presence to rush at her from a corner, but nothing moved as she hugged her chest and hurried to the attic.

Zett was asleep on the sofa with Opal beside her. With her hair in two tight plaits over her shoulders and the lime Tweety Pie T-shirt she wore clashing with the red plush sofa, she looked very young, too young to be dodging someone as unpleasant as Jude Moran.

Miri touched her shoulder. 'Zett? Wake up!'

'What.'

'Jude's been here.'

Zett sat up, her elbow pinned by Opal's head. 'Where is he?'

'It's okay, he's gone.'

Zett eased her arm out from underneath Opal. The baby's cheeks were flushed and her mouth was open as she snored gently.

'What happened? What did he say?'

Miri picked up the cigarettes from the floor and handed them to her. 'He said he had a court order to stop you taking Opal away. He's applying for custody.'

Zett's hand shook as she took the cigarettes. 'Custody!'

'He'll never get it.'

'Fuck! You don't know Jude.'

With biscuits and two mugs of tea balanced on a tray, Miri climbed the stairs to the blue room. The outer bedroom door was ajar and, when she pushed it open, Aziz stretched out his hand towards her. He had crawled from the mattress and was sitting just inside the door.

She set the tray on the floor and slipped an arm around his shoulders. 'You shouldn't be out of bed.'

He twisted into a kneeling position and she supported his weight as he struggled to his feet. With her arm around his waist, he hobbled to the mattress. She went back for the tray and set it down beside him. When she passed him the mug of hot tea he wrapped both hands around it, avoiding her eyes as he inhaled the steam.

'You're walking now,' she said.

He shook his head, and she wondered if he understood that she was encouraging his effort. She handed him a biscuit and settled into her customary place against the wall. The sight of him sitting up sent a sudden shiver of achievement through her, although he looked anxious and depressed.

'What's the matter?' she said.

He put a hand to his head as if it ached or was filled with painful thoughts.

She was seized by the urge to cheer him, and the snowy scene on Con's old tin tray reminded her of the snow domes downstairs. 'Wait,' she said.

A small cry escaped him as she lurched towards the door, but Miri shook her head and held up a finger. 'I am coming back.'

In the parlour, an enormous speckled mirror swung on chains above the fireplace, and she saw herself reflected, a tall thin dark-haired woman with a feverish look about the eyes. Below the mirror stood the row of water-filled globes — snowstorms with tiny Christmas and alpine scenes moulded in coloured plastic. Miri picked up the largest, shook it, and watched the snowflakes whirl and settle under the dusty glass. She gathered them into a wastebasket and, in the kitchen, piled the ornaments into the sink beside the dirty coffee mugs and turned on the hot water. The wet glass sparkled as she wrapped them in a tea towel and hurried towards the blue room.

'Close your eyes!' She caught his hand and pressed the fingers across his eyes.

He waited while she arranged the snow domes on the floor beside the mattress. When they were lined up she selected the largest globe and shook it. Gold flakes surrounded a snow-covered tree laden with tiny multi-coloured gift boxes.

'Look, Aziz!'

He lowered his hands and stared.

'Snow!' She shook it again and held it in front of him.

He looked surprised for a moment, then a smile spread from his mouth to his eyes. It was the first smile she had seen from him, or anyone, in days.

He touched the glass as she held it to the light. 'Snow?'

'Snow.' Miri gently pressed the dome into his cupped palms.

MIRI

Miri had known her mother was sick before anything was said from the way Candela stayed in bed longer each morning, in spite of the summer heat. Sometimes she had stayed there all day.

'Just too lazy to move, sugar,' she said, whenever Miri tugged at the sheet and asked if she would come downstairs and play. 'Maybe tomorrow, after school.'

But when tomorrow came, Candela still felt lazy. In the afternoons, Miri brought homework and sat cross-legged on the square of carpet beside her mother's bed.

'What are you doing down there?' Candela said.

'Geography.'

'So, ask me a question.'

'Okay, what's the capital of Peru?'

'Peru.' Candela thought for a long time as Miri doodled on a page of her exercise book. 'Is it Lima?' she said at last.

Miri shrugged and wrote down Lima. 'And what's the capital of Denmark?'

Long after the homework had been handed in, Miri and her mother continued to name distant cities. They picked out their favourites from an atlas and threw them back and forth like exotic jewelled balls: Constantinople, Kathmandu, Paris, Rome and Cairo. Miri made lists of countries and they memorised the capitals. Candela loved the cold countries: Finland, Sweden, Norway, Iceland. In the afternoons, cushioned from the thudding heat by heavy velvet curtains, she counted capital cities like worry beads – Helsinki, Stockholm, Oslo, Reykjavik – unstringing and rearranging them in a memory game that carried her through the day and far into the night.

Miri consulted another atlas for more countries and produced small remote gems. Panama, Paraguay, Guatemala and Bolivia. When she had exhausted Central and South America, she unlocked the treasure chest of Africa.

Lists of countries fluttered from her schoolbooks; they wadded to pulp in the pockets of her uniform in the wash. After class she interrogated her geography teacher, who was perplexed by this sudden passion, and at night she slept with the latest list tucked underneath her pillow. Geography had become a battleground, Miri's lists against the sickness that was overtaking Candela. If only her mother could memorise enough cities, it might anchor her to the earth.

One afternoon, with a new list of Russian cities in her pocket, Miri found Candela with her handkerchief pressed to her mouth and tears sliding down the slope of her cheek. That night the flash of Con's torch woke her as her aunt paced the upper floor, throwing open windows and doors to funnel any breath of air into Candela's bedroom.

An ambulance arrived before breakfast and took her mother away; after school her aunt picked three perfect nectarines and a bunch of grapes from the garden and they carried them to Candela's room in the hospital. They did this every day, but Candela never touched the fruit. Her sustenance was drawn from bottles of colourless fluid suspended above the bed, and Miri wondered what happened to all the fruit they picked. Perhaps the nurses buried it in the grounds of the hospital so as not to hurt Con's feelings.

One Friday afternoon, her aunt drove Miri straight from school to the hospital without stopping to pick fruit. While Con spoke to the doctor, Miri sat on the floor in the waiting room chewing her nails. She could see her aunt and the doctor behind glass, Con lifting her hands, imploring, the doctor shaking his head. If Miri stood on tiptoe she could see the hospital gardens. In the still, dead air of the hospital, the bodice of her school dress, brown-checked cotton, new that term, suddenly felt too tight. While she waited, Miri counted the people on the lawns. When she ran out of people she counted flowers. There had been a dust storm in the night and frangipani and hibiscus blooms littered the grass and the concrete paths like scraps of pink and white paper.

Two nurses walked towards her along the corridor. White laced shoes squeaked on the polished floor. White gauze veils masked their hair. As they drew level, one nurse touched the other's arm and they stopped and stared at Miri. The prettiest asked if she would like a glass of lemonade. She bent over Miri, and her voice was softened by an Irish accent. Miri shook her head. As they walked away, the Irish nurse crossed herself, and it was in that rapid pass of hand over starched white cotton that Miri read her catastrophic loss.

Her mother's face was ice-white and waxy and her black hair spread across the pillow in ripples where it had been plaited and undone. There was a chemical smell of violets, and the soap and starch smell of hospital bed linen. Con's cheeks were wet. Miri had never seen her tough aunt cry and it frightened her more than the stillness of her mother in the bed.

'Give your mother a kiss, Miri,' Con said.

The unexpected chill of her mother's cheek travelled through Miri's lips and settled around her heart. Her hands and feet grew numb. She felt frozen, glacial. But as she stared at her mother's remote smile, a tiny lava bubble of fury erupted: Candela had set off on a journey to the cold countries without even saying goodbye.

AZIZ

He understood surfaces, for there was no texture on earth he had not covered. Snow, ice, clay, wood, stone, shingle, mud, ancient lava flows, the scaly skins of dried-up river-beds, grasses and grains in all their moods and seasons, Aziz knew them intimately. What he had lost was depth.

When the woman had gone downstairs, he picked up one of the snow globes, turned it in his hands and peered through the glass. In the white plastic landscape, a tall narrow house stood between a lamppost and a pine tree, while children in coats and hats played with a tiny black dog. He stared at the cut-out figures standing in a whirl of snowflakes; like his own world, this one was flat.

He leaned back against the pillows and gazed at the sky-coloured walls, at the window ledge where dust gathered, imagining the foundations of the house piercing the earth. Just as the garden had taken root, so had the house, and he envied the woman her home.

For him, home was elusive. He could no longer point to

a patch of soil or a tall mud-brick wall with a door of a certain shade of blue. Home was always tugging at him, but when he turned there was only blank air, the shifting clouds, traffic sounds. While his mind accepted that home and all it once contained was lost, his body refused to relinquish it. Home might be nothing more than the scent of crushed cardamom, a red kite twisting and falling, or the sticky juice of a pomegranate trickling down his chin, yet with all his being he craved it.

Even as he fled Afghanistan he never doubted it was his home. Later, in detention, people overwhelmed by the grief of exile beat their heads against walls in despair, sometimes until they were subdued with drugs. The only way to endure the ordeal of imprisonment piled upon loss was by clinging to a belief in a better future, but living with uncertainty made that difficult. Cruelty was the same in all languages. In Afghanistan he had witnessed floggings, hangings and the destruction of his family. In the camp, persistent cruelty combined with loss had driven a gentle girl of good upbringing to cut her own throat. That act alone seemed to prove to him that for all the distance he had covered he had only swapped one terror for another.

MIRI

After Jude's visit, Zett kept to the attic, only emerging to warm Opal's food. Each time she appeared in the kitchen her anxiety was contagious, and although the back door was kept locked Miri checked it constantly.

'Jude'll be back,' Zett said. 'You can count on it.'

Miri fumbled in her bag for cigarettes. 'No law says we have to answer the door.'

Zett shook her head. 'Last night I dreamed I stole a speedboat and took off down the river. It was so easy. Then I woke up and remembered that I never even learned to swim or drive. Can you imagine it?'

Miri shook her head.

'Anyhow, I phoned my brother in Cairns. He's sending me some cash and as soon as it comes we'll get going.'

But there was something about Zett, a wavering uncertainty in her voice that made Miri wonder whether she had lost her nerve.

Now that his foot was healing, Aziz made up for Zett's absence by coming into the kitchen half-a-dozen times a day. He usually pretended to want a mug of tea, but by the way he moped about the scullery, fingering utensils and peering wistfully into the gloom of the cellar, she guessed that what he really yearned to do was cook. With Jude Moran in mind, Miri tried to shoo him back upstairs. While she was washing dishes one afternoon he appeared again, descended the cellar steps and emerged a few minutes later with an onion in each hand. As Miri wiped down the counter with a dishcloth, he set the onions on the table and pressed his palms together in a pleading gesture. When she put down the cloth, he mimed chopping, stirring, and presenting with a flourish an imaginary plate of food for her inspection.

The enforced bed rest had eased the pinched look around his nose and mouth. He looked almost light-hearted as he hovered, waiting for her decision. When she hesitated, he repeated the performance.

'Okay,' she said, 'if you can find anything worth cooking.'

Aziz grinned and vanished into the scullery, and soon she heard cupboard doors banging and pans rattling.

Later, when she came downstairs with her handbag, he was squatting on the lino poking newspaper and kindling into the wood stove. Beside the sink, the onions were peeled and diced in a creamy mound on the chopping board.

'I could shop,' she said.

He turned towards her, puzzled. She mimed picking groceries off a shelf and putting them into a basket.

'I will go to the supermarket,' she said, 'so that Aziz can cook.'

'No.' He waved away the offer. 'Plenty, plenty.'

Miri shrugged and called up the stairs to Zett that she was going to visit Con. The answering shout was followed by a muffled shriek from Opal. Miri shook her head in dismay; ever since Jude's visit, Zett clapped a hand over the child's mouth if she made the slightest sound, paranoid that her high-pitched squeals could be heard from the road.

Aziz was seated on a kitchen chair with a newspaper spread across his lap when Miri returned from the hospital. Vegetable peelings were piled on the paper and he was prising the skin from a lemon with his long brown fingers. A rich scent of curry wafted from the oven and, with the fire crackling, the kitchen was overheated and stuffy. Miri watched as he shaved slices of peel with a knife. Half-a-dozen garlic cloves were lined up beside a handful of thyme and spikes of rosemary. In the centre of the table, a glass jar overflowed with stems of red hibiscus.

'Smells good,' she said as Aziz brought a slice of lemon to his nose. His face lit up as he inhaled its scent. She wondered what he had found to cook that could produce such an aroma. He must have risked going into the garden in daylight.

She frowned at him. 'Outside?' she said.

He looked up and flashed such a radiant smile that she hadn't the heart to persist.

In the bedroom that she was beginning to think of as her own, Miri opened the wardrobe and felt for the gypsy blouse and black dress Nell had left for her to find in Sydney. The dress was crumpled but she looped her fingers in the straps and held it against her body. The hemline finished midway up her thigh. With shoestring straps and a plunging neckline, it would expose plenty of flesh.

What had Nell been telling her with this — that she was no longer young enough to carry off such a dress? She raised the fabric to her face and sniffed: there was a heavy oriental perfume, Nell Bardot's foxy smell. She let the dress flutter to the carpet, stepped over it and picked up the blouse. It was ruby with panels set into the sides, hand-worked with flowers, leaves and tiny birds with long curving beaks. The sleeves were full, the neckline scooped low and caught in front with narrow silk ribbon. She held it to her face and detected the faint chemical scent of dry-cleaning fluid. Miri peeled off her T-shirt and slipped the blouse over her head, unpinned her hair and let it fall forward over her shoulders. At one time she had wanted to cut the clothes to shreds and post them back to Nell, but now it felt like a greater revenge to wear them, take them on and turn them into her own. Like eating the flesh of the enemy.

In the mottled glass, with her eyebrows raised, she looked foreign, guarded. This was the surface of her; this was what other people saw when they looked across a room, this woman with the dark hair and oval face, with the long neck like a Modigliani woman, with her angular hands looking as if they needed something to hold. This was what Jack saw, this unpainted mouth with its downward slant, which in time would gather all the sadness into a permanent pattern of lines and make a new and unfamiliar landscape of her foreigner's face.

From her mother's wardrobe she chose a long black taffeta skirt, bias cut so that it tapered to nothing at the waist. In her purse was a red lipstick. She coloured her mouth with careful strokes, combed mascara into her lashes and ran a dampened fingertip over her brows. As she touched her own skin she thought of Aziz, of the way his whole face had glowed with pleasure as he held the lemon. She tried to imagine such a moment of personal pleasure and found herself stepping into the fizzing white light of a summer afternoon with the weight of a child on her hip, their two shadows joined and falling away from them across the sand as they moved towards the bright dazzle of water.

She turned from the mirror. That day, all those days, were so far behind her. She was in a different place now. She was in a different place, and with Alice gone the light had changed.

She had collected Alice from the Firth Clinic on a day gritty with exhaust fumes and city smells that were intensified by approaching rain. In the room where they had struggled through so many meals together, a woman in a blue uniform had stripped the bed and was wiping down surfaces with anti-bacterial spray. Miri paused on the threshold; the room already looked less familiar, and now that Alice was about to become an outpatient the bare walls and discreet iron window grilles had shed their menace.

Alice waited in the day lounge while Miri said goodbye to Laura.

'Is it really over?' Miri said.

Laura's face was serene. 'I think it is,' she said. 'But I'll see her once a week for the first few months.'

Miri badly wanted Alice to move back home after leaving the clinic, but didn't push it when she resisted. Instead, they drove to the flat in Glebe where Alice's flatmate, Jessica, and two girls with thin brown bodies and sun-streaked hair sat at the kitchen table smoking and drinking coffee.

Jessica introduced the girls to Alice. 'Louise and Tara

came down from Brisbane last weekend,' she said. 'They're crashing on the sofas. Just until they get a place.'

Alice nodded. Dance music boomed from a speaker balanced on top of the fridge. Jessica got up and opened the window when she noticed Miri in the doorway, while Louise, or perhaps Tara, leaned into a cupboard and turned down the music. The girls from Brisbane seemed faintly embarrassed, but Jessica offered to make fresh coffee.

'I still don't do caffeine,' Alice said.

Jessica grinned. 'I forgot.'

Miri shook her head. 'Thanks, but I have to go.'

She followed Alice into her bedroom. There were flowers in a jar on the desk: sweet peas which seemed doubly fragile in Alice's black-clad presence.

Alice sat on the swivel chair and rested her elbows on the scarred wooden desktop. 'Jess always buys flowers for people. Her parents have shares in Interflora.'

Miri closed the door. 'They were smoking dope out there.'

Alice shrugged. Her face was suddenly very white with shadows deepening underneath her eyes, as if the car journey and climbing the stairs with her suitcase had exhausted her.

'So? They were drinking coffee, too, but that doesn't mean I have to.'

'It's ten o'clock in the morning.'

Alice rolled her eyes. 'Is there a particular time of day when it would be okay by you, Mum?'

'Alice, promise me—'

'I promise, okay!'

She should have packed up her daughter's belongings then and taken her home. Maybe she should have quietly threatened to call the police. Underneath Alice's veneer of cool, Miri saw that she was not keen on two strangers camping in the flat. If only she had been able to summon the right mix of anger and concern, Alice would have gone with her. But she had been afraid to rock the boat, afraid of pushing Alice out of reach and, as so often happened when it really mattered, she had misjudged the moment.

The scent of curry penetrated to the upper floor of Havana Gardens, where Miri was curled on the candlewick bedspread; she still wore Nell's blouse and picked with a thumbnail at the embroidery on the cuff. Perhaps her rival had worn it when she came to their flat. Perhaps she had worn it when Jack led her to their bedroom. She pictured Jack and Nell tumbling on the blank canvas of the king-size bed, their bodies casting shadows on the duck-egg walls. Mosquito netting drifted overhead like smoke and Nell's limbs were smooth and gilded, each tiny nail glistening with polish and those buttery hands of hers, so busy.

Miri rolled off the bed and stood before the mirror, squeezing the hairbrush with both her hands to stop them trembling.

When she came into the kitchen she watched Aziz's eyes widen and his reaction gave her a small rush of pleasure. She had made an effort with her appearance. God only knew why. And she was still wearing Nell's blouse. In this hot and shabby house miles from Sydney, without her even knowing it, Nell was being swallowed by the enemy.

Miri put the food Aziz had prepared onto a tray — five small dishes, a large bowl of rice, flat bread wrapped in a cloth — along with the jar of hibiscus, and carried it up to the attic. Aziz followed with the hot stew pot and one of Con's tablecloths tucked under his arm. In the attic he darted forward to spread the cloth over the Persian rug, then sat back on his heels and pointed to the centre where she was to set the tray.

Zett came in with her hair wrapped in a towel and Opal damp and wriggling from the bath. 'Something smells amazing.'

Aziz didn't meet Zett's eyes, just grinned at the bowls of food. He had arranged cushions on the floor and gestured to them to sit. Zett produced two white candles jammed into empty wine bottles.

'Mood lighting,' she said, as she flicked her cigarette lighter.

Earlier in the day Zett had rooted around in cupboards and found some ancient Christmas decorations, pinning faded paper chains across the ceiling of the attic, while silver baubles and a length of gold tinsel were looped above the window.

When she saw Miri looking at them she said, 'It's Opal's first Christmas — let's drink to it.'

Miri went downstairs for wine and heard Zett shout after her to bring plenty.

When she returned, Opal was cooing quietly on the sofa and Zett was rubbing her wet hair with the towel.

Zett grinned when she saw the bottles and nodded at Aziz. 'He probably doesn't drink,' she said. 'Let's corrupt him.'

Miri set down three tumblers, picked up the corkscrew and opened the first bottle.

The stew was rich and slightly oily with slivers of fine-grained meat. Aziz must have caught a rabbit in the gardens. She hadn't eaten rabbit since she was a child, when her uncle Dig would appear with a pair, freshly gutted, dangling from his belt. She had seen Con skin rabbits on the back verandah, peeling back the fur with deft strokes, exposing the defenceless flesh until the skin lay ruffled behind the neck like a satin-backed cloak. When her aunt took up the kindling axe to cut off the heads, she had always closed her eyes.

They ate without plates or cutlery, sitting on the floor with the food, between them. Aziz showed them how to squeeze rice into a ball between their fingers and transfer it to their mouths, how to tear chunks off the flat bread and scoop stew from the pot. Miri's fingers became tacky with rice, but the soft grains felt good between her fingers. Gravy rolled down Zett's chin and she mopped it with a piece of bread.

'Notice it's only the one hand he uses,' she said.

'Both mine are sticky,' Miri said.

'Mine too.' The candlelight flickered, pressing shadows into Zett's face. She was flushed with the wine and the spicy food, and her long hair, which had been wet when they sat down, was drying in ripples. 'Let's get wrecked,' she said, and raised her glass. 'To escape artists everywhere!'

Aziz lifted the glass of wine.

'Go on,' urged Zett. 'It'll put hairs on your chest.'

He paused, his brown eyes puzzled.

'Oh never mind.' Zett took a gulp of wine. 'Just drink up!'

Miri watched Aziz tip the glass against his lips, saw him flinch as the claret cut through the richness of the stew and surprised his tastebuds.

The slow fire of chilli spread from Miri's tongue to her lips and down her throat. As well as rice, the side dishes contained a pungent fresh lemon and herb chutney, spicy dhal and a rich sweet mixture that looked like chopped raisins. She watched Aziz eat without haste and without mess, while Zett gobbled chunks of curry-soaked bread.

Lemon juice seeped between Miri's fingers and her palms were slick with oil as she lurched down the narrow stairway from the attic to the bathroom.

She returned to find Zett with a joint poised between thumb and forefinger.

'I've been saving it,' she said. She took a long drag and held it out to Miri.

In the corner, Aziz looked up. He had drunk little more than half a glass of claret but took the joint when Miri passed it to him.

Zett patted the small mound of her stomach. 'I haven't gorged like this in months.'

The attic was hot and smoky and the candlelight beat against the pink walls like waves breaking. Sweat broke on Miri's forehead as the joint passed back and forth between the three of them. When it was finished, Zett reached for the bottle and refilled the glasses.

'Muslim man thinks we're wanton,' she said.

'Shh,' Miri said. 'He understands.'

Zett lifted the hair from the back of her neck with both hands. 'If he understood, he'd have more to say,' she said.

But Miri had the feeling Aziz followed their conversation. She watched as he carefully gathered up the tablecloth and brushed stray crumbs from the carpet into his cupped hand. They were long, narrow hands, the palms roughened, and he had a scattering of small white marks scarring his forearms. When he had emptied the crumbs into a bowl, he ran his palm across the pile of the rug, a slow considering stroke, and for the first time she noticed its pattern of small medallions, regularly spaced across the faded blue background.

Aziz smiled, as his fingertips outlined the central motif. 'Is from Isfahan,' he said.

Opal woke with a snuffling cry and Zett rolled up onto the sofa beside her. A candle guttered and Aziz quickly pinched the wick. Miri opened another bottle and settled against the cushions to gaze at the remaining flame. After a while she closed her eyes and dozed. When she opened them again, Aziz was hunched with his chin on his knees and Zett was dancing with her arms above her head and her shirt tails tied in front to expose her midriff. Her red hair drifted about her and she hummed as she swayed and swivelled her hips.

When Zett noticed Miri watching, she let out a tipsy giggle and swooped down to sip from her glass. In the wild dips and turns of her dance, the silky skirt she wore flared in a hoop around her knees. The flesh pink walls sloped inwards as the candle flame wavered in the draught and Zett's hands cast animal shadows. Her dance was Arabian nights crossed with rave. There was not enough air in the attic and Miri wondered if she was about to be sick.

Sometime later, she woke to find Zett flaked out on the sofa beside Opal.

Miri was not sure how much time had passed, but she now lay on her back in the cool shell of her bed. A shout had woken her. She sat up, propped on her fists, as it came again. Her arms and legs felt spongy with sleep as she slid off the bed. Bumping into furniture and cursing softly, she fumbled her way to the door and along the hall to the blue room.

On the mattress beneath the window Aziz slammed his head into pillows. A slant of moonlight showed her his eyes screwed shut and his cheeks streaming wet.

Miri stooped and clasped his shoulders. 'Shhh, shhh.' She was on the mattress with him, squeezing his arms to wake him, still uncertain if she herself was awake or asleep.

Her head felt woozy as she touched her palm to his mouth, hushing the keening sound that resonated in his chest. His skin was warm as she stroked his arms from shoulder to elbow, setting up a rhythm, and thinking, in a muddled way, that rocking and rhythm worked with children. It had worked when Alice was small and woke up crying in the night.

He was naked under the sheet, his body tense and tight as a spring. As she bent over him her hair tumbled forward and brushed his cheek, and when she drew it back behind her ear the strands were damp. Words flew out of him, a wild sorrowful sound spiralling around them, but it was impossible to know what he was saying. 'It's all right,' she said. 'Sh, shh, shhhh.' Sounds to soothe him.

When he fell back against the pillow she fell with him, trying to think who had been with her after her own collapse. There had been shifts of strangers, mostly women in cool starched uniforms. They had not bothered with 'sh, shh, shhhh', only offered disembodied hands to clasp as the needle punctured her vein.

He was a little quieter now and, when she put her arms around him, he burrowed blindly into her shoulder. The swift response caught her by surprise and her own eyes filled with tears. He felt so thin and brittle in her arms; his bones might break if she squeezed too hard. She leaned against him, rocking, until his shudders eased. When he turned his face towards her in the moonlight he had a famished look.

He was quiet as she laid her head against his chest, but his arms slid around, pulling her close. As they clung together, her body began to tingle with such heat that for a hallucinatory moment she was back in the room at Bird's Hotel, Jack's solid limbs entwined with her own, their joined bodies rising and falling.

She no longer knew exactly where she was, no longer cared. It was enough to be clasped in these wiry arms, enough to feel this warm skin pressed against her. He found her mouth and brushed it hesitantly with his own. The faintest scent of lemon juice on his lips, of mint and cloves on his skin. Her head felt light as she kissed him and, as the kiss became more urgent, she had an image in her head of sunlight penetrating the stitching on the ancient roller blind in the blue room; hot white pinpoints danced over the bedclothes and their bodies, and suddenly the gloom was sprinkled with marcasite-bright dots as she pressed along the length of him. In some calm part of herself she remembered where she was, remembered quite well that the room where they lay together was filled with the subtle violet light that fills all space in the minutes before dawn.

She woke with an overpowering thirst, fresh from a dream in which Jack squeezed fleshy pink guavas for her until the juice ran into a frosted glass. The persistent buzz of a blow-fly butting the windowpane drew her eyes upwards. It was past daylight. She turned her head, reluctant to relinquish the guavas, and found Aziz's cheek, shadowed with stubble, half submerged in the pillow. Waking alongside him was not a surprise; she remembered leaving her bed and stumbling towards his room, although her head began to ache as details of the night solidified. For a while she watched the rise and fall of his chest where the skin was flecked with scars, perhaps a history of boiling water or cooking fat. In sleep, his face was soft. He looked young and strong, sharply drawn against the white pillowslip. Her own body felt tender, and empty as a beach with the tide far out.

For the first time since she'd come back to the town she felt rested after sleep. Jack had been there in her dream but, for once, he was a benign presence, less important in the scheme of things than the sweet pink guavas. She eased off the bed without waking Aziz, found her nightdress and shrugged it over her head.

Zett was in the kitchen eating Weet-Bix with Opal perched on her knee. When she turned, her expression was diamond-hard and disapproving.

'So,' she said, 'I flaked out and missed the orgy.'

Miri shrugged. Her head throbbed and she drank a whole glass of water as she waited for the kettle to boil. 'I'll help bring the debris downstairs,' she said.

Zett frowned, pushed the spoon into the cereal and stirred it around. Her hair was clamped into a knot on top of her head, and the chewing-gum cheekiness she normally exuded was missing from her scrubbed face. For reasons of her own, Zett was miffed.

Opal banged her fist on the table, scattering grains of sugar.

Miri turned her back. She was too old to be accused of sluttish behaviour by anybody except herself.

While Zett busied herself buttering a slice of toast, Miri thought of Aziz curled on the mattress upstairs, delivered from whatever demons had leapt out of the wine and taken hold of him in the night. In the process of soothing him, she had soothed herself.

'I take it he'll be staying?' The edge in Zett's voice grated.

'Isn't this the home for stray dogs?' she answered, and, with the mug of coffee in her hand, she pushed through the back door into the slow-burning morning.

The side path curved around the corner of the house, past a rotting tank stand where ivy and white geraniums spilled from rusted buckets and on towards the feed shed and the stables. As Miri crossed the yard to a row of upturned crates, Con's horse made snuffling noises on the other side of the fence. The feed shed door was hanging off its hinges. She stuck her head inside and was hit by the mingled scents of chaff and dust, molasses and mouse droppings. A pile of empty sacks was stacked to one side, and along the other was a workbench littered with an assortment of tools. Everything was covered in a crust of red dust. Cobwebs in the rafters sagged with it. Miri dipped her hand into an open sack; the oats were sharp and shiny and the feel of them took her back to childhood when she had played there with litters of stable kittens.

Among the jumble of old veterinary bottles and assorted junk on the workbench were strips of oiled leather that had once been part of a bridle. She fingered a buckle, poked at a rusted tin containing horseshoe nails; when her hand brushed something moist she pulled back, peering at the still-damp bundle with distaste. It was rolled professionally, fur to the inside and the greyish mucous of the skin, where it had been peeled from the flesh, still streaked with blood. A pattern of tabby stripes was visible. Miri wrinkled her nose.

The lumps of pale meat in Aziz's stew flashed into her mind. She turned and stared at the skin. With a survivor's skill, Aziz had cut herbs in the gardens and afterwards hunted up meat in the shed. She wondered if she was cross enough with Zett to tell her.

The silence inside Havana Gardens built all day until it felt almost solid, so that the sound of the telephone was as shocking as a sudden blast from a burglar alarm. Miri had the childish impulse to clap her hands over her ears and ignore it, but then she thought of Con and ran down the stairs, gasping as she reached the bottom step and picked it up.

'Miri, you there?' Jack's voice hit her like a slap.

She opened her mouth, but no sound came.

'Miri?'

A meteorite shower of static on the line and then his voice again, close and irritable. 'Under the circumstances, I think you might have told me where you were going.'

Circumstances. She felt herself sinking and clamped the telephone to her cheek as if it could keep her afloat. The old-fashioned handset was weighty and smooth; she could see where dust had collected around the grid of holes in the mouthpiece. Her eyes shifted to the cable which disappeared into the wall and snaked away under the floor-boards, spanning the desert all the way to Sydney.

'What do you want?' she said.

'Whiley asked me to find you. There's some big-deal gig and he's breathing steam that he can't raise you.'

There might have been something, she couldn't remember.

'Lunch,' Jack's voice ebbed and flowed in the current of white noise, 'with some guy he's been nurturing for months.'

Whiley's apple cheeks puffing cigarette smoke. Miri remembered, as if in another life, how he had telephoned to ask if she was up for meeting some American director. He had kept his voice pitched low but she could tell he was wagging harder than a dog with two tails. At the time she had agreed to go, but surely no-one expected her to keep appointments she had made back when Alice was still alive.

She picked a flake of cream paint from the skirting with her thumbnail. Whiley would have found someone else for the American, someone younger. Probably Nell Bardot.

'Where are you?' she said.

'I'm at home,' Jack said. 'The apartment's covered in dustsheets.'

She imagined their sitting room with Jack pacing up and down. The bleached light at the windows would be hammering hot panels into the parquet floor, palm fronds rubbing against the railings of the balcony. He might be there or he might be in some room she'd never seen; he might be with Nell. When Miri closed her eyes she pictured a room with blood-red walls and a black lace shawl draped over the lampshade. There was velvet and fur and sequins and the light was greenish and flickering, the sounds harsh and rasping, like in foreign porno films.

'I'm at home,' Jack said again.

She saw a dish of polished stones poised on the breakfast bar like a nest of exotic eggs, with Jack, a tarnished shape, against a background of neutrals and naturals. Havana Gardens' high cool rooms full of a pale grey light, its generations of shabby clutter, made the Sydney apartment seem coy and featureless, tainted by failure. Miri squatted on the bottom step and leaned her head against the newel post.

'Listen, Whiley says this guy is genuine,' Jack was saying. 'He can stall him until the New Year if you—'

'Tell him not to bother.'

'What does that mean? That you've given up work for good?'

'It means Whiley shouldn't bother.'

'But work could be the thing that saves you right now, you know?'

In a sudden band of quiet, she could hear Jack's breath. She closed her eyes, listening.

'You still there?'

'Yes.'

'You and I should talk,' he said.

She gripped the telephone until her knuckles cracked. What made Jack think he knew what would save her? She could still hear his voice as she hung up and a tingling sensation crept along her arm and settled in her chest, as if Jack had touched her.

AZIZ

The house smelled of lemons as he made his way downstairs to the kitchen. When he opened the back door, the
dry night air was hot and still, sucking moisture from his
eyes and mouth as he peered along the empty road.

The garden gate opened soundlessly. Before him the
path wound away into the dark, but the map of the gardens
was stowed in his memory and he followed the shallow
curve of flowering shrubs to the far corner nearest the
river. Cicadas rasped in the long grass as he stood beneath
a fig tree and looked up to where a new moon, hard and
bright, gleamed between the branches. Figs ripened by the
moon, his mother had taught him. On the lower branches
the fruit was green, but he pulled himself up from branch
to branch until he could reach the few ripe figs at the top
of the tree. He stripped off his shirt and used it as a sling
to hold the picked fruit. When it was full, he slithered
down and back along the shadowy perimeter of the garden
towards the house.

In the little room behind the kitchen he found a bowl and climbed the stairs with it cupped between his palms like something precious. As he opened the door, the figs shyly held before him, she sat up in bed.

Later, sitting naked in a square of moonlight in the blue room, he took a fig from the bowl and held it to her mouth, the sticky juice running between his fingers as her teeth sank into it.

He knew it was wrong but he could not stop looking at her; his astonished eyes wandered like hands over her skin as he tried to memorise the long soft map of her body. Nothing so luxurious had ever been lavished on him and, as he touched her, some part of him drifted outside and above his ecstatic senses. In the dawn light he peeled back the sheet and raised himself on an elbow. She stirred but did not move to cover herself. Their thighs, slick with sweat, pressed close on the narrow mattress; against his skin she appeared almost fair. When he brushed his fingers lightly across her nipples they began to pucker. He ran his hand over the curve of her hip as a sigh eased out of him.

'What is it?' she said in a voice thick with sleep.

He was silent, wishing only to gaze at her until the shape and texture of her body was embedded in memory.

Later, when she woke, he came from the bathroom holding a stump of black kohl pencil.

'This, *sormah*,' he said, steadying her chin with a hand while he outlined first one of her eyes and then the other.

'It makes me look old,' she said, pulling away from him.

'No!' With thumb and forefinger he turned her chin towards him. He knew about cosmetics, knew *haft-rung*, the seven colours. Even saying the words brought sharp memories of his sisters, their warm flowery scent. They would practise drawing intricate patterns on their hands and feet using *hinah*. Indigo, *wasmah*, was for colouring their eyelids and there were red and white powders for the faces, gold for foreheads, and musk-scented oils to perfume their bodies. The packets and jars were kept hidden behind a loose brick in the washhouse, but sometimes, after they'd been dressing up, Aziz could smell the cosmetics in the hallway outside their bedroom. His mother smelled them too, and there were arguments and tears. She threatened to throw them away but, as far as he knew, the precious colours were still hidden when the house burned.

The smell of burning. In the aftermath of the fire, life was suddenly without structure. No mother to shake him awake for morning prayers. No sisters to cook and clean. No carpets to barter, no house to return to at the back end of the day. His fingers shook as he smudged the kohl upwards at the corner of her eye. Simultaneously, his mother flashed before him, her mouth open in a soundless shriek, hands raised in horror at the sight of him sitting naked beside the woman. But Nadira was dead – and didn't he deserve one soft moment after all the hard?

The woman traced his upper lip with her thumb. 'Do you have a wife, Aziz?'

He understood and shook his head. 'No.'

If things had turned out differently he might have married his young cousin. Later, in detention, he had promised to marry Jamila. It had started as a game, a distraction; he had kept her entertained for hours with intricate descriptions of their wedding and the more details he invented the more she desired, as if ritual held the possibility of safety.

'And will I be covered with seven veils?' Jamila had asked again and again.

'Of course you will,' he said each time. 'And in the corners of the veils, small objects will be sewn.'

'What objects?'

Aziz had remembered this part from his sister's wedding and gave it to Jamila.

'Saffron, for happiness,' he said, 'cloves for purity, crystalline sugar for prosperity. There will be coins, of course.'

'Silver or gold?'

'Gold, for sure,' he said.

When his sister, Amal, was married, she and her husband sat on a platform of gold and silver cushions and, as her veil was lifted, a mirror was placed before them so that each saw the other's face for the first time. It was a moment of great romance; that and the sound of the old wedding song, *Ahestah-buro*, go slowly, had made him cry. It was such a short time ago and yet so much had happened. He was in a strange town with a naked woman beside him, yet on the day of his sister's wedding such a thing would have seemed impossible.

He nuzzled the top of her head where it rested in the crook of his arm. There was a custom of temporary marriage by which a man could take a wife for a specified time; it kept men happy when they were away from home. In the circumstances, a temporary marriage might placate his mother. He shook his head again. Nadira was dead. It was a mystery to him, this need not to disappoint his dead mother. He gathered the woman's hair in his hand, testing the weight of it.

She opened her eyes. 'Where did you come from?' she said. 'Who are you?'

He shook his head. 'My mother is dead.' He lifted her hair and held it out behind her head.

'An accident?'

Again he shook his head. 'No!'

The effort of reaching for the English words overwhelmed him and as he switched to Dari the woman moved closer. With his hands still tangled in her hair, the story poured out of him, how it had been so cold in the house that night, so draughty, with a wind that swept down off the mountains carrying flakes of snow and tiny pellets of ice, so that his mother had slept in with the children to keep the young ones warm. She had made them wear extra layers of clothing and bundled the little ones in blankets, and he had heard them laughing together in the dark before they went to sleep. The flames had reached the women first and he woke choking, coughing up smoke, saved from certain death by their high-pitched screams.

He could not forget the cracking sound of the house as the fire took it. The heat was immense, snapping at his back as he scrambled through a window to stand gasping in the yard. His father had crashed into him, shouting, holding two metal buckets that slopped water as he ran. He told of the sudden flourish of flames at the corner of the house, of sparks flying from the windows and the hopeless sight of his father flinging the buckets of water as wind fanned the fire upwards through the roof. He described how he had watched a door slam open and seen the women running, their arms flapping, beating at their clothing, dripping flame, their long hair ablaze. How his father ran after them, shouting, while he stood dumbly staring into the night that was stained with the afterglow of their fiery passage.

He could have grabbed the metal buckets and filled them from the yard pump. Instead he had stood covering his nose and mouth against the noxious black smoke. Stood numbly in the icy wind until he fainted and was pulled clear by a neighbour.

On and on it flowed, his torrent of sorrow that had never been expressed to anyone, not even his father. And the woman must have understood because, when he had finished, she was crying. He caught her hands and held them to his cheeks to stop them trembling.

She pulled back and looked into his face. 'I was not the right one, Aziz,' she said. 'You should have waited for the next car.'

He kissed tears from her face as she wept and when she turned her head he kissed her wet mouth. As his hand moved down between her legs he was startled to see his mother in the doorway, her face half turned away. He could tell by the tilt of her chin that she was angry with him. Then the shadowy figure was gone as suddenly as it had appeared and his body settled into a long slow aching rhythm that nothing, not even his mother's presence, could arrest.

Afterwards, he consoled himself with the thought that his father would understand. Aziz could raise one thousand and one reasons for what had happened with the woman and all of them cast a pure light on his actions. That was the way it had always been for men. That was the way it was. But his mother's opinion continued to torment him. Nadira, who in life had always deferred to her husband and her sons, in death had become all-powerful.

PART THREE

Scattered Light

TEN EXPOSURES

Most of the time she looked unremarkable, unless a camera was present. In front of a camera, something special happened, some subtle shift of cells that realigned her features and drew what passed for beauty to the surface. It was an involuntary conjuring trick performed with light, mirrors and shutter speeds. Sometimes this transient beauty shocked her, as if she had found a stolen object in her handbag, something glittering and expensive, something borrowed from a stranger without asking. But even as the altered curves and angles startled her, this woman who metamorphosed before cameras was tiresomely familiar; Jack had drawn her out in countless images created in a variety of media. As Alice had pointed out, it was the real Miriam Passmore who was more elusive.

Aziz's eyes opened and closed like a shutter. From his expression she saw that he had transformed her as the camera did. He smiled with his eyes closed.

'What's the joke, Aziz?' she said.

His eyes opened again and he was silent — either he did not understand, or did not want to struggle with words this morning. In the warm crease beneath his chin the scent of oranges lingered from the soap she had given him, and beneath the citrus, his own spicy fragrance. His body was young and smooth, with a charge of restless energy ticking in the muscles like the rapid eye movement of a dreamer. Miri allowed herself to sink under his gaze, felt his mouth brush her forehead lightly, and then skim each eyelid and cheek. As his warm breath settled in her ear she wondered how long she might stay like this, drug-limbed and lazy, wondered how long before her luggage of woe came bumping after her.

He would remember forever the moment when she first came to him, the balm of her cool hands on his skin. As she knelt beside him, her scented hair had fallen across his cheeks. Then, as she rocked him in her arms, her body underneath the thin nightdress had flattened against him, smoothing terror from the surrounding night as simply and completely as if she had switched on a light. He had never been so close to anyone, never felt so close to breaking the dark surface of himself and swimming into light. He was overwhelmed with the desire to hold her, to be attached. Yes, yes, he had known other women, a few needy creatures who had hooked him out of the crowd and emptied his pockets before taunting him with their scrawny bodies. It had all been so quick. He had learned a little about the shape of women but nothing of their true taste and texture. Never had a woman come to him of her own will, and the small tight pain at the centre of his pleasure was exquisite. He wondered if it was the same for her, wondered how he could find the words to ask her.

She combed her hair without looking in the mirror, letting it slide through her hands in a long smooth skein. A green slip with fine straps that she had found in her mother's wardrobe released a scent of camphor as she rose and crossed the room. She had stopped wearing her own clothes and now dressed from the drawers and wardrobes in Havana Gardens, feeling in the worn garments a fragile but comforting connection with her mother and grand-mother.

She sat on the edge of the mattress and touched his mouth, following the soft line of it with her fingertips. With regular rest and food his face had filled out, but he was still too thin. With the sheet folded down, she could see each of his ribs, the soft hollow of his stomach. How long could she keep him safe? Was it possible to put him in the car and head south? And then what? Set him adrift in the netherworld of homeless people?

He caught her hand, tugging her away from these thoughts and down onto the mattress until she lay curled around him. 'I forget where I am going,' he whispered.

Early evening, tobacco-brown light inside the house. He watched as she removed her shoes, tucked the legs of her jeans into socks and pulled on her aunt's old green gumboots.

'I'm going down to the river,' she said, 'to pump the water.'

Aziz pushed his feet into the battered riding boots she had found to fit him, and as she moved away from him towards the back door he followed.

She shook her head. 'You stay in the house.' But when she stepped out onto the verandah he was close behind her.

They stood in the cool shadows under the grapevine watching night clot in the treetops, listening to the first cicada. With his warmth against her shoulder, Miri's resolve crumbled. 'We'll be careful,' she said.

The garden survived on Con's rotation plan, a yellowed sheet of butcher's paper thumbtacked to the scullery wall. But in the hot dry week before she had arrived, many of the drought-tender plants had become dehydrated and the pawpaws had begun to drop their leaves. Last night she had watered the roses and the circular beds of gardenia and hibiscus. Tonight it was to be fruit trees and the vegetable patch.

The hose was stored in a forty-four-gallon drum hidden behind lantana bushes at the far edge of the garden. As they fed it down the slope towards the river, Aziz touched her shoulder and pointed at the sky. Thunder rumbled over the broken-backed hills and a drop of water landed on her cheek.

He waved at the hose, a question.

She said, 'Let's wait and see if it rains before we start the pump,' and heard him repeat the sentence under his breath.

They stumbled down the slope towards the river, parted the curtain of overhanging willows and entered a narrow tunnel criss-crossed by branches and padded with leaves.

'Listen.' Miri tipped her head towards the music from a radio that drifted across the water. The river channelled other sounds towards them: muffled shouts, someone picking out a tune on a guitar, the fretful cry of a young child.

Along the riverbank was a place where a broad low-hanging bough formed a natural seat. The willows were less dense here. She watched him untie the corner of a length of cloth he wore slung over his shoulder, stepped closer to see what he held out to her. A handful of raisins. She took some and slipped them into her mouth, then pulled off her boots and paddled the shallows. Raindrops came more thickly now, warm as they trickled over her skin. When she turned back he was absent-mindedly twisting the length of cloth around his head. She came close to him and took his damp hand, touched by this unconscious revelation of who he was, who he had once been.

He smiled at her. 'You swim?'

She thought of the sluggish grey-scaled fish, the slippery black eels she had seen pulled from the river, flapping and wriggling in nets or at the ends of lines. 'Not tonight,' she said.

Leaves rustled around them as he stripped off his clothes. She held his shirt and trousers and watched him wade in where moonlight pooled on the surface, watched the black water lap his waist as he pushed away from the bank. Within seconds, he had vanished and she leaned out over the water's edge, suddenly aware of the unpredictable current and the submerged roots of the trees branching in the silted water.

She cupped her hands around her mouth and called softly across the unseen river, 'Be careful.'

As she listened for him, rain drilled the water's surface, pattering in the willow leaves and dripping down through the branches, soaking her hair and clothes. With her bare feet sinking into the soft clay of the riverbank, with the hiss and smack of raindrops, came a memory of a summer holiday, years ago. Alice in blue polka dot bathers, holding her nose as she jumped into a swimming pool, climbing out to leap again and again. Even when it had begun to rain, Alice kept it up, leaping until she had conquered her fear of the deep end.

Aziz surfaced, and as she stretched out a hand to pull him from the water she shivered. Alice and Jack were far away from her now. This was partly because her body had fallen so willingly into this pocket of forgetfulness, partly because she knew she was approaching the deepest part, the part where all the blame for what had happened to Alice belonged to her.

Rain made their hands slippery as they struggled to roll the long coil of hose into the drum and lock the wooden lean-to that housed the pump. Trees rustled and swayed as they walked back through the gardens and when they reached the fountain they heard the steady trickle of water filling the dry stone basin. It would evaporate in the heat of the day, but the leaping pink stone salmon would be wet tonight.

Aziz tugged at her arm and they broke into a jog, pausing in the shadows at the edge of the garden to catch their breath before crossing the open ground to the house. The intoxicating scent of rain was all around them as they ran, drops exploding on their heads and shoulders as they unlocked the back door and pushed together into the kitchen. Miri dragged handfuls of wet hair from her face and felt the run-off glide down the back of her neck. She was heading for the pantry where a towel hung on a hook beside what Con called the flower sink when Aziz caught her hand and tugged her towards the stairs. In the dense darkness of the hall, she felt the heat of his hand leading her towards the blue room.

Rain smeared their arms and hands as they peeled off damp clothing. Her fingers found the delicate indentations between his ribs. Then the dampness of their bodies, pressing together. The musty river taste of his skin. Rain against the glass. Thunder rolling across the sky, moving closer. Miri licked rain from her lips and kissed his mouth.

When he tugged her towards the mattress there was a moment of weightlessness, before they fell together.

He held a sugar cube in his mouth and sipped hot tea. Her name, Miriam, was so close to the name of his dead sister, Maryam — a little shallower on the tongue, but otherwise the same. He said her name softly as he waited for her to stir. Miriam had cried in her sleep, deep gasping sobs, the sound so unsettling that even when it stopped he had stayed awake. Now she slept with her arms flung out beside her like a child, hands squeezed into balls. He lifted a long strand of her hair with his finger and watched it tremble in the draught swooping under the door, touched with his fingertip the soft pulse at the side of her neck and knew that he could watch her sleep for hours.

In a glass cabinet in the dining room she found an album with tiny sepia-tinted photographs fixed into slots in the pulpy black paper. *Esperanza Mendez, Habana 1929* was written in faded script on the inside cover. Her grandmother had not brought Cuba's landscape with her, only its people — children with tight plaits and scrubbed cheeks, couples in Sunday dress, complete with hats and gloves, a dark-haired woman holding a cake, an old man planted bolt upright on a kitchen chair with a dog at his knee, his features indistinct under a panama hat. Miri turned the pages, marvelling at the stiff backbones and sober mouths, the fearless gazes directed straight into the camera lens. In these austere faces it was possible to detect traces of her mother, her aunt, herself and Alice.

Aziz studied the photographs and gently touched her cheekbone. Slowly, she explained how her grandmother had married and left Cuba knowing that she would probably never return. Esperanza had tried to carry Cuba to Australia in her trunks of ornaments and photographs, in the statues of saints with their sad eyes rolled skywards.

She took his hand. 'Do you have a photograph from before?'

A wistful smile hovered on Aziz's lips. He pushed his hand into a trouser pocket and pulled out the pear-shaped stone she had found when she undressed him. 'From my house,' he said, 'this.'

In the early morning, with the day gathering light outside the window of the blue room, she set her camera on a tripod and photographed him as he sat propped against the wall drinking tea. The zoom lens moved in on his fingers wrapped around the white cup, his mouth and eyes still blurred from sleep. He laughed and shook his head at her, ran his hands over uncombed hair and pulled the crumpled sheet up to his chin.

'Don't move,' she said as she pressed the shutter, capturing his luminous eyes and shy smile in frame after frame of 35-millimetre film.

In the gardens, they lay in the cool grass. The full moon, bright as daylight, washed over them; she rested in the curve of his arm, his gaze fastened on the tiny chocolate mole that hovered above her top lip. As he stared at it, the weight of the night garden pressed, hissing, against his back. Beads of sweat broke out across his forehead and he swiped them away with the back of his hand. Just the rhythm of her white cotton blouse rising and falling was something to live for.

Shadows fell from the blue walls and gathered in the folds of the sheets, in the curves of her body. Golden and unkempt, full of unimaginable secrets, her beauty was of the same calibre as a rare antique carpet his father had once owned, its silken surface busy with hundreds of flower motifs, honeybees, butterflies and tiny hummingbirds. His father had prized this carpet for the beauty of its dyes infused from walnut husks, pomegranates, autumn apple leaves, chamomile, saffron, cinnabar and indigo, and, for its holy image of a garden, an intricate blue and gold paradise, *behesht*.

She came from the bathroom wrapped in a towel. In the bedroom, light pooled on the varnished floorboards leaving the corners of the room in shadow. Air flowing through the open window was potent with the scent of rain, and as she towelled her hair and combed it smooth, raindrops pattered against the window glass. She put the comb beside the hairbrush on the dressing table without looking in the mirror. When she moved to the bed and turned back the sheet, the pillow and bottom sheet were strewn with star jasmine flowers so freshly cut that they had not yet begun to wilt, their scent high-pitched and sweet.

The door swung wide and Aziz leaned in the opening, his hands braced against the chipped woodwork. Miri gestured towards the pillow and he smiled. As he walked towards her she let the towel fall.

The cotton pillowcase was cool and scented. At first they moved together as effortlessly as swimmers gliding in calm water, then faster, and faster still, until they were gasping.

Afterwards she picked crushed flowers from her hair and curled against Aziz with her eyes closed. Beside him, she was able to sink straight from wakefulness into sleep, descending without effort to a place of profound rest, a place where the pain of remembering was suspended and neither Alice nor Jack penetrated her dreams. Beside Aziz, she dreamed of knot gardens and mazes, of her feet padding over warm, richly patterned floors, while a yellow-ochre sun inched across an expanse of bare white wall.

PART FOUR

Diffraction

MIRI

On Christmas Eve a desert wind sifted red sand, fine as talcum powder, over the surfaces inside the house. It rattled the sash windows and roared in the chimneys, yet despite the currents of air circulating around her, Miri found it difficult to breathe. She was easing ice cubes from a freezer tray when she heard the postman's motorbike. A few minutes later, Dig appeared at the back door with a batch of mail. He stood on the threshold of the kitchen turning the letters in his big scabbed hands. 'This was in the box,' he said. 'Junk mail and something for you from Queensland.'

Miri frowned. Wind gusted past him and shook the roller blind she had drawn against the heat.

Her uncle dropped the mail on the table. When he took off his hat, dust drifted from it and settled on the linoleum. 'Lois cooks hot lunch on Christmas Day,' he said. A fly buzzed about his head and he batted it away. 'She wanted me to tell you. Everyone's welcome.'

Miri dropped ice into a jug of water. 'Thank you, tell Lois,' she said.

When her uncle had gone she slit the packet with a knife, stared for a moment at the contents and then hurried upstairs to the attic.

'This came inside a packet addressed to me,' she said to Zett.

Zett's hands shook as she grabbed the letter and ripped it open. Inside, Christmas wrapping paper was folded around a wad of hundred-dollar notes.

She counted them quickly. 'Two thousand dollars! Good old Cam to the rescue.' Zett grinned, suddenly radiant. 'We're all set, now.'

By the afternoon, even the cellar felt warm and stuffy when Miri went down to bring up wine. She stood with a bottle of Con's claret in her hands, remembering how her mother used to sit on the cellar steps shaking chemicals in a plastic canister to develop rolls of film. It was down here that Candela had kept light-sensitive materials: photographic paper in heavy cardboard packets and silver salts – bromide, iodide and chloride, which were also the names of streets in the town. The street names had never sounded odd when she was a child, but now it struck her that the grid of the town was like a great photographic plate, thousands of ghostly images of their lives etched into its dusty surface.

In the kitchen she spread thin slices of bread with cream cheese, pâté, pale circles of cucumber, and pressed them into sandwiches. By the time she had finished, the wind had dropped a little. It was time to water the garden.

She was on the verandah tugging on a pair of her aunt's riding boots when she looked up and saw Jude Moran. It was the time of day when Zett would be thinking about warming a jar of baby food for Opal; at any moment Aziz could step through the back door ready to help her pump water. Miri's stomach flipped as she pushed her foot into the boot and straightened. The back door was partly open, and she could see through the kitchen to the bottom of the stairs.

Jude's hands were jammed in the front pockets of his moleskins as he crossed the verandah. 'How've you been?'

'I've been okay.'

'Fancy a drink?'

In a single fluid movement Miri shut the kitchen door and stepped away from it, closer to Jude. 'Can I go like this?' She lifted her arms, indicating her jeans and T-shirt.

'Fine by me.'

She seemed so anxious to go with him that it was sending out the wrong signal, and he had that silly look on his face some men got when they thought they were going to score – if not immediately, then soon. She followed him to the car without glancing back at the house, wanting to hurry but forcing herself to move at his pace.

Jude opened the car door for her. 'Up you go,' he said.

She felt his eyes sliding over her as she climbed in; as they pulled away from the house she told herself that the true purpose of beauty, if she had it, was these moments of distraction.

They drove out past the racecourse with its ancient wooden grandstand. Past the derelict Starlite Drive-in, where rows of white posts set in concrete still dotted the red soil, and the peeling surface of the big screen gathered sunlight and bounced it like an SOS into space. Jude flicked on the radio. It was a Sydney station, smooth drive-time music that made her picture cars gliding in slow motion through the hot winding streets of the city. She glanced at him and then away out the window, irritated by the smug half-smile on his blunt face. Tomorrow, or even later tonight, he would tell his mates how she couldn't get in the car quick enough. But there had been no choice.

The pub was tucked into a curve in the river, an old-time watering hole that had been done over for the tourists. Jude steered her towards the ladies' bar, where middle-aged couples sat silently over glasses of beer in a slush of piped music. Tinsel garlands swayed overhead in the breeze from the air conditioner. Through the window she could see the flurry of willows lining the river, the thin leaves bronze-tinted as the wind tossed them in the last of the day's sun.

'Beer?'

She nodded, studying Jude under her lashes as the barmaid poured their drinks.

'Inside or out?' he said.

She looked away from the static couples towards a door that opened onto a deck. 'Out there?'

As they sat down with their drinks the sky was rapidly losing blue, but the pub's limestone walls still radiated the day's heat.

'Do you work weekends?' she said, not interested but needing to break the silence.

He took a swig of beer and sucked froth from the moustache that concealed his upper lip. 'Sometimes. But I'm off work right now.'

'Will you go away?'

He shook his head. 'It's not a holiday. I've been relieved of duties indefinitely. Waiting on the outcome of an inquiry.'

The glass was cold and slippery in her hand, but she managed a sip of beer without spilling it.

'Sounds like trouble.'

'Yeah, trouble for nothing. For a bloke who knocked himself off in the cells. I just happened to be in charge at the time. Apparently I'm supposed to have eyes in the back of my head.'

'What was he in for?'

'The usual: drunk and disorderly. If he'd been white, there wouldn't have been a fuss — but it's a black kid, so there has to be a big investigation. A journalist from Sydney's been poking around trying to stir things up. You might have read about it in the local paper.'

She hadn't seen a paper. 'What will happen?'

'Nothing much. It was just another day at work, far as I'm concerned. So what if one more solvent-sniffer tops himself in jail? How bad can it be? Time was the cops would've held a party. One less larrikin to deal with on Saturday nights, one less hot-wired car to chase. But now we have to go through the charade of an inquiry. Have to put up with all the "where did we go wrong" stuff in the papers. No skin off my nose, though. I'm still getting paid.'

Jude took a long swig of beer and tapped her glass with his knuckle. 'Drink up.'

She took another sip. 'I'm a slow drinker.'

'What I hear, you're a wine drinker.'

Miri kept very still, the only trick she knew to conceal her agitation. 'It's nice to know my habits are being discussed in high places.'

Jude laughed. 'There are no high places round here. Low as it gets for miles and miles and miles.'

Her body felt damp inside her clothes as she watched him go to the bar for more beer.

When he came back he said, 'I didn't think you'd last here until Christmas.'

'I don't care about Christmas.'

'Nice Catholic girl like you?'

'I'm not a Catholic.'

'I thought all the Kissack women were Micks.'

'My grandmother was, but that's as far as it went. Where will you spend Christmas?'

'That an invitation?'

Miri stared at him helplessly.

'Actually, I always go to my mother's,' he said. 'Practically the only time I see the old girl.'

'Does she live in town?'

'About two hours up the river. She used to be a housekeeper and when the old bloke died last year he left her the property.'

Somehow she managed to keep the conversation moving, spinning out her second beer while Jude polished off two more. As they talked, the last light of the day gathered thick and golden around them and she noticed how it burnished everything, even ugly fence posts and sheets of corrugated iron and the curves of cars in the pub's car park. She watched a family tumble out of a beaten-up Commodore and head towards the pub, a broad-waisted woman in a shapeless floral dress, a man with his face as brown and wrinkled as a raisin, and two towheaded kids with bare feet. It was the still, silent, sinking moment of the day when she felt most raw, when anything, even a pleat of light striking the stem of a wineglass, the swoop of a bird or the sound of children's voices — especially children's voices — could undo her.

'It's six-thirty,' she said, her voice softer and weaker than she would have liked. 'Hospital visiting starts at seven and I promised to see my aunt.'

Jude's disappointment was almost comic, but he recovered quickly. By the time they drew up outside the hospital gates he was putting on a show of good humour.

'Well, thanks,' she said, forcing a smile.

Jude leaned his head out of the open window and grinned at her as she backed away. 'Next time, we'll grab a meal.'

ZETT

She was almost at the bottom of the stairs when she heard Jude's boots cross the verandah. The staccato tap of his heels was unmistakeable; she would know that arrogant strut of his anywhere. And then, as if to confirm it, she heard him say something to Miri. The sound of his voice rooted her to the spot, toes gripping the threadbare runner of carpet, as the back door clicked shut. Opal was in her arms, pink-cheeked and dozy after an afternoon nap. Sometimes the baby stayed quiet when she woke, but other afternoons she screamed the house down until she was fed. Opal's mouth stretched in a delicate yawn as Zett turned and scrambled up the stairs. Adrenalin pumping into her calves pushed her up two steps at a time.

She opened the attic door and stood for a moment, jiggling the baby, listening for sounds from below. Opal recognised this attempt to lull her, and as her eyes and mouth crumpled in resistance Zett wrenched up the front of her T-shirt and eased a nipple into the open mouth.

The sudden sight of her fading bruises and the certainty that Jude was close by set off a painful fluttering in her chest. As the panic zone around her heart tightened she willed away the feeling, concentrating on the rhythm of Opal sucking, the tiny mouth circling her nipple and her daughter's eyelids, like waxy flower petals folded over the sapphire eyes. With her free hand she covered her nose and mouth and breathed cautiously into her cupped palm; she'd read somewhere that breathing into a paper bag helped, and the last time she'd tried it, it had.

When she could move again, she squatted beside the sofa and reached underneath for the gun. It was wedged into the upholstery webbing, and the smooth handle felt enormous in her palm. Jude had taught her how to load the old double-action revolver, how to line up an empty chamber at the top under the hammer because she was worried about it going off by accident. She still kept it that way out of habit, and the gun was already loaded as she drew it out and eased back onto the sofa facing the door.

With Opal in her lap and the gun resting on the arm of the sofa she felt a fraction calmer. The bad feeling in her chest ebbed as the baby kicked her feet and made small milky noises in her nose and throat. Opal's sounds were loud in the attic but dispersed among the ticks and groans of the house. Zett strained to pick up any noise from below, and in another minute her body sagged with relief as Jude's car started up and drove away.

She let her head flop against the sofa and closed her eyes. The weight of the gun in her hand brought back hot afternoons before they were married, Jude driving her out into the desert with a cooler full of beer and a wild eager look in his eyes. Back then he drove a rusting white Chevrolet with burgundy leather seats and had taught her how to shoot empty beer cans off its bonnet. One long afternoon, parked in a shallow depression on the old towpath beside the river, he had taken her picture while she was sleeping off the beer. They'd made love before she'd fallen asleep and when she woke she was naked on the back seat, her skin tight with a film of dried river water, and Jude was holding a bulky Polaroid camera. When she asked what he was doing he said he wanted to look at her that way when he was bored at work. He said she was so beautiful he never wanted to stop looking at her body.

Even after everything that had happened between them, the memory of that afternoon filled her with a spreading warmth, made her want to throw down the gun and run after her husband, to pull his face down towards her one last time. It made her think that maybe they weren't so bad together, that they could get help, or she could learn to hold her tongue when he was on edge.

On that first afternoon, with the river water tugging at her skin and a blanket of sky and willows muffling the out-side world, with Jude looking at her with his eyes so hot and bright, a strange electricity had surged through her. She had been curled sideways on the seat. Maybe it was the beer — they'd certainly drunk plenty of it — but the black eye of the camera excited her and she rolled onto her back, pulled up her knees and opened them wide, staring up into the camera. Jude groaned and moved in closer. She slid two fingers inside herself, moving her hand in slow circles that quickened as she heard the shutter click, then the soft whirr as the print slid out of the camera.

Afterwards, they drank a lot more beer, and Jude pleaded with her to do it again. He wanted the perfect picture, he said, and he handed her his gun. They'd been shooting the last of the beer cans and the handgun was still warm, with a powdery, metallic smell clinging to it, when she knelt on the back seat and eased down onto the barrel. Jude was leaning in through the open door, the hot sky behind him and the camera making wavering circles in front of her. Polaroid prints were spread out on the ground around him. Her long hair floated around her; she felt it crackle with static electricity as the alcohol buzzed in her veins, speeding everything, blurring everything. She was panting, moving up and down on the gun, little lightning flashes of heat exploding in her body, as Jude's camera clicked and whirred, clicked and whirred.

'Pull the trigger, Zett. Pull!'

Poised on the edge of coming and about to tumble, she faltered.

Jude cajoled her. 'C'mon, Zett, do it for me.'

She didn't want to stop, but she always had to please him. They had just emptied the gun; there was no danger. This flashed through her head as her thumb, warm and sticky, hooked around the trigger. She heard the simultaneous clicks of gun and camera above the rasp of her breath as she came.

Later, Jude showed her the single bullet nestled in the chamber. He'd slipped it in when she wasn't looking. She couldn't believe he'd done it.

'You stupid crazy bastard fuck!' Suddenly sober, she lashed out with her hands and feet, but he just lifted her off the ground and kissed her. And his face when he looked at that picture was so weird, like he'd just seen God or something. That was the beginning of their photographic sessions in the desert, the beginning of something that neither one of them seemed capable of ending.

The first time she'd left him after they were married, he had found her inside an hour, booked into a room at the Astral Hotel. His knuckles were soft against the wood.

She'd pressed her cheek against the cool plaster and heard him breathing on the other side of the door. After a while, he gave up knocking. The sound of the revolver's well-oiled chamber spinning, followed by the hammer click when he pulled the trigger, made her open the door just a crack. She thought he must be joking, until she saw the barrel pressed to the side of his head.

His eyes had a dazed look. 'Tell me you love me, Zett,' Jude said, lowering the gun again and spinning the chamber.

When she didn't move, he pointed it at his head and pulled the trigger.

'I love you. I love you,' she cried, before he could do it again.

Jude always carried everything too far, and alcohol pushed him to extremes. But the scariest part about that night at the hotel was that Jude had been stone-cold sober.

Thinking about him made her whole body hot, as if her blood boiled and bubbled beneath the skin. Bubbles of fear. Bubbles of love. Zett shivered. They might have been good together once, but Jude was crazy and for Opal's sake she was never going back. Never.

When Opal was full of milk, Zett rubbed her back, easing out a series of small windy burps and smiles. She laid the baby on the floor while she jammed nappies and toys into the rucksack, then scooped her onto a hip. As she skittered across the road that divided the house from the gardens, she wondered where Jude had taken Miri, what would happen when they came back. The main thing was, she wouldn't be there. Lois Kissack was a good sort and would probably take her in, but as a place to hide it was too obvious. Instead, she headed for the plaster statues and tin lollypops in Artie Rose's front yard. Artie could keep a secret. He might even help her get away.

JUDE

He watched her walk away between the tall wrought-iron gates of the hospital, feeling that prickling in his crotch he used to get when Zett came bouncing towards him wearing just her slip, and with a can of beer in her hand. The way this woman moved made him wish he had a video camera handy. Matter of fact, he'd just been looking at one in the photographic shop. His digital camera took good pictures, but that long unhurried stride, like she was gliding on wheels, her peachy arse swaying from side to side in a mesmerising rhythm, all that delicate friction would be wasted. He imagined her walking away from him naked, walking with that same sway spreading into the gorgeous width of her hips. He imagined her long legs opening towards him. Even the shape of her feet was beautiful, as he'd seen when she pulled on the socks and riding boots. Feet supple as fish, with long, bony toes; the memory unsettled him, made him sigh for action, as if all around him everything was solid and static and he needed to stir the air in order to breathe, needed to kick-start some reluctant motor deep inside himself.

He glanced at the dashboard clock, then peered along the street. The pubs would be filling and he couldn't face seeing people he knew, people hoping he'd go down for the count over Billy Martin. Well, whatever happened, he wouldn't give them that satisfaction.

More than anything he wished Zett would stop fucking about and come home. Wished he could lay his head in her lap and feel her small, warm, freckled breasts tickling his face as she leaned over him. She was somewhere close by; he could feel her. He'd always been able to feel her, as if her red hair spread a heat that his radar was specially tuned for. He knew she was around, that she'd come home soon, or he'd find her and tell her he was sorry, that he'd turn over a new leaf. Once the inquiry was over they'd take a holiday. Maybe up to Queensland to see her brother. If he could just talk to her, convince her he was going to behave himself from now on. He didn't know what got into him. Something just took over. And Zett was the mouthy sort, like her mother.

Jude shoved the car in gear and headed out along the Sydney road. It was only a short run to Castaway and with any luck that little waitress, Chandelle, or Chantelle, would be finishing up at the roadhouse around about now.

CHANDELLE

Moths as fat as sparrows flopped against her cheeks and her bare white arms as she dragged the bulky sandwich board towards the diner. It was the blunt end of the day. There had been no traffic in either direction for over an hour, not a single truck. In that time her only customers had been two kids who'd walked the mile and a half from home to pick up cigarettes for their mother. Above her head, stars pulsed. She felt their cold sheen seeping through the pores of her skin, felt their glitter circulating and tingling in her blood and knew that later, in her hot little bedroom with the sheets folded back, starlight would spread through-out her overheated body like a rash.

In the dry creek bed behind the servo a couple of stray steers shuffled and bumped against each other in the rusty dark. Every so often one of them would stretch its throat in a bellow as forlorn and ghostly as the twice-weekly hoot of the overland express. She stumbled and knocked her ankle against the wooden board, cursed, and bent to rub the skin. When she straightened, she saw the interior of the servo pressed against the hot night like a picture torn from a magazine, blue-tinged, empty, with the racks of gaudy snack foods and bottled drinks, and the ice-cream fridge with its smeary glass lid, and sparks fizzing in the creepy light of the mozzie catcher, and plastic streamers looped back in the kitchen doorway as if held by an invisible fist. A cardboard Coca-Cola sign dangled above the till. Wiped-down tabletops glowed with a greasy lustre, and the lead-coloured light gathered around serviette dispensers, salt and pepper shakers and chipped white sugar bowls. A Christmas tree with plastic icicles and multicoloured fairy lights stood at an angle inside the door.

Christmas Eve. Chandelle pressed her forehead against the window glass, feeling panic beat in her like wings. What if this was all there was? What if this was the length and breadth of the world, her life forever and ever? In ten years' time, when those kids were coming in for their own cigarettes, she could still be here behind the counter, filing her nails, waiting. She was hit by a wave of clammy nausea; when she leaned against the building for support it seemed to slide away from her. The black sky, with its pin-points of light, pressed the breath from her and held her pinned against a vast emptiness. In the distance a yellow light shone in the window of the Murphys' kitchen; Mickey's scrawny wife would be feeding baked beans to their kids, while he sat in front of the TV in his socks. Chandelle felt like she was suffocating, until a faint hum from the bitumen distracted her. A single white light separated into a pair of headlights. Someone was moving towards her from beyond the junk-filled cave of the servo. She dragged her fingers through her hair and smoothed the front of her shirt. Someone beside herself was alive out here. They were coming towards her, and she could only pray that whoever it was would stop.

LOIS

The Virgin Mary had first appeared after a dust storm. She'd been there on the kitchen window when Lois came to clamp it shut against the weather, a serene face with the robes covering her hair undulating as the red outback dust drove against the pane. At the same moment, her kitchen had been suffused with the scent of roses. Not a synthetic smell like the plastic room-fresheners in Bi-Lo, but the pure perfume of the old-fashioned roses in the nuns' garden at her convent school in Sydney. And the face of Mary on her windowpane had the same chaste lines as the face of the plaster Virgin that had overlooked the school playground, her arms extended in mute blessing. Lois had stood transfixed in the middle of her kitchen as the dust face of Mary spoke in a slow sad voice that detached itself from the whine of the wind and settled in her ear, an audible yet quiet caress.

'Now, I don't want you to worry, Lois,' the Virgin had said, 'but I've got a few things to tell you.'

Mary's voice had a faint Irish lilt, like Aileen Ryan on the corner who had taken in washing during the great miners' strike to keep the seven Ryan children from starvation and later opened the town's first laundrette. But Aileen was a big woman with coarse black hair who went without a brassiere, whereas Lois's Virgin was finely moulded, her dust-coloured eyes tilted upwards at a holy angle.

Since the storm, Mary had visited her kitchen once or twice a month. Lois had heard of the Virgin appearing to people in other parts of the world, but no-one in the town had ever seen her. In the library she read of visions in far-away places like Guadalupe, Lourdes and Fatima, which was in Portugal. In the United States, the Virgin had visited a woman in Georgia and another in Colorado, the latter a blonde named Theresa Lopez. Sometimes Lois wondered how she measured up against these American women. Americans always had a lot to say for themselves on the TV. Whenever she thought of Theresa Lopez, Lois brought out the bleach; if she was not the most intellectual of Mary's chosen then she would keep the cleanest floor. Oh, there were outlandish sightings, too; the faces of Mary and Jesus spotted in such unlikely places as a Texas tabletop, a screen door, a linoleum tile, a tortilla chip, not to mention a plate of spaghetti on a billboard. Surely that was blasphemous.

Lois clucked her tongue and reached for her pink rubber gloves. Those foreign sightings had a tendency to escalate into sideshows, with thousands of pilgrims camping and cavorting nearby, turning the garden of the chosen one to mush, tracking mud across their clean linoleum. Lois wasn't having any of it. She had kept Mary's visits to herself and planned for it to stay that way.

When she had heard that a dust storm was forecast for Christmas Eve, she had bought a spray of miniature carnations from the florist. The arrangement was in the fridge covered with cling film, and after Lois had transferred the flowers to the windowsill, she lit a stick of incense. An orange propped on cocktail stick legs stood on the sill, and she pressed the incense into the rind. Red gingham curtains pulled back on either side of the kitchen window exposed the darkened pane and reflected the room, neat and ordinary, with Lois in her housecoat.

She crossed herself and addressed the windowpane. 'I heard some terrible news today, but I guess you already knew about Alice.' As she stared at the glass, her eyes began to water. 'It all makes sense now, Miri coming home. Dig and I were beginning to wonder, and if Con hadn't said something we'd have put our foot in it over Christmas, for sure. So, you being a mother and all, maybe it wouldn't be too much trouble to show Miri some consideration, if you're passing.' She sniffed. 'Her own poor mother was a sweetheart, bless her, and I know she'd have wanted me to ask.'

Lois poured vodka into a glass, topped it up with orange cordial from the fridge and propped her hip against the sink. After a couple of sips, she addressed the windowpane again.

'Not that it's anything by comparison, but the front step's finally collapsed. White ants. Like I said before, at this rate the house won't last till Easter, and the cash I saved for the pest extermination man has gone. Dig just saw it as a lazy five hundred and the bookies have had it off him, so you're my last hope.'

Two streets away, a car engine coughed and then accelerated with a screech of tyres. The windowpane reflected the plastic cone of the overhead light fitting and the painted kitchen cupboards. Peering past the reflections, Lois saw a sprinkling of stars. She switched off the light and leaned closer, concentrating, as the wind gusted against the pane and the curtains stirred in the draught sweeping under the back door. The kitchen reeked of bleach and jasmine incense and the hot night curving in from the desert. Lois swayed a little as she rose on tiptoe to straighten the framed picture of the Madonna that was tacked to the wall above the toaster. From this angle, a cloudy shape was visible on the glass and she held her breath as she waited for the Virgin to appear.

MERVYN

The black dog pressed her rib cage against his legs. She was a good quiet dog, and fast, too. Even without the money he'd slipped to the steward to help her out of the starting gate ahead of the field, she'd have romped home. Could've saved himself thirty bucks, but he wasn't complaining. With what he'd picked up from different bookies he could pay off Sharkie and start the new year with a clean slate – or at least keep his front teeth. All he had to do was slip her back into Dig Kissack's kennel and retrieve his own dog. He had planned to quietly get rid of his own useless mutt once he'd paid off his debts, but now he thought maybe he'd keep her, leave the door open for another swap sometime.

His bicycle towed a dogcart. That was another thing. This dog walked to heel, but he'd brought the cart to save wrestling with his own silly bitch. He smirked into the darkness; it was a bit of luck that one black dog looked exactly like another, and out at the track they hadn't been too fussy about checking ear tattoos. He wheeled the bike with its dogcart along the hedge at the side of Con Kissack's old garden. The headlamp showed a length of hose running down the slope and under the fence, and he cursed softly as he pushed the bike over it. Then he was at the north-west corner, at the back of Dig's house. The dog whined softly and wagged her tail. An hour earlier he had seen Dig disappearing through the front door of the Criterion Hotel. Half the town was headed there for a Christmas Eve barbecue and booze up and, as he had expected, the Kissack house was in darkness.

LOIS

The wind had dropped and the vodka bottle was almost
drained by the time Lois came out the back door with a bag
of rubbish. Diego's old blue heeler, Tania, wagged her tail
and unfolded from the dusty hollow her body had worn
beside the dog kennel. Lois dumped the rubbish in the outside bin and was just turning back towards the house when
she heard someone moving about near the concrete kennel
where Dig kept his racing dog. Tania growled as something
landed with a thunk beside her kennel. Lois saw the heeler
sniff at it, then pick it up in her jaws and settle in the dust.
A bone. Someone had chucked a big meaty bone at Tania.

A piece of pipe left over from one of Dig's abandoned
plumbing repair jobs stood in an empty flowerpot. Lois
picked it up and moved cautiously along the side fence.
She heard the clink of the chain on the gate of the racing
kennel and the soft whine of the greyhound. Someone was
definitely fiddling around down there, and Lucky Tikki
was a soppy dog; she'd go to anyone.

Lois saw a bulky shadow. As she edged forward, gripping the pipe, her heel jammed in a crack in the concrete path and she staggered. Her hand shot out, grabbing air, and a shooting pain in her ankle made her shriek as she tumbled sideways into the weedy ditch beside the fence.

Tania barked once and strained at the end of her chain, pointing her muzzle to where Lois sprawled with the wind knocked out of her. A lightning bolt of pain zigzagged up from her ankle to her thigh and receded, leaving a dull throb low down. Her housecoat was rucked up round her neck, and the gritty dirt of the backyard scraped her back and shoulders. When Lois flexed her ankle the pain whacked her again. She swore softly and lay still.

From the kennels came a muffled curse. The back gate clanged shut and footsteps passed on the other side of the fence. Lois was tempted to call for help, but as she opened her mouth she remembered that she hadn't shaved her legs in a week. If she ended up in hospital it would be around town like wildfire that Lois Kissack had legs like a gorilla. This realisation gave her the impetus to roll over, and as she braced herself for the crawl towards the house, she tugged at her housecoat and suppressed a groan. There was no way that anyone, not even an intruder, was going to see her in this condition.

MERVYN

He listened to the grunts and groans as Dig's old lady crawled towards the house. She'd interrupted him before he'd made the swap, and the dog was tugging at the lead to let him know she wanted to go home. If it hadn't been for Lois appearing in the yard like that, he'd have been on his way to the pub by now. Mervyn ground his teeth and swore silently. He had to dump this dog and retrieve his own before Dig noticed the difference. The longer he left it, the more likely that was, and it wouldn't take the Kissacks long to figure out whose dog they'd been walking and feeding for a week.

From the sound of it, Lois was out of action. He was about to try the back gate again when a car pulled up in front of the house.

Mervyn cursed again as he headed back to his bicycle. Give it an hour or so to quieten down, then he'd slip back and try again.

MIRI

'Lois's gone and broken her ankle,' Con announced as Miri sat down beside the bed. 'She's in casualty, getting it set. Dig had to drag her in kicking and screaming. She wanted Artie Rose to slap a bandage on it.'

Miri took her aunt's hand in her own. Lois must have had an accident while she was out with Jude. 'What happened?' she said.

Con's mouth twitched. 'According to Dig, she heard someone fooling around in the backyard. Like the idiot she is, she went to have a look.'

'Poor Lois.'

'Oh, Lois'll give as good as she gets. How's the garden, is everything dead?'

Miri shook her head. 'It loved that bit of rain, but the dust and wind will have dried it out again.'

The lines around Con's eyes deepened as she examined Miri's face. 'You look a little rested but still kind of white around the mouth. I'm glad you've got some company, like the old days.'

'The house guests are no bother.'

Con said, 'Suzette Moran's nice enough, but like her mother, she's a magnet for trouble.'

Miri leaned close to Con. 'Zett's husband turned up suddenly tonight. I had to go for a drink to get him out of the way.'

'Don't get too cosy with Jude,' Con said. 'He might be police, but you'd be safer going out with Sharkie White and that's saying something.'

'I didn't want to go,' Miri said, 'but there wasn't any choice.'

Con pouted in disapproval. 'Well, you look out for yourself. Jude Moran plays rough.'

Miri remembered Jude's parting remark and shivered. It had reminded her of Jack's voice on the telephone, his insistence that they should talk. From the corridor outside Con's room came the steady *bleep bleep bleep* of a pager. Footsteps hurried past, and the telephone at the nurses' station began to ring.

Miri sat holding Con's hand, swamped by dread. Jack's voice in her ear had opened up other conversations, like the one she'd had on the telephone with her agent, Whiley, his nasal brightness setting her nerves on edge.

Right after Alice had come out of the clinic, Whiley had called to tell her about an American who was casting a film called *The Whaler's Daughter*. Miri knew she wasn't the only actor Whiley was pitching, but at least he let her think she was at the top of the list.

'The part is a peach,' he said. 'Wear something special.'

She was jotting down the time and place of the audition in her diary, mentally sorting through her wardrobe, when she realised Whiley was still speaking.

'. . . quite how to say this, under the circumstances.'

'Say what?'

There was a long exhalation and she guessed he was puffing on one of his thin brown cigarettes.

Whiley told her in a rush. 'I wanted to get in first before you heard it from someone else. There's a rumour little Nell's got herself knocked up. It's rubbish, of course. Don't lose any sleep over it.'

'Who's going to lose sleep?' She had said it too quickly, knowing instantly that the story was true. Nell was not like other women Jack had fooled around with. She played dirty and seemed to be playing for keeps. If Whiley felt he had to tell her, then Nell was definitely pregnant.

After she put the phone down, Miri wondered who else he thought would have told her. Only Whiley knew her well enough to break the news that her husband had made another woman pregnant. And once she knew, it was impossible to think of anything else.

She drove through the city making slow aimless circles in the traffic. Eventually, she found the feeder lane onto the expressway and crossed the harbour, staring down at boats bobbing on the dark moiré surface, wondering why she was always looking at her life from a distance, as if there was no private shortcut to her emotions but only the isolating eye of the camera, Jack's eye, to give her presence. She was astonished at her ability to absorb new blows, to take in bad news, turn it around and make it part of herself. She had been in a stage play once, a domestic drama in which the husband was having an affair. There were so many scenes of confrontation between her character, the wife, and the philandering spouse that after each performance she had gone home exhausted. Exhausted, and amazed, too, that this mild little woman with flour-dusted cheeks had such resources, such fire. The play had run for six weeks, and every night she had shouted at her husband on the stage then gone home and curled quietly beside Jack.

On the north side of the harbour, she parked outside a corner shop with a table and two plastic chairs set on a narrow strip of pavement. As she stood outside wondering what to order, sparrows swooped down from a tree and hopped towards her, scouting for food. A man came out of the shop with a paper under his arm and looked as if he might speak, but she straightened her shoulders and peered at the cards blu-tacked inside the window.

The conversation with Whiley had thrown her into a new orbit. Miri ordered coffee, and while she waited for it doodled egg shapes on a paper napkin, tadpoles swimming, swarming spermatozoa. She tore the napkin into tiny pieces and stowed them in her pocket; later she would open the car window and let them flutter away on a street above the harbour.

Within the bitterness of the black espresso she found a moment of clarity, a moment in which she recalled Keiko standing in the street below their window with her blue-black hair glinting, the moist red slash of her lipstick like an open wound. With the caffeine buzzing through her, Miri knew what to do. She lit a cigarette and pressed Whiley's office number into her mobile phone.

As she had hoped, his new young receptionist picked up the call and Miri asked for Nell Bardot's address. The girl hesitated, but before she was able to pose any awkward questions Miri launched into the lines she had rehearsed in her head.

'I've just had lunch with a friend of mine who has a script he wants Nell to read. He asked if I would drop it in the post.'

The receptionist held her breath. The girl was green, but maybe not too green to guess what was going on.

Miri plunged in deeper, projecting enthusiasm she hadn't felt for anything in weeks, with the exception of feeding Alice. 'I've read the script myself. It's a fabulous part and Nell's going to fall in love with it.'

The perfect part for Nell Bardot would be a blood-sucking baby, a vampire with dimples, a Venus flytrap. And if Jack had flaunted his affair at the agent's office, the receptionist would know she was lying. The thought made her flush, and she held the telephone away from her mouth as she drew smoke into her lungs. Miri was counting on her husband's preference for secrecy, and as the receptionist hadn't yet challenged her story, she had probably judged it right.

'If I were younger,' she narrowed her eyes against the drifting smoke, 'I'd fight her for it, but this part is just so Nell, there wouldn't be any point.' Self-loathing washed over her. 'If you just flip open that telephone index on your desk, I'll jot down the address and put the script in the post.'

The girl reeled off the address, and Miri disconnected with a twisted little smile of triumph. She went to the car for the street directory, was thumbing through it when her mobile phone rang.

Alice said, 'I've got a sore throat. I think I'm getting a cold.'

Miri wanted to ask what she'd eaten and if she'd slept, but resisted. 'That's no good. How did it go with Laura yesterday?'

'I was late, but it was okay.'

'How late?'

'I missed the bus. It was twenty minutes till the next one came. Laura was fine about it. She's always running late herself.'

Miri chewed her lip. They talked on the telephone every day, and she had permission to ask about Alice's weight, but in return she was compelled to believe the answer.

'Did Laura weigh you?'

'Mum,' Alice said, 'don't start freaking me out.'

It must have been her tone of voice. She dropped the subject. 'What you need is echinacea drops. See if you can get some from the chemist.'

Miri found Lois in a cubicle in the casualty department, her right leg encased in plaster from ankle to knee.

'I swear it's just a sprain,' Lois said. She waved Miri towards a chair. 'But now I've got these bloody crutches, and I'm waiting for someone to show me how to walk with them.' She fumbled in her handbag and pulled out cigarettes and a lighter, then groaned. 'Can't smoke in here, either.' Beneath the make-up her face was haggard.

'It's best to get it set,' Miri said, 'otherwise you could have problems later.'

'Yeah, yeah, I know. Anyway, sit down and tell me what's been going on. Dig saw young Zett with her baby under her arm go flying past the house as if her knickers were on fire. He said she went to Artie's place and didn't come out. What's up?'

Miri wrapped her arms around her chest and leaned forward in the chair. So Zett knew Jude had been to the house. It had been a close thing, then.

'Zett's husband came round this afternoon,' she said. 'Maybe he suspects she's there. He wants custody of their baby.'

'Custody? If you left Jude Moran in charge of a dog you'd get back and find it with six broken ribs. Speaking of dogs, we had a snooper in the yard, which is how come I'm stuck with this busted foot. Whoever it was had brought a bone for Tania. Dig said it must be someone tossing bait, but Tania's still scratching her fleas. The greyhound is none the worse, either. Just acting kind of quiet and droopy.'

'Maybe some lost drunk on the way home.'

'Yeah, and he just happened to have a big bone in his pocket.' Lois coughed and shoved the cigarettes out of sight in her bag. 'Now you tell me Jude Moran's hanging around. Something weird is happening. Tell Suzette to take the baby and go while she can.'

Miri said, 'I think she's waiting on the collective hang-over on Boxing Day.'

Dig appeared in the doorway as Lois said vehemently, 'Tell her not to waste any time. If you hadn't come in, I'd have sent Dig with a message.' She looked at her husband. 'I told you, didn't I?'

Dig hovered at the foot of the bed. 'Lois gets these hunches. I don't know where they come from, but she's usually right.' He grinned at Miri. 'Just a pity they're not more useful, like Lotto numbers, or the names of a couple of winners.'

Lois frowned irritably at her husband then closed her eyes; she looked as if she might be going to faint.

Miri touched her arm. 'Are you okay, shall I call some-one?'

Her aunt's eyes opened. 'Tell Artie to get that girl and her baby out of town tonight. Everyone's so used to seeing his old rabbit truck that nobody'll bother him. He can take her to the truck stop at Castaway and fix her up with a lift to the coast. Artie knows all the drivers. He's patched up most of them over the years. They'll be safe then.'

To please Lois, Miri nodded. Now that Zett had the money, there was nothing to stop her going. And if someone was snooping, they would soon find out where she was.

She ran her fingers through her hair as it struck her that they could also be looking for Aziz. 'I'll go and see Artie,' she said.

A tea trolley rattled along the corridor and a woman in a striped overall appeared in the doorway with a cup and saucer. Miri sat up straight on the chair. For his own sake, Aziz ought to go with them. The town was too small. Eventually someone would see him and word would get around. It was the right time to go. With Zett and Aziz gone there would be nothing to worry about if Jude Moran or his cop buddies came calling. Nothing to worry about, nothing to hide, but the house would be unbearably empty.

Tomorrow was Christmas Day, her first without Alice. Miri closed her eyes. She wondered if Jack was still at home, or if he was spending Christmas with Nell.

Nell's flat was in a residential hotel in a suburb reached by ferry from Circular Quay. A scummy residue surged around the struts of the jetty as the ferry docked. When Miri asked at the kiosk on the quay she was directed to a street that ran uphill opposite the ferry terminal. Her heels clicked on the pavement and the sun struck the back of her neck as she walked away from the harbour. The Santa Fe Hotel was mock adobe with an unlit neon sign over the entrance. Letterboxes filled the wall behind the reception desk and smoked-glass mirrors reflected leather tub chairs and cactus plants in terracotta pots. Nell's flat was on the fourth floor. Miri faltered between the mirror-covered pillars. Her calves and ankles felt weak as she subsided into a chair.

'Help you with anything?'

A young man lifted a flap on the reception desk and approached her across the pink marble floor. He was sandy-haired and freckled and looked as if he would be more at home in board shorts than the shirt and tie imprinted with the hotel's logo.

'I'm waiting for someone,' Miri said.

He smiled. 'Is it one of our residents?'

She nodded. 'Yes.'

The telephone on the reception desk rang, and the young man smiled again as he backed away. She wondered why he'd come out from behind the desk, and turned to the mirrors for confirmation that her make-up was not smeared or her hair dishevelled. In the smoked glass her smile was painfully tight, but her clothing was in order. The chair she had chosen, circled by the succulent discs of cactus plants, was positioned in front of the lift. Everyone who came and went had to pass her, and with only a half-turn of the head she could study traffic in the street beyond the double glass doors. On the wall above the lift was a stainless steel clock on which she watched the minute hand tick towards evening.

The lift doors opened and closed as people came and went, and from time to time the young surfer behind the desk cast a puzzled glance in her direction. At six o'clock a woman with fiery auburn hair and black eyeliner flicked up at the corners of her eyes came in from the street and moved behind the reception desk. The surfer nodded in Miri's direction and whispered in the woman's ear. Keys jangled, and when the young man departed swinging a squash racket the woman approached her.

'Was someone expecting you?'

Miri turned from her study of reflections in the lift doors and her eyes locked with the woman's beady gaze.

'I don't think so,' she said.

'If you give me the name of your friend I can ring upstairs and see if they're in.'

Miri's voice was slow and vague. 'I don't mind waiting,' she said.

The woman stepped closer, and her voice was firm. 'There's no point, if your friend's not here,' she said. 'What was the name?'

Miri shrugged. 'Nell Bardot, fourth floor.'

The lift doors opened and Miri turned hopefully towards a blur of pink tracksuit as a young woman headed for the main doors. It was not Nell. Behind the desk, the receptionist stared at her as she lifted the telephone.

Outside, the entrance of the Santa Fe glowed in the headlights of cars as they came up from the harbour. Lit in this way, the building looked so secretive and smug to her, so warm and conspiratorial, that the impulse to smash and batter was overwhelming. This must have been how Keiko felt. Miri shut her eyes and imagined the weight of a shovel in her hands, the heavy square-bladed tool Con would lift to kill a snake. Her elbows stiffened and locked as she pictured the shovel blade slicing the swollen moon shape of a cactus. She would grip with both hands and slam it into the Santa Fe's plate glass windows. Pellets of glass would ricochet across the rose marble; they would crunch underfoot and tumble from her hair as she battered the fake adobe archway to rubble. Pain branched up her arms, pinning her eyes closed, just as if she was demolishing the four floors of the hotel single-handed.

'No answer from upstairs.' The woman's voice was spiky with irritation.

Miri opened her eyes. Her fists were still clenched and her knees had begun a palsied tremble. She spread her hands in her lap to mask the shakes. 'Thank you for trying,' she said quietly.

The woman came out from behind the desk and peered into her face. 'You don't look at all well,' she said. 'Let me call you a taxi.'

Miri straightened. 'I don't want a taxi.'

'Look, I don't wish to be unpleasant, but you can't stay here.'

A figure pushed through the door from the street, and as Miri leaned forward in the chair, the woman pounced. 'Okay, I'm asking you to leave.'

'But I'm waiting for someone.'

Jack's head snapped around at the sound of her voice, and his expression wobbled from surprise to wary recognition.

'Miri?'

The woman bending over Miri straightened. Looking down, Miri watched the brown hammers of the woman's toes tense against the soles of her high-heeled sandals as Jack inserted his bulk between them.

He glowered at the receptionist and when she retreated to the desk he squatted beside Miri. 'What're you doing here?'

Jack's voice was husky and gentle. It was the first time she'd seen him since she'd gone for him in the flat, although they had spoken briefly on the telephone of Alice's recovery, a cold, stilted conversation that might have been between strangers.

'Just waiting,' she said.

'Is it Alice?'

Miri's hands fluttered in her lap. 'No, Alice is okay.'

'That's good.' He glanced around the foyer, following her gaze towards the stainless steel lift doors. 'Were you waiting for me, or . . .'

'Not really.' She settled her back against the curved leather. 'You carry on.'

He stared at her for a moment, then put his mouth close to her ear. 'We need to talk.'

Reflected in the gleaming surfaces that surrounded them she saw the umbra of her hair, the polished toes of Jack's loafers, the dull bloom of his denim shirt.

'It's too soon to talk,' she said. 'You go up. I'll just wait.'

He shook his head as he backed away from her. In another minute the lift doors slid shut on his baffled stare.

Numbers blinked as the lift climbed to the fourth floor. If Nell was not at home, then Jack must have a key. Or perhaps Nell was at home and had asked the woman at the desk to fend her off. If they were there together Jack would be too shaken for the sex he'd come for. Perhaps Nell would pout and flounce, or perhaps Jack's desire would overcome the image of his wife sitting patiently in the foyer.

She almost didn't care if Nell and Jack had sex. What she wanted was for the weight of her discomfort to press upon them, to fill them with dread, the way the sight of Keiko waiting underneath the window had once filled her with speechless terror. Five minutes later, when Jack strode from the lift with his face set in a bitter scowl, Miri saw that she had succeeded.

The reception staff changed every eight hours. Most of them were young, like the boy with the squash racket, and at handover they simply shrugged in her direction and got on with their work. But the woman with the tiger-striped eyes took Miri's presence as a personal affront. Each time she came on duty she threatened to call the police, but called Nell's flat instead. Miri hunkered down into the chair, letting the woman remind Nell of her presence. In two days, she only abandoned her position to walk to the toilets that were tucked behind a bank of hairy cactus plants to the right of the lifts. In the cold tiled washroom she drank water from the tap, splashed her face and wrists and patted them dry with a paper towel. In the mirror, she was white-faced with exhaustion as she pulled her fingers through her hair and tucked stray strands behind her ears.

Late on the second day, Jack came in from the street and walked straight up to her. He dragged another chair across the floor and positioned it between Miri and the lift, sat down with his elbows on his knees so that his exasperated face was level with her own. 'Look, laying siege to this building is a waste of time. I've come to take you home.'

She shook her head. 'I won't go home.'

'Well what then?'

She shrugged. 'Just bring me some cigarettes. I'm out.'

Jack reached into his jacket pocket and, as he handed her his own pack, their reflections on the pink marble floor overlapped and joined. She lit a cigarette and watched him through the smoke.

It was odd that as Jack's discomfort grew, her own pain magically subsided. This was what Keiko had known. Already she felt lighter.

The front door of Artie's house was locked. Miri knocked and waited, watching the moonlight reflect in the polished tin of his cut-outs. A few moments later, his tall stooped figure appeared at the screen door.

'Thought I heard someone.'

Miri followed him into the kitchen, where Zett stood at the stove stirring something in a frying pan. She grinned when they came in, but her face was as tired and crumpled as her green cotton shirt.

'I've been showing Artie how to make bubble-and-squeak,' she said.

The old man smiled.

The baby sat on a rug on the floor with a plastic spoon in her fist. Miri knelt beside her. 'Opal's sitting up!'

'Yep, she's so proud of herself.'

Miri brushed her fingertips against the child's creamy shoulder; with the touch of dewy skin came a surge of memory. She turned her face to the wall as she struggled to compose herself.

'So where'd you go to with Jude?' Zett held the wooden spoon, covered with coloured mash, in midair.

Miri stood up. 'A beer at the Five Mile pub.'

Zett pulled a face. 'Jude fancies you, then. He thinks it's smart there, with its carpet and flushing toilets.'

Miri felt the need to apologise. 'I didn't want to go, but I had to get him out of the way.' She watched Zett's face, wondering how she would feel in her shoes.

Zett dropped the spoon back in the pan with a shrug and her voice was tense. 'He's getting close, isn't he? Next time we might not be so lucky.'

Miri said, 'Lois has had someone snooping around her place. She's got a bad feeling about it and she thinks you should go tonight, before anything happens.'

'Yeah?' Zett looked from Artie to Miri. 'Jude'll be going up to his mother's around now, he always does.' But her voice faltered and she glanced nervously at Artie. 'So what does Lo know that we don't?'

Artie said, 'I, for one, would not disregard the advice of Lois Kissack. 'If you want to go, I'll take you. It's up to you.'

Zett pushed the frying pan to the back of the stove and stooped to pick up Opal. 'All this talk of premonitions and people creeping round in the dark is giving me the willies.' Her freckled face was apprehensive. 'But maybe Lois is psychic or something.' She turned to Artie. 'So, let's do it.'

'Looks like I have to cook my own Christmas dinner,' Artie said.

'You can eat it with me,' Miri said, surprising herself with the invitation.

Artie smiled suddenly. 'Thank you,' he said. 'That would be my great pleasure.' He put out his hand and she took it, his dry touch remaining like a warm penny in her palm when he released it.

AZIZ

The blue room was stuffy and his dead mother and sisters nagged at him as he tried to sleep until, with the ease of practice, he led his memory away and back over older anecdotes. These were the small moments of family life that had worn smooth with telling, like the day his youngest sister was separated from them in the crowded bazaar and how his mother, flapping back and forth between the stalls in panic, had imagined her lost forever; like the time when he was sick with fever and his father had rolled him in a blue silk prayer rug and carried him to the mosque, and how on the way home the fever had broken and he had slept for days.

Ah, his father! Aziz pictured the old man playing *falash* with his friends, the cards grey and their edges furred with use as they turned them in their hands. Before the Taliban, his father had often stopped after work to play a game of chess under the trees in the public gardens. Aziz would wait beside him on the grass, eating pistachio nuts and watching children run over the rooftops and walls to recover fallen kites. He remembered how he loved the sharp salty flavour of the nuts, how he would pick them from the *qabli pilau* his mother made when guests came to eat with them.

Aziz understood that he had become a storyteller, carrying in his head the secret history of his family. The history was a precious private language that connected him with his father, his mother, his brother and his sisters in a way that could never be spoken or learned by others. The process reminded him of carpet weaving, of chanted rugs from Tabriz and Isfahan, where the weavers recited the colours, or of tribal rugs with their patterns constructed again and again from memory.

If his mother was here she would nod her head over the episode of his sister. 'Yes, yes, I thought she was lost,' Nadira would shriek, wringing her hands and pulling faces in imitation of her distress. 'And then suddenly the child was perched on the wooden bench outside the lamp shop, with a fresh peach in her hand!' At this point his mother would beam a smile that was the mould of his own smile. 'And being overjoyed to find her, I did not ask where she got that peach.'

Already he had begun to make new stories, stories of his journey and the boat with its cargo of sad frightened people, stories of the sea, of those who survived it and those who were lost. Soon he would make stories with Miriam, how on hot nights they had pumped water to the garden, how the smell of the river lingered in their hair and clothing and the water soaked into the soil leaving a red stain. He smiled at the sudden aptness of the astrological sign he had been born under, *Dalwa*, the water bearer.

With Miriam, there would be stories of mornings when

mauve shadows lay trapped in the bed sheets, when daylight inched down the wall until it warmed their faces. There would be stories of nights, and the soft friction of skin against skin, the electricity that roared in his blood and exploded in a hot gushing liquid that by morning had settled in silvery trails, like snail tracks, upon their thighs. These brief moments of asylum had become their private history, stories to be told in a language his family would never understand.

MIRI

Aziz called to her from the upstairs verandah. She guessed he'd been watching the road for her.

'Where is Zett?' he said, as she eased into a chair beside him.

She pointed across the gardens. 'Gone to Artie's house.'

He took her hand and turned it, brought the inside of the wrist to his mouth. She closed her eyes, almost too tired to get up and do what had to be done. The sour taste of stale beer and cigarettes lingered in her mouth; the outing with Jude had left her feeling soiled. She wanted to run a bath, fill the tub with tepid water and soak. She was hungry, too. Hungry for the food Aziz had cooked, the little dishes of spicy lentils, the lemon chutney. Even the curry, though she wished it had been chicken. She heard Alice's voice, heaping scorn on vegetarians who ate fish. *So fish drown in air and people drown in water. Why would a watery death be more painful? It's smug and convenient to say fish don't feel pain.*

Alice had been a vegan until she went into the clinic, when she had reluctantly agreed to small amounts of dairy in an effort to regain her health.

Those days of spooning ice-cream into Alice's mouth seemed so far away. Miri recognised her own hunger as a sign of something. Perhaps the grief counsellor had been right; perhaps she was moving towards a kind of acceptance, although it felt very like betrayal. What she wanted now was to eat and then to lie down in the blue room with Aziz, to fold into him and lose herself.

'Zett's leaving tonight,' she said. At once she felt his attention sharpen, and his head swung towards her. 'You could go with her. It would be safer for you to go.'

He was silent. She listened to him breathing beside her and wondered what he was thinking.

After a few minutes he said, 'I took water to the garden. Very thirsty.'

She guessed he was saying that he wanted to stay. It would be easy to agree, to move him into the attic and, for a while, keep him away from the town. But Con would recover and come home. Even after Zett had gone, Jude Moran might not give up. Sooner or later, there would be trouble.

'I had to go out because Zett's husband came. He is a policeman. Not a nice man. That is why Zett has to go away.'

Aziz took her hands and squeezed them, a silent plea that she could almost hear above the noisy trill of the cicadas. If they had a common language she wondered what he would say to her. Wondered how she would answer. Would she be prepared to find a bigger town, one that could embrace them both? She didn't know. Not yet.

Miri said, 'Think about it while I pack Zett's things.'

She was kneeling on the floor of the attic folding Opal's

baby clothes into a suitcase when Aziz appeared in the doorway. He glanced at her uncertainly and then stretched out his hand to show her a small green peach. The peach was about the size of the stone he carried in his pocket. The trees in the garden were laden, but the fruit would not ripen for a month or more. Then, it would come in a rush and they would not be able to eat it all before it rotted.

'What is it?' she said.

He passed the peach to her and pressed it into the curve of her palm. Her hand closed around the unripe fruit, sensing the stone inside as well as the tough knot of memory at her own centre. *You can't solve a problem until you can say it out loud.* It was time to crack it open before she shrivelled around it. She knelt on the rug where the three of them had shared a meal and tugged at Aziz's hand until he sat beside her.

'Listen,' she whispered. 'This is how it was.'

On the third day, Nell Bardot rushed from the lift carrying a suitcase. She wore a floral cotton skirt with the wrong shoes, a lacy cardigan badly buttoned. Her face was pasty behind dark glasses as she hurried towards the street and a waiting taxi. Then, and only then, Miri uncurled from the chair, stretched her numbed limbs and stumbled out into the humid street. She was gazing at the pastel haze above the harbour when a taxi pulled up at the kerbside and she recognised Jack's face pressed against the rear window. She stretched her hand towards him in surprise; *you've just missed Nell*, she started to say. But as he opened the door, his mouth and eyes buckled and she saw that Jack was crying.

'What is it?' she said.

He staggered from the back of the cab and reached for her hands. She thought it must be this haunting that she had visited on him and Nell. His stricken look even made her feel a little ashamed of herself.

'Jack, I didn't mean—'

'It's Alice,' he said.

Alice? For a moment she couldn't connect what he was saying with his distress, and then her fear kicked in. 'Alice?'

He put his arms around her and his tears wet her face. Her legs almost gave way with fright.

'Please, Jack—'

His voice was muffled against her cheek. 'The police tried to reach you.'

'What?'

'It looks like hit and run, but there might be more to it.'

Hit and run. Alice. She clung to him so as not to fall. After a moment, he led her to the taxi. Squashed in beside him on the back seat with the nauseating swirl of traffic speeding past the windows, she read in Jack's face that Alice was already gone. She felt the sharp snap inside as some part of her perished. Whatever happened next, whatever the details, on that ride across the harbour with the bruised sky flashing between the massive steel struts of the bridge, she had felt all lightness leave her, felt it drain away through the pores of her skin, through her hair, her breath, her dulled eyes, through her wild scattered thoughts. The lightness that was generated by her love for Alice had left her, and by the time they reached the far side of the harbour every cell of her body was weighted with despair.

ZETT

She poured a glass of white wine, slid the bottle back into the fridge and sat astride one of Artie's kitchen chairs. Only another day and she'd be so far away it would feel like another planet. Only one more fucking day! She drank quickly, feeling the buzz in her blood as the alcohol circulated. The money Cam had sent meant a fresh start; she could even change her name if she wanted. Ever since she'd opened his letter she'd been giddy with relief. From Adelaide she could head to Cairns. Her brother had two kids. Opal could grow up with family around. Otherwise there'd always be just the two of them, and the thing she dreaded was getting sick, dying young of something awful and leaving Opal. She'd make arrangements, just in case. Her sisters were useless, but Cam was a decent bloke. He'd look after Opal if it ever came to that. She'd have to let him know it was what she wanted, make sure Jude didn't get first say. That meant going to a lawyer. Would there be enough money for a lawyer and to keep them both until she got a job? Hell, she wasn't sick; the lawyer could wait.

The bag containing Cam's letter was on the floor. She pulled it onto her lap and slipped her hand inside. When she brought the envelope to her nose and inhaled, the crisp banknotes smelled of freedom. It was good to feel happy for once, to be sitting here with a lap full of money and this bubble of pleasure round and bright inside her. She pushed the envelope to the bottom of the bag. The gun was down there, heavy and cool in her hand. Zett drew it out and put it on the table.

The old Colt revolver was Jude's favourite and she had taken it, if she was honest, so that he wouldn't be able to play those stupid games after she was gone. A few years back, when her mother was sick, Sadie had talked for the first time about that bloke who'd shot himself in front of her, how she'd seen him pull out the gun and hadn't lifted a finger to stop him. If they were going to do it, they'd do it anyway, was her mother's view. It wasn't long after that conversation that Sadie had pleaded with Zett to get a gun so that she could escape the cancer that was eating her. Like her life, Sadie's death had been tough. Zett sniffed back tears. Her mother would have told her off for being soppy. No use crying over spilt milk, she'd say when anything went wrong, no matter how disastrous. Especially now, with money in her bag, Zett should be looking on the sunny side.

Opal stirred. Zett had put her down to sleep using Artie's plastic washing basket as a makeshift cot. She leaned over and stroked the baby's cheek with her free hand, then checked her watch. Artie had taken the truck into town to fill up with petrol. The waiting around was making her nervous. Miri was bringing her things from the attic, but it was too bad if she didn't get back in time. As soon as Artie showed up they'd be off.

Opal opened her eyes and cried harder for a moment, then trailed off into sleep.

MERVYN

He pushed his bike and dogcart along the track towards the gardens. He was approaching Dig's house from the other side now, eyes and ears wide open for trouble. Everything was in darkness, but as he passed Artie's back fence he heard a baby crying. There was only one place it could be coming from. Mervyn stopped and listened, wondering what old Artie Rose was doing with a baby.

ZETT

Artie hadn't come back yet. She was biting her nails between trips to the front window to look out. To keep her spirits up, she drank another glass of wine and then needed to pee. Artie's toilet was outside and infested with spiders. She thought of squatting beside the back doorstep, and after crossing her legs for a while, she slung her handbag over her shoulder and picked up the clothes basket; there was no way she was leaving Opal alone even for a minute.

The back doorstep was bright and exposed under the moonlight. Zett cursed and followed the concrete path towards the toilet. She could smell the old brick dunny well before she reached it, a tiny space, too narrow to fit the washing basket.

She set the basket on a patch of grass, skittered in and was out again in under a minute. The night noises were spooking her. Why was Artie taking so bloody long?

MERVYN

Mervyn stuck his head through a gap in Artie Rose's fence and saw a woman coming out of the shithouse. She had her back to him, but he had no doubt it was that freckled floozy, the copper's wife. Her head gleamed in the moonlight and he heard her talking to herself as she picked up a washing basket from the lawn. He'd been in the pub with her old man lunchtime before last, heard him asking all and sundry if they'd seen her. Apparently she'd bolted with their kid.

As he watched her walk back to the house, a plan was forming. He would pass on the wife's whereabouts to Jude Moran, and Jude would be so grateful he would trade favours and order Sharkie to lay off. The gambling debts were old and cold. Sharkie would be happy to forget them if it kept him in good odour with the cops. And with Sharkie squared, he could hold onto his winnings.

Beside him, the black dog folded her legs and lay down on the grass. The important thing was not to scare off the wife.

When she went inside, he crossed the yard and crept closer to the kitchen. There was no blind on the window and he watched her pour a glass of wine, pace up and down the kitchen and look at her watch like she was waiting for somebody, or in a hurry. The kid was in the basket. Mervyn stepped away from the square of light falling from the window, wondering just how grateful Jude would be if someone was to pluck the baby out of there and take it to him.

ZETT

The racket of the truck's engine drowned out the sound of possums scratching on the roof, the creaks and groans of Artie's house. The shoulder bag with the money was hugged tight against her body as she watched the truck swing into the driveway. She felt light-headed from the wine, nervous but happy, ready for another drink, even more ready to hit the road.

When Artie got out and slammed the driver's door, she heaved a sigh of relief and turned back to the kitchen. Then her blood leapt as she saw a bulky figure in a checked work shirt squatting beside Opal's basket.

MIRI

In the stillness of the gardens, the gunshot was as sudden and as random as a lightning strike. Birds flapped and shrieked in the treetops. The cicadas fell silent. Miri staggered and dropped Zett's suitcase. Aziz scrambled to pick it up and, in the brittle silence, they tripped and stumbled over the knotted roots of a fig tree as they began to run.

When they reached Artie's front fence Aziz caught her arm and dragged her to a halt, put a finger to his lips and edged forward into the shadowy front garden. At first it looked as though nothing had happened. The truck was parked beside the house; the front windows were unlit. But then they saw that the front door was swinging open and, from inside, Opal began a high-pitched wail.

ARTIE

In the kitchen, little Zett Moran stood hugging her baby. 'I've killed Jude,' she said. 'There's so much blood. I've killed him.'

The pan with the remains of the mashed potato was splashed with blood. Artie grimaced as he leaned over the figure on the floor. The light was bad, but she was right; there was a lot of blood. The other two appeared from the front of the house then, and he asked Miri to hold a torch while he assessed the damage. She took the light and aimed it steadily.

When he looked up at her he saw in her eyes the anxious expression of a swimmer who has drifted too far from shore in rough weather. 'This fellow is not dead,' he said. 'That is the good news. Bad news is that he must go to the hospital before he bleeds to death. That means there will be questions to answer.'

Dig appeared then with a black dog cavorting at his side. 'Jesus Christ!' he said. 'I heard a shot. What happened?'

From far away in the town, the thin high whine of a siren started up.

Artie fished a bunch of keys from his pocket and handed them to Miri.

'Dig and I will take him in,' he said. 'You better drive the truck for these two.'

AZIZ

Once more the road stretched before him, like a sword tilted, or a silver river, tranquil and deceptive. His heart hammered in his chest. There had been no time to do anything but accept the coat the kind doctor had thrust at him and clamber into the truck. Zett, still weeping, had climbed up beside him. Now, as they bounced and swayed on the wide front seat, the vanilla scent of Miriam's hair swirled around him and he touched his throat where it felt knotted with anxiety and dread.

Thrust into motion by the gunshot, he had recovered the momentum of his journey as well as its purpose. Remembering his father and sister and small nephew in the goat shed in Peshawar, he was ashamed that his own comfort and pleasure had distracted him from his duty and he imagined their patient faces turned away in disgust.

'Dip your lights, you stupid bastard,' Zett shrieked suddenly, as Miriam slowed the truck.

Headlights had appeared. It was the first sign of life they'd seen since they'd left the town, but he wasn't reassured. The glare dazzled them and he felt as if they were pinned in the beam of hostile searchlights. Zett ducked below the dashboard as the car passed in a whoosh of light and road noise. Ahead of them, the ribbon of road melted into night. He remembered the shape of his father's hands holding a book, felt in his arm muscles the weight of his nephew's small body as he slept.

This is My Straight Road, so follow it . . .

MIRI

The old truck bucked and roared and shuddered as if it would fly apart. Miri imagined hot blades of metal carving the desert air; saw a fusillade of worn screws, nuts, bolts and pellets of glass, particles of wood, chrome, leather, steel, fur and bone being catapulted into the night and swallowed by the broad porous darkness.

At the Castaway roadhouse, she eased off the accelerator. When she cut the engine, Aziz turned towards her. On his other side, Zett hugged Opal in silence. With the headlights extinguished, the cab became a raft, adrift and isolated. His arm brushed her side as he peered through the bug-spattered windscreen. Three trucks were parked nose to tail along one side of the servo. In the blue light of the cafe a group of men sat drinking coffee at a table.

As the tick of hot metal replaced engine noise, a weight settled behind her breastbone. There had been no time to talk, no choice but to get the two of them away before the police arrived.

Miri said, 'What do we do now?'

Zett was still shaking as she opened the passenger door. 'You go in and order a coffee. See if you can suss out the drivers before we agree to ride with them.'

CHANDELLE

She was filling a metal teapot from the hot water urn when she glanced out the window and saw Jude's wife lifting a suitcase from the back of an old blue truck. Chandelle almost dropped the pot of boiling water on her feet. There were three of them getting out of the truck, but it was Zett Moran she noticed. She covered her confusion by wiping down the work top. It was only a couple of hours since she'd had that funny turn — it had been Jude who'd stopped and sorted her out. She busied herself with the till roll so as not to seem to be staring. Jude hadn't been gone long. He must have passed his wife going the other way.

Chandelle smothered a smile. Things were moving along just fine with Jude. One night, about a week ago, he'd even slept over, the first time she'd ever done it in a bed with sheets and time to think. He told her how his wife had buggered off. He sounded gutted, but men got over wives leaving. She'd been disappointed when he left so early in the morning; she'd barely woken up. But the way he held her to him as he slept had reassured her. Jude was definitely coming back.

As she was spooning Nescafé into cups the dark-haired woman came in and the drivers starting flirting with her. Jude had given Chandelle his mobile number. Actually, he'd left his phone on the table and she'd written the number down while he was in the toilet. But she knew if she called and told him his missus was in the servo he'd be back like a shot. They'd have a big bust-up and that'd be it forever. He'd spend more nights with her. After a while he'd ask her to change her job, move into town to be near him. Through the window, she watched Zett fold a pink rug around the baby and kiss the top of her head. Then again, she'd seen people make up just because it was Christmas time and they had a kid.

After Chandelle had served the coffee, she fished her mobile phone out of the drawer under the till and found Jude's number. She was tempted to call him, get a divorce happening. She looked up from the phone, still uncertain. The woman had organised for her friends to hitch a ride with one of the drivers. It was a bloke called Ted Everton, and even from a distance Chandelle could see he was disappointed that the woman wouldn't be riding with him herself.

She slipped the mobile phone into the pocket of her apron. Zett Moran was lugging a suitcase. In fifteen minutes she'd be gone. If Chandelle forgot she'd ever seen the wife, eventually Jude would do the same.

MIRI

The moment when she heard the precise details of Alice's accident was easily the worst of her life. She and Jack sat in the hastily tidied sitting room of the flat in Glebe while Jessica held her parents' hands and wept as she described the last time she had seen Alice.

'A few people turned up and a party started,' Jessica said. 'Louise and Tara had just found work and were getting their own place. They wanted to celebrate.'

Miri sat with her hands folded in her lap and watched the girl blot her eyes with a tissue.

'Alice wasn't well. She had a cold starting and said she would go and see her mother. She told us not to worry if she didn't come back because she was probably going to sleep at home.'

Jessica's mother stroked the back of her daughter's hand with a thumb, a small loving gesture. Their identical blonde heads were close as they huddled together on the divan bed. On Jessica's other side, her father the lawyer sat with a straight back.

'Anyway,' Jessica sniffed, 'Alice rang home but there was no answer.' She raised puffy eyes to Miri. 'I think she tried your mobile, but it was switched off.'

Miri bowed her head; she felt as cold and senseless as a stone. Later, when the reality of Alice's death sank in, she would hurl her phone from the window of a taxi, sickened to recall how the power had died after twenty-four hours in the lobby of the Santa Fe Hotel. One missed call. And there would never be another.

'So Alice went to bed and the party carried on.' Jessica's parents squeezed her hands protectively as she spoke. 'Most people were pretty much out of it by the time she came out of the bedroom and asked if anyone had something for her headache. I didn't see what happened, but the others said Louise put a couple of pills into Alice's hand and she swallowed them.'

'Was Alice in the habit of taking drugs?' Jack said.

Jessica shook her head. 'Alice didn't do that stuff.'

Jessica's father bent his head towards her. 'Honey, Alice's parents have to know the truth. If there was anything—'

'That *is* the truth, Dad.' Jessica's eyes overflowed again. 'There wasn't much light in the room. Just a couple of lava lamps, you know? Alice didn't see what Louise had given her. She probably just thought it was . . .'

Jessica's father stood up and took a few steps towards them. His face looked grim, but an expression of barely suppressed relief passed across it as he regarded his daughter's bowed head. 'The police have sent some pills for testing—' he cleared his throat, a sad apologetic sound, 'but they seemed pretty certain what the results will show.'

So they had been high on a cocktail of drugs and alcohol, and when Alice had asked for aspirin, they'd given her ecstasy. Miri remembered the girls in the kitchen, their brown muscled bodies and sun-streaked hair. Their shrewd blue eyes. Maybe they had even thought it was a joke. With her low body weight, Alice would have been in trouble. As it was she had stumbled out into the street in front of a car. The driver hadn't stopped.

Jessica's parents shook their heads and expressed their sorrow. They wrung their hands and hoped the police would trace the driver. They hugged their daughter as she cried.

There was nothing else to be said.

She walked beside them to the truck. Through the window of the servo she saw the waitress filling a thermos for their driver. Miri had judged him to be the most sensible of the three, and when she'd asked for a lift to Adelaide for her friends he'd told them to get in the truck and wait.

Miri fumbled in her handbag, searching for a pen. 'Here.' She grabbed Aziz's arm and peeled back the sleeve of his jacket.

Not on the hand, where anyone might see, but higher up on the weathered skin of his forearm, she pressed the point of the biro. As she cupped his elbow he pulled her close and she burrowed in, inhaling the scent of him. A wail of protest welled inside her, but she suppressed it. If he was to get away, they must part company.

She pulled back and focused on the point of the biro. What would she write for a man who could not easily read her language? Over his shoulder she saw the driver move from the counter towards the door. Aziz covered her face with quick hot kisses. The driver was walking towards them. They should've done this sooner.

'Wait!' She held his arm steady and forced out the letters of an address in the city, the telephone number of a friend, pressed them into his forearm like a tattoo. Her fingertips lingered in the soft crook of his arm as she spelled out the street name for him. Then she pulled down his sleeve and slid a hand inside the jacket Artie had given him. The wad of a map was tucked into the lining; she'd found it in the truck's glove box. The jacket would keep him warm in the desert, and the map would guide him if he left the truck. It was more than he'd had when they met. And perhaps he would make sense of what she had written.

The driver stood with the thermos cradled in his arm and a woollen cap pulled low on his forehead. 'You changed your mind about coming?'

She shook her head and watched Aziz climb up beside Zett. The first drops of rain smacked the windscreen, drops the size of quails' eggs that exploded against her cheeks and hair and obscured their faces behind the glass. She turned and ran to Artie's truck, and by the time she slid the key into the ignition the big Mack was pulling out onto the highway. She waved and thought she saw an answering flutter before the truck moved away from her into the night.

APPENDIX

Undated Photographs

1

The river flows from left to right, its mirrored surface flashing dimples of light where it conceals fallen boughs and the roots of willows. The old man stoops slightly as he treads the dry, cracked strip of bank, his boots leaving no footprints. Light refracts off the lenses of his spectacles, masking his eyes. Beside him, and closer to the water, a woman with dark hair tilts her chin towards the sun. Balanced on a slender neck, her oval face resembles a portrait by Modigliani; her feet are bare and muddy as she steps over a hose that disappears into the river. In one hand she carries an old-fashioned Box Brownie, while around her neck a Nikon camera dangles on a strap. Her free hand is bunched in her skirt, lifting it clear of the mud. The man's hand lightly cups her shoulderblade, and as she leans into his touch, a hesitant smile radiates pleasure and relief.

2

White cups up-ended in stacks on an espresso machine. Tiny glasses, green-tinged, in a leaning tower beside the till. Customers suspended over plates of scrambled egg and bacon. An elderly woman with her legs plaited under the table and a latte at her elbow holds a pen poised over a magazine cross-word puzzle. Streamers loop across a doorway which reveals a cross-section of scrubbed stainless steel kitchen where dirty dishes wait in piles. Cutlery drains on a rack. He wears a long black apron tied around his hips. Sleeves rolled back reveal forearms speckled with ash-coloured scars. On the wall beside his cheek, in a photograph of a garden torn from a glossy magazine, a stone fish leaps in the spray of a fountain.

3

Brown paper held in place with packing tape obscures both light and view from a kitchen window. The room is spotless under the glare of the overhead light bulb. Racing trophies adorn the top shelf of a dresser, and a pair of marabou-trimmed mules are parked beside the doormat. A cut-glass ashtray gleams in the centre of the yellow pine table. Cigarettes and a lighter. On the wall beside the sink, a picture hook juts from the plaster, and the paler rectangle defines the space on the paintwork where a small photograph or picture frame has recently been removed.

4

Her auburn hair is pulled back into a ponytail that exposes freckled cheeks. A lime-green uniform with *Majestic Cinema* embroidered on the collar shows signs of wear. *Jack and Jill Child-Care Centre, 45 Montgomery Street, Cairns,* outlined in rainbow letters above the door. From the garden, a toddler with marmalade hair waves a chubby hand and the woman smiles.

5

The Castaway Service Station sign is in the bottom left-hand corner of the photograph. Twenty yards away, in the scrub, a blanket obscures the windscreen of a red four-wheel drive. Police cars line the track that cuts from the highway to Castaway Creek and, at the back of the servo, the doors of an ambulance gape wide. A young woman burrows into an oxygen mask held by a paramedic. A police officer kneels beside the red car as two colleagues spread a plastic sheet over a body. Flies gather on a blackened pool of blood. A boot heel protrudes from one end of the sheet and a ginger-haired policeman holds up a shotgun wrapped in plastic.

6

Swann's Pharmacy is written in swirling black and gold script above the door. The windows are cluttered with faded displays of hair accessories, children's plastic bath toys, and a range of equipment for the elderly available for hire. A young woman rearranges a pyramid of shampoo bottles in the window to the right of the door. Her white coat falls open and she raises manicured nails to the chain with silver letters that nestles in her milky cleavage.

7

The young woman and the baby are caught mid-waltz, their features slightly blurred as they twirl against a background of kitchen cabinets and a table littered with the remains of a meal. The woman's face is a smooth golden oval broken by a brilliant smile. The baby grasps fistfuls of her long blonde hair. Pinned to the wall behind them, a poster advertises *The Whaler's Daughter*. In the poster, the woman's face looms against limestone cliffs. A summer skirt balloons around her legs; her feet are bare and a lace blouse slides from her shoulders as she swings the child into the dance. Pink balloons bunch above their heads and two lovebirds, flying loose, perch on the curve of a wrought-iron cage. On the table, a butterfly cake with pink icing and a single candle has been cut with a bone-handled knife.

8

People walking, heads down and faces frozen into the grimaces they pull in rain. The underside of a jetty pushes out from the beach and at the end of the street a pair of ragged palms frame a lozenge of sand. A woman walks along the kerb, dark hair falling away from her cheekbones; her eyes search the street numbers of the cafes that line the strip. The woman's mouth is open and the cloud of her breath hangs in the air. A side door is propped wide to allow the salt breeze into the steamy kitchen and, as he catches sight of her, he propels himself through the narrow opening, eyes alight and mouth stretched wide in a shout of joy.

#9

She cradles the violin on her left shoulder, and her right arm blurs in a graceful arc as she raises the bow. Vintage lace outlines a slender body. Jet beads dangle from her earlobes, and blue-black hair is parted in glossy wings. The young man at her side clasps a cello between his knees, and his spiky hair is dyed the colour of aubergines. Overhead, sunlight pierces the tumbling clouds in broad golden shafts; it strikes the heads and shoulders of the two musicians like theatre spotlights. On the damp pavement, pedestrians turn uncertainly towards the two as if searching; some of them smile. In the open violin case, scattered coins glitter. The air trembles. The pavement is blue with fallen jacaranda flowers.

Acknowledgements

I am indebted to Isobel Dixon for her patience and faith and to Sam Humphreys, Jane Palfreyman, Ali Lavau, Meredith Curnow and Elizabeth Cowell for editorial advice and support.

At the University of Adelaide: Dr Jan Harrow, Katherine Doube, Christy Di Frances, Blake Jessop, Robin Potanin, Emmett Stinson, Dominique Wilson and Sean Williams.

I first learned of the woman who gave birth aboard a sinking ship from an account of the *SIEV X* by the late Amal Basry. Amal survived the tragedy, which claimed the lives of 353 asylum seekers on 19 October 2001, and was courageous in speaking publicly about her experience.

I would like to thank Sheik Solaiman Noureddine of the Al Khalil mosque in Adelaide, South Australia, and Ghulam Hazrat Beedar, for their advice on Arabic and Afghan languages.

Of all the good fortune that has come my way the greatest was to have been nurtured within a creative and loving family. Peter and Beverly Hiscock can never be thanked enough for all their years of effort, for leading by example, for always including me in their projects and encouraging me to dream. Also it is with enormous affection that I acknowledge the debt of gratitude owed to the aunts and uncles who shared my childhood, boots and all, and in the process passed on so many skills: Sheila Hiscock, who introduced me to the mysteries of the darkroom and let me help when she hand-coloured photographs; Joyce and Murray Heinicke, who were endlessly generous with their stories and knowledge of greyhound racing, and who read the manuscript; Louis 'Tiger' Hiscock, for starting the storytelling while I was still in nappies, and his wife, Loraine, for her kindness. For all else I am indebted to Christopher, Lorena and Rafael Lefevre.